BIOGRAPHY

Martin Goodman's first novel was shortlisted for the Whitbread Prize, and his most recent biography won 1st Prize, Basis of Medicine in the BMA Book Awards 2008. Other nonfiction writings explore the extremes of the spiritual life: shamanism, sacred mountains, hallucinogens, and self-proclaimed goddesses. Other fiction focuses on the aftermath of wars. A BBC New Generation Thinker for 2012-13, he is Professor of Creative Writing at the University of Hull, and Director of the Philip Larkin Centre for Poetry and Creative Writing.

ECTOPIA

MARTIN GOODMAN

BARB
ICAN
PRESS

Published by Barbican Press in 2013

First published in Great Britain as a paperback original by
Barbican Press
1 Ashenden Road, London E5 0DP
www.barbicanpress.com

A CIP catalogue for this book is available from the British Library

ISBN: 978-0-9563364-5-3

Typeset in 11.75/15.5pt Garamond by Mike Gower
Cover image: 'Malchus' Ear Healed' by Ian Pollock
Cover Design by Jason Anscomb of Rawshock Design
Printed and bound by Lightning Source UK Ltd., Milton Keynes

JAMES

Bender –
Clock Zero

0.00

Others have sisters. Older sisters. My sister's the one they all want though. She's older than me by a couple of hours. She's me with a slit and tits. We boys sit in a semi-ring of chairs on education-and-reporting night. The light from the vidscreen makes our faces shine like we've rubbed in radiation. Best would be to get a ladder and perch behind the vidscreen. I could look down on em. See their faces pale with longing. Pretend they're looking up at me.

I don't though. I join in.

A film's just started. Teensquad puts up with the beginning coz they know how it ends.

It's my film. I made it a year and a bit ago as my entry piece for teensquad. We have to make a film about our family home to show the truth behind family values. That's the official shitline. Statesquad preaches crap like that and we all go numb and blank. We don't run the streets to keep our homes safe. We run the streets to get away from home. We keep the streets clean coz that's where we live. Home's as full of shit as ever.

I call my film Fuck All, coz that's what happens at home. I hate watching it but it's teensquad's favorite. They outvote me every time and set it running.

The film starts on the street facing our fence then goes in through the gate of the house. It's a basic film. I kept the camera running and walked till the five minutes were up.

The gate opens and there's Dad. He made us call him Pop when we were little. I'm Steven Sickel. He was Alan Sickel. Pop Sickel. Popsicle. It was a joke. A pet name. You give names like that to things you love. We grew up and let the name drop. I call him Dad when I call him anything, though it's a lie. That old father son thing's a dead concept. If he's like a Popsicle at all, he's like the stick that runs up through its center.

Dad's in the garden. He's stripped himself down to a pair of baggy shorts. What's on show is a freak. His body's white coz he protects it from the sun, with baggy pants and shirts with sleeves that hang over his wrists and hats with peaks.

Today he's showing off for the camera. He says he's got a six-pack and displays it indoors when he's drunk but what we see are ribs. He's tall, and walks in that loose way skeletons walk in vidgames, the limbs hanging or swinging. His bones should rattle but they don't. He can go about dead silent, letting breath hiss through his teeth sometimes to show he's still living. Grey hairs curl on his white chest, but the hair on his head is shaved with some grey fuzz showing like his head's out of focus. His head's a skull and the skull's grinning. He's wearing round steel spectacles, and boots on his feet. He waves an axe in the air. The muscle flexes in his right arm. His muscles are fine but they don't suit him. He thinks he's lean and fit but he's sick. The muscles don't impress me. I think of em as tumors. He's about to chop down our apple tree.

Dad made money in lumber. He worked in the timber industry, before trees were protected and when they still grew. A statesquad inspector came and drew the white cross on our tree's trunk. It's officially dead. Dad can chop it down. He's got a chainsaw but he's saving all his fuel for some big gig so he raises his old axe. It's his big moment, the last strike of the lumber man, and he wants it caught on film.

Well fuck him. Fuck that. I turn the camera away.

This isn't his film. It's mine.

I pan the garden. It was still a garden in the film, not the mantrap Dad's been making of it since. Everything's dead. Mom stood by the fence once long ago and said the other man's grass is always greener. It was an old saying. It maybe made sense when grass was green and didn't powder under your feet. The grass is brown, flowers and leaves brittle on dry earth, roses in the shape of the sticks and thorns Mom pruned em to when they died. It was her garden. She pressed its last flower, a yellow weed, between the pages of a book, and hasn't come outdoors much since. In the film

I walk the camera to the back garden and her silhouette blots the kitchen window.

I finish the garden and point the camera up at the house. It's a red brick nothing house, dead ivy stuck to the walls, a door and a window downstairs, two windows upstairs, one of em mine and my brother Paul's, the other Mom and Dad's.

Back round the house and in through the front door. We turn right into the front room. Paul's plugged into the console in the corner and doesn't look up. He's not changed much in the last year. His sweat stinks but that doesn't show and if he stood up you could see he's grown, but he stares into the screen as intense as ever.

Mom's in the kitchen with her hands in soapy water. Maybe she thinks it shrinks em. It's funny to see her just a year ago. You wouldn't think she could grow bigger than she was then but she has. She still has a neck in the film. She can turn her head round without turning her whole body. Her walnut mouth is open, her lips forming words as a song comes out. She turns full round when she sees the camera, so she can give a real performance. She was a singer before the swelling started. She stood by a piano and sang songs. It's one of these nonsense songs she's singing now. She says they're in German but who knows. She makes things up.

I don't wait for her to finish. There's no soundtrack in any case, just a pulsing beat someone's added in the editing. I go back through the front room, into the hall, and start up the stairs.

Teensquad stirs. Hands slip down the fronts of their shorts. It's a group thing. A group jerk-off. I don't join in. I don't pretend. I don't like what's coming though I don't mind sneaking glances and the smell of come's a turn-on.

Here's my memory of making the film. Karen's sitting on the floor of her bedroom when I walk in. It's before she got her treadmill, when she was into yoga, so she's dressed in silver spandex and lying on her back. Her arms are to her sides, and her right foot is pressed against her left thigh. Her ginger hair's hanging over her right eye but she opens her left one, stares at me, and tells me to fuck off. I back away slowly. End of movie.

On the vidscreen things are different. Her fifteen year old breasts expand and the spandex melts away. A broad and naked body grows on top of her slight and dressed one. The breasts are so big they flop. The triangle of pubes between her legs isn't ginger like it is but a bush of black. She lifts a finger with bright red nails and beckons the camera closer. We draw near and she licks her finger then slides it down her naked body.

It's a digital remastering. Some image from pornbank's been cloned onto Karen's body. The work's crude. Teensquad wants Karen coz she's the youngest girl on the planet, but they've switched that fifteen-year-old body for this plump and heaving twenty-five year old porn has-been. She fingers herself, they jerk off, everybody comes.

Fuck All's a hit. It's a film about my life and I'm not even in it.

I turn the lights back on while the rest are wiping down, and head out for a solo run.

No-one's banned solo running at night. You do it if you're crazy.

I get crazy sometimes. The air's still but the sun's gone and I can run up a breeze. Go fast enough and runsweat dries off my face.

Old couples grunt. Baby boys wail. Teenagers scream their way out of nightmares. Sounds from houses I pass tear me up sometimes. You can't run from being an empath but you can smudge out the sounds. I set the headphones to runpulse and turn up the volume. My strides grow longer and I reach the edge of town.

Town is lit by solar strips. Orange arcs of light leak out at night. Beyond the town, beyond the fencing, Cromozone blazes.

I take off the headset to hear it. The place has its own pulse. They say they run generators but generators roar and this sound is soft like a heartbeat. The place glows, from the sheds at the outskirts to the towers at the center. It's a halogen glow that gathers in a dome as white as the moon.

This voicecard came from a statesquad unit inside Cromozone. The card came with the teensquad rations. They've made me the teensquad scribe. What happens in teensquad, what happens in my days and nights and thoughts and dreams, anything I want to say about my life, I can say into this card. It's secret, they tell me. The card is encrypted and I must make my unique code. Whatever I write, only I can read. I am scribe and keeper of our teensquad records.

That's a shitline, Cromozone. You're listening to me now as I sit right here and watch you glow. Bet you are. Listen on. I've got no secrets. Secrets are treasures or secrets are guilt.

I've got no treasures. The world gives me nothing.

I've got no guilt. I'm young. It wasn't me who fucked up the planet. Nothing I can do can make things any worse.

I'm scribing for the future. There is no future. So scribing's pointless. Life's pointless.

So scribing is the meaning of life.

Reading this is the most redundant activity in the world.

You'd be better off doing what I'm going to do now.

Run.

Karen's Book

'Mom' – a competition essay by Karen Sickel (age 16), to be judged by the Council of Women

Mom sprogged me and I was a girl so that was nice, then some hours later she sprogged Steven and he was a boy so that was terrific and Dad got drunk on whisky and lost consciousness and when he came round good news was bad news and he wasn't a proud father any more. It didn't last long for him. Other boys got born between me and my twin Steven because Steven's like that, he sees the future and doesn't want any part in it so he took his time coming, but no girl in the world was born after me. I'm the last girl in the world. That makes me a statistic and a freak. It's freakish to be normal in a world that's gone sick. It's sick to be a statistic. I don't like the world but I do like my Mom. She's mad but that's normal and at least she's different. She's mad in her own way.

I don't think Mom wanted kids, at least not with Dad. They were just husband and wife, bitch and buck before that, him telling her she was loud and she telling him he was useless, they had their understanding and they lived their disappointment and that was OK because that's what people did but they weren't yet Mom and Dad. The universe hadn't linked them in that weird unsexy way. Then we two twins came along. We marked triumph and disaster, the beginning and the end.

"What did you ever see in him?" I asked when I was about ten and Mom was still coherent.

"Your Dad loved wood," Mom said. "Other timber merchants don't. He was hands-on, never bought off the Net. We went to furniture outlets together and he stroked wardrobes and chairs like he loved them. He pulled tablecloths off tables when we ate in fancy restaurants, so we could share the bare surface. He counted the knots in spruce ceilings like he was counting stars. The feel of oak made him teary with nostalgia, the grain in walnut made him poetic, mahogany and teak made him speechless though I don't know why. He was passionate about wood. It seemed a bit artistic. I thought he was a homemaker. I thought he was a safe bet." She blinked a bit but no tears came. "I wasn't all wrong," she said. "The house isn't stuffed with cheap plastic. We've got nice things."

If I got to run like Steven runs I'd see stuff like ours, wooden lamps and wooden frames and bedsteads and cabinets made of wood, and stuffing puffing from sofa cushions like it does from ours but the sofa's got arms of ancient elm so we're meant to love it nor chuck it out like normal people do, so the sides of the streets are lined with the stuff that clutters the inside of our house. Mom's not a homemaker. Dad's a collector. He gets the run of the house.

Mom doesn't do homemaker and she doesn't really do Mom. Motherhood started to stink before they tossed out my placenta. People bred for the future, and now there's no future and babies are drains.

Mom was a diva. She's given up now but once upon a time she played Mom as a stage role. When Steven and me were tucked up at night she placed a chair, a wooden chair, between our beds to face us both. A candle on the hickory bedside table cast shadows up from her high cheekbones to darken her eyes and soften the red of her lips. She had a face then like mine is now, with a shape to it that wasn't just a balloon, but older than mine and painted with makeup. Mom dressed for her lullabies in a long white gown and lit the candle for effect. She sang us Brahms's lullaby, which she called *Wiegenlied*.

> Guten Abend, gut Nacht, mit Rosen bedacht,
> Guten Abend, gut Nacht, von Englein bewacht

The door slammed back against the wall and Dad came in.

"I won't have that kind of language in my house!" he said.

That's my first memory of Dad and Mom together. He didn't shout. He just delivered every syllable like a slap round the face. It frightened us. Mom held a silence, just long enough for our fear of Dad to register, then she spoke.

"You remember who pays for this house," she said. "And you remember what pays for it."

We were little and didn't know what they meant or what language was or that Dad was a xenophobic bastard who didn't like German or anything foreign and houses had to be paid for. We knew Dad had frightened us but Mom spoke and that dealt with him. Dad withdrew and we were safe again. We were a family split into two camps. Mom opened her throat wide like the new gulf between Dad and us and her lullaby bloomed into a concert.

Our little brother Paul wasn't family. He was his own thing, a blob of baby. We played with him. We picked him up and turned him around and built him mazes of furniture for him to crawl through and find his own way out. Mom never noticed him much. He was like a stain you got used to. Dad dressed him and bathed him and put him to sleep in his cot and picked him out again. His first word was dada so Dad had someone that talked to him at last. He took Paul's hand and they walked around together, Dad calling him my little mate and looking at us sideways and them giggling like they were in on the joke and the joke was us. They were sad but it was OK because Steven had me and I had him and Mom was in a world of music and herself. When Mom was gone with her bedtime lullaby Steven or me climbed down, crossed the space between the beds, climbed up, and we slept not so much together as around each other.

In the mornings we woke and parted but that wasn't enough for Dad. It wasn't right, he said, a girl and a boy sharing a room like that, it wasn't healthy to be so close. He dragged Steven's bed from our room and put him with Paul in a separate place. I've not slept since. I just coast the night, hearing sounds.

Planes used to fly over our house and their roar was like being with Mom. She moves around slowly but carries the threat of sonic boom. Our house is worth lots because it's a 3 bed detached but Mom needs a stage not a domestic box. We saw her on the stage once, Steven and me. She was dressed in stripes of vertical rainbow and sang more Brahms, a requiem, and the orchestra massed and stroked and struck and blew away like they were playing up some wild ocean yet Mom's voice, the voice of one single woman, just fed on that sound and rose above them all like a high tidal wave.

The hall was packed and silent when the singers and players finished, then everyone rose and shouted and clapped. We stood on our seats and watched Mom gather bouquets into her arms. She stepped away from the orchestra, from the conductor, away from the other singers, and walked into the wings. It was her last concert. Her performance was glorious and fatal. She had risen high on one line of song and simply kept on rising. The orchestra went quiet as she left them behind and they waited for her to return. They tell me a singer can't do that, that it's not allowed. Well she can and she did and it was amazing.

She sang to a program in our front room, sometimes with orchestras but she liked the piano best, the piano sound coming from speakers mounted in special wooden boxes. I worked the controls of the computer, choosing Alfred Brendel or Gerald Moore or Michiko Hichita, always one of those greats from the past, and set Mom's voice to be the dominant factor. As she stretched a line to the close of her breath the pianist would pause in awe and respect. The program attuned to Mom's solo flights and then found the right mix of recorded piano notes and sent waves of cadenzas to chase after her. Mom sang from the heart of the music, not from the score.

Mom's famous in the world beyond our street, and people pay to download her voice. That's what buys the life in our house, the boxes of food that come to the door, the oak-barreled whisky down in Dad's cellar and his illusion of earning a decent wage. I play her songs still. Mom goes solo now, so deep into the land of invention and loss that no computer accompaniment can ever follow her again, but her recorded voice is like a neural link to the power that still floods inside her.

Mom's everything and nothing all at once. She's a raft bobbing lost in an ocean and she's the ocean too. She's being lost and being found both at the same time. It starts off safe when she holds you in her arms then it feels like sinking and drowning. Her womb held me and Steven while she sang us into life. Then the world went sour. The songs drew on old hopes then lost their way.

What do I get from Mom?

She taught me German. She gave me music to analyze and appreciate and she's made me want to keep control. Mom's filled with power and I am too but I try to keep the surge inside.

The Book of

Paul

;O(

101110001010100101010101010101010101010101010101010101001
010101010111101011101001010101101111100010101010101010101
010110010101010010101010101010101010111010101010100101111
001010100001010111010010101111010100001110010010101010110
010101010101010101010110010101010000111101010010101011000
101111010101000110100101010101010101010101010000111001111
010101010100100110010100101010101010101010101111111000111
111101001010010101010010001110010010011011010101010101010
101010100101010101010101010101010101010010110101100101010
10101001001010110101010101000101010001000000001011

110000000000011110100110101111000010001010101001101010101
010101010111000101010110101101010010101010101001010101001
011010100100101001001010101110101010110101010010110111010
101010101010110101010001111010100101101010100101010101100
101010101000111010100110011101001010100101010101010101001
010011110101001111010111001101011100011110001010101010101
001010101011010101101010110101101111010101011001010101001
010100010000101010110010101010010101001010

10100100110000011

Bender's Book

0.01

2.10am

Bugger Dad. I slope in, click shut the gate, wake no-one. Two steps in and the path gives way. An edge collapses inside a hole and I'm over.

- Shut the fuck up, Dad says – Don't move.

I'm on my face, a line of barbed wire stretched under my chest, the blade of a spade pressed against the back of my neck. Dad's been digging again.

- We don't want you hurt, he says – Not more than we have to. I'll hold the wire. Press down with your hands and lift straight off.

He sets down the spade and stands over me, one foot on the wire to either side. I get up. Three cuts. I can feel em, feel where the barbs stuck in. A new shirt fucked.

- What do you say, boy?

His voice is a whine plus a hiss. Licker's on his breath. You don't answer back to Dad. Not when he's in drek mode. The drink turns to fire in his stomach and the fire smokes his brain. You can watch his brain pulsing in his forehead, a little bump that makes his skin throb. On the streets we chase down dreks like him. At home I avoid him.

Now he's got me. That's enough. That should see him happy for the night.

- You think you rule those streets, Steven? You rule nothing. You can't even walk down your own garden path without getting creamed.

We've not got a dog. No-one's got a dog. Dogs are extinct. Dogs are history. Dad's our dog now. We let him out at night.

He's had it though. Shagged out. Soon be time to put him down. My chest will scar. Fuck him.

7.40am

Boards crack as Mom crosses the floor to my bed. She strokes my hair then licks her finger to wipe it round the barbed wire cuts.

- Your Dad been playing with you again? she asks.

You don't answer back to Mom in the mornings. You let her have her way and get it over with. She grips hold of my nipples. I look up. Pimple eyes button nose and walnut mouth on a ball of fat. Moonface, Paul calls her. She's his Mom too but there's no love lost between em. He turns over in the other bed so he can't see her.

Mom nods, the folds creasing in her neck, and stares down. My early-morning hard-on's poling the sheet.

- Lose that, she says - There's enough cock in the world. Tits are what you need. I'll pull em bigger.

Her fingers are so pudgy she gets no grip. Tweek tweek.

She wakes me tomorrow my hair'll be gone. She wants to stroke something she can stroke my dick.

8.30am

I shaved my head. Did it myself. Cut it first so it was jagged on my scalp then took a blade to it. Picked handfuls of ginger hair off the floor and chucked em out the window.

Dad's out there.

It starts, this thing I do. It came on when I was seven. I look out at the present and see the future. I don't know if I just see these things or make em happen. My cut hair falls and looks like flames and I know Dad's going to burn some day soon. I let the pictures run in my head. Lick him, I tell the vision of flames. Fry him. Burn him. Catch light at his ankles and burst out of his skull. I want to hear him pop. I want to smell his fat fry as it spurts out.

Dad's strutting the perimeter, checking his defenses. Crabs go sideways. Snakes slither. Dad struts. Thinks coz he squeezed a last-gasp girl out of his cock he's got hero tattooed on his balls.

Think again Dad. Fire's coming.

It'll shine your bald spot like a sun. Then bubble and burn it black. Black like craters. Your scalp'll be a planet of black craters, black and edged with purple.

I see it. That's what I see coming.

Paul says nothing when he sees my baldie. Just wipes his finger over the cuts on my scalp, sticks the finger in his mouth, and sucks off the blood. It's like the taste sets his mind working. Ping. His eyes widen. He trots off for a piece of clear plastic, wipes his finger over my razor cuts again, and smears the finger clean on the plastic scrap. He's got himself a sample.

- Great, he says – Karen's promised me some from her next curse. I'll do a comparative analysis. The blood of two twins, you and Karen, one a boy just about and one a girl. See if the computer can tell me the difference. Build a program on the results.

- You're fifteen, I remind him – Nearly sixteen. It's time you knew the difference between boys and girls. It doesn't take a computer to do it.

- Fuck off, he says.

Fuck him.

Karen's working her treadmill and sees me through her open door. - Cool, she says – Hang on. I'll shave my hair off and we'll be identical. Twin maggots.

- You wait, I tell her – Fire's coming. The big one. I've seen it. Do you know what happens to redheads like you, with bushes of hair like yours? Whoosh. Your scalp'll burst like a volcano.

She lets the treadmill go idle and stops still to look at me. I don't speak the future as a rule. It freaks people out. The sight of burning Dad's got me excited though. It's the kind of news to cheer Karen up. I don't feel like doing that.

- You seen something? she asks – For real? You see me? Something happen to me?

She knows that's not how it works. I don't see her future, like I don't see mine. We're too linked. The most I can do is lie down and know what she's going through. I experience her nosebleeds. I know when blood's trickling down her inner thigh. I know when girlchat gets hot with fancy and makes her flush. I know when Dad revolts her.

- You have, she insists — You've seen my future and you're not telling.

- Yeah, I say, and make my eyes bulge and my voice go all trancelike. Serves her right for thinking she's special, thinking her future's worth a fuck. I'll save news of Dad's burning for later — I see bad juices bubbling. A body swelling. Clearer, clearer, it's coming through. I see it now. You're as big as Mom. No you're bigger than Mom. This is it. This is ultimate. You're swelling, you're growing. You're becoming the perfect sphere.

- That happens, she warns - That happens to me, maggot head, and you'll know it. I swell like that, I get that round, and I won't stop till I find you. I'll find you and roll you till your guts squeeze out of your nose. I'll roll you till you're flat as dirt. Then I'll piss on you. Piss to water all the weeds that'll grow up through your body.

She ups the notch on her treadmill and starts running.

11.30am

This bed's a cesspit. The sun belts in through the window. I lie here, I leak, I melt. Most of my body's water and most of my water's sweat. What's left of me lies on a sodden mattress.

I get up.

Dad's crashing round the garden, drilling spikes into fenceposts. Fencing us in coz he can't get close to Karen and won't let no fucker else close. He'd have Karen's slit under lock and key if Karen'd stay still for him. She's the meaning of his life, that girl. He keeps looking up from the garden, making bug-eyed longing faces at her window.

Clank clank, the treadmill goes round. Keeping herself trim. Mom says she had a hamster once that did the same job. Hamsters were creatures that looked like mice only fatter and fluffier and stupider. Mice lived in houses and hamsters in cages. Fat lot of good staying trim did hamsters. They went extinct before I was three.

Dad's on his steps. Gloves up to his armpits. Coiling razor wire between two spikes.

- It's my duty, Dad says. He's stuck on what he calls the good old days when men had duties not details. - A man's got a daughter then he's got to take care, he says - Keep her safe till the right time comes. Civilization's counting on it.

Civilization counts on a prick like Dad, it might as well pump artificial intelligence into worms. It might as well burst and be done with it. Karen won't wear out. She could sprog five times and not wear out. Keep her lubed, keep her limber, keep her hot for the big day, that's a good way to treat Karen.

The big day. The right time comes. I'm forcefed so much crap I'm spewing it out myself.

I'm outta here.

10.40pm

Mom's grunting up a wind. Snoring a breeze. Snatches of her breath work under the door and touch my skin.

The electric's off. I'm speaking this by the moon.

I see the face in the moon sometimes. The man in the moon Mom calls it. It looks like Mom. Mom staring down with that puzzled popping vacant look of hers.

Day One's a bummer.

I'm really outta here.

0.02

7.20am

Mom's fingers are sponge. She chews the skin around her nails. She pulls on my tits.

- Tits on boys, she says - God fucked up from the beginning. Dicks on girls, that'd be a miracle. That'd set the world straight. God should pull his finger out and give us a miracle like that.

I look at her....

And I look at Dad....

And I think if they're the sum of a world set straight, they can stick it.

1pm

My teensquad's been on details all morning. Street cleaning. All 24 of us. 6 abreast, 4 rows deep.

Fuck load of use that is. Dreks scarp. Streets go clean before we turn em. The breath of us, all our lungs breathing as one so a wind blows down the road, the stamp of 24 in sinc, no drek'd wait on that. We crunch their bottle litter and steam on.

Who cares. Dreks can spoil a good run. It's like running has a purpose more than running. Sniff the trail of a drek and a run turns into a hunt. Hunting's reaching out of yourself, chasing something more than you've got. When we're running and not hunting we've got everything there is. We're churning power and living inside it.

Then running ends.

The uniforms get piled in a heap by each team. We put on one-size skinner shorts wet with the last kid's crotchsweat. Muscle-strap shirts, olive stained brown. Pumping shoes still pooled in their inners. It gets me, slinking into damp castoffs. Gets us all. Stuffing boners into skinners, we're aching for it.

Then at the end when we peel em off, leave the uniforms in a heap for the next crew, when we put on our own stuff and get set to leave, it's not like we're back where we started. We're changed. Running changes things.

Details are OK.

Put me in charge of drek hunting and I'd change the rules.

They say you can't hunt dreks in their homes. You have to let em step outdoors.

That's what I'd change. I'd say target homedreks first.

Starting with Dad.

Dad's the saddest fuck of a drek there is. He's always dribbling licker of some kind down his throat. He calls it whisky, claims they're malts, but anything will do. Here's what we'd do on our first drek hunt. We'd take him down his cellar. Maybe drag or maybe shove, I haven't thought that bit out. We'd break his bottles. Make him dance barefoot on all the shards. He drinks so much that it fills his veins so when he begs for a drink we'd force him to his knees. He could lap up his own lickered blood from the floor.

9.40

Paul's on the scanner. His head's held in the padded headclamp Mom knitted out of orange wool then stuffed with scraps of foam. It keeps his face stock still so the probe can count every dilation in the pupils of his eyes.

Dad's pressing keys on the IQ card, upping the level of questions that stream across the screen. Figures flash in front of Paul's eyes. The recognition count zips up the scale. Nothing tricks him. He stares a blank at every dud. His pupils dilate at every bingo.

He's good. I've tried. You can't fake scores like that.

Paul snaps off the visor.

- Trig scores, Dad smirks - Off the chart. Genius and rising. Well done Paul. No teensquad streetcleaning for you.

- I'll get the prize? Paul asks.

- Rates like these? You'll get to jerk your load into every tube in the lab. We're going to clone some girls, they may as well be geniuses. It's a new start, boy. A new race. Your sperm's going to seed the next universe.

Dad begets Paul. Paul begets the whole fucking universe.

I get to teensquad.

One more day not worth a repeat.

0.03

4.20pm

Just back from the undertow.

It's good fizz, the undertow. We're the same team as teensquad, only dressed in our own clads. No uniform, no record, no rules, just our own. Our rules are made up, not written down. Till now.

Rule 1

Alcohol stinks. Target dreks.

Rule 2

Women are soft. They can be herded not hurt.

Rule 3

The undertow's a democracy. Mob rules.

Rule 4

When in doubt, take qual.

Rule 5

When things need to stir, run up our own wind.

We came across a drek on the reckie – a loner. No pass-out. Full mind, full of chips, bright burner, turned on.

- Yo! he shouts.

We're hanging not running. Dreks are teensquad stuff. You get scores for a drek in the teensquad rankings so you can't just run em by even when the running's great and you're flying. You don't want a drek when you're in your undertow clads. But you do what you have to do.

- Bumfluffs, he yells.

The drek's shaved his head, but his beard's five days of real stubble. Some of us have beards and some don't. The beards we've got are soft. That's what he's getting at.

- Your heads are so ugly you've swapped em for asses.

You don't challenge a boy's beard. Some shave, some don't, that's it, no sweat. You can't tell a boy by the softness of his beard.

You can't do that. You don't do that. Do that and you make a big mistake.

- Soft beards and soft in the head. Fuck off, bumfluffs. Run back to your mammies. They'll give you a good wipe and put you to bed.

Teensquad or undertow, we're a unit. We share brains. Some of us have em, some don't. Those without, the more brainless ones with the soft beards, are impulsive. It'll be hard to keep em back while we perform our inquo.

The drek goes eye-on-eye with me. They do that, the bright ones. It's a crash choice, zoning me for support. I listen, but it's not my job to spare em. They want a pet empath, they can go clone a dog.

He's bug-eyed, this drek, but the bug eyes shine.

- How old? I ask.

In teensquad we card em for their age, making sure it's official. In undertow we go on instinct. 21's the cut-off for release. Younger than 21 we give em count-down, give em the chance to run for home. Older than 21 and they're ripe for the cull. This one's worn. He's old. I'd guess 23.

He gives no answer.

Malik's our prime examiner. He's the one who scans the evidence, comes up with the questions.

Here's the evidence:

The drek's kneeling like he can't stand.

Six bottles, all wine, are screwed into dry earth in front of him so they stand up.

Evidence is clear.

- You're a drek, Malik announces.

The drek smiles. Most dreks smile like a newborn, a bubble of gas bursting through soft lips. This drek's smile is tight and shows white teeth.

- Yeah, he says.

No dreks admit to being dreks. It's not what they call themselves. I see that now. Too fucking late to see it but I see it now. I was too lazered to see it then.

- You know what we do to dreks?

- I know what you want to do. He drawls like the licker's weighing heavy on his tongue. His lips are wet with it. His voice is trying to sing but there's no music in it. Just a whine - Doubt you can do it. Fucking Bumfluffs. I hoped for better than you.

Malik's no bumfluff. His face is clean. Still, you don't have to listen to crap. He picks up two bottles and smashes one against the other. They're half-full. Wine splashes on Malik's legs and pumps. The drek is wearing an old button shirt. Its white turns red as the splashes hit it. He pulls the shirt open so the buttons burst off. His body's thin, his chest is pale. It's an invite.

- I've analyzed you bumfluffs, he says - In my job. I'm a teensquad analyst. I feed in the figures, feed out the results. I've done it for years, but never met you. Least now I know. There's no future for me, and no future for you. I ran the data and factored you out. Good to meet you, bumfluffs. Good to take you out. Clearing the streets of pricks like you, it's worth a man's life.

He throws aside his shirt, pulls off his pants, and stands there. His little cock's blazing away.

He's a stagey. He's asking for it.

I get it. Malik gets it too. We're mainbrain for the group.

Brain won't stop em now. It's gone too far. It's time for mainbrain to numb itself and go dumb.

- I'm meat, the drek says — Fresh meat. You know what that makes you?

He's calling in the butchers. Malik holds his broken bottles to the sides for others to take. He's prime examiner, not butcher. We've got butchers. They move in. Bottles smash on bottles. The first slice is to the throat. It's ritual. When the throat's gone the drek's safe. No more licker can pass down it. We can drain his body, purify it.

This drek gurgles but never shouts. He turns his head to watch the blood soak into the earth till his eyes glass over. His limbs kick but in spasm not attack.

We don't react. It's a dance of death. It's a show. It's a good way for a drek to go.

I don't slice, examine or butcher. I watch. Watching's my role. I stand close and witness without blinking.

Malik penscans the drek's card at the close.

The drek's ass is still heaving as we leave. His death throes are cute in their way. He got what he wanted.

One less I suppose.

One more for the bodysquad.

This journal's worth a squirt for once. Writing about the drek, it's like he gets to leave a suicide note.

I took a short break. Had to throw up.

We let the drek get to us. He tore us apart. OK, we tore him apart but he started it.

We sliced him coz we could. Coz he got to us. Coz it's easier to go animal than bright. Coz what's a boy meant to do when you call him bumfluff? Grow up?

Killing changes you though.

Do it once and you get the taste.

11pm

Malik's texted a message.

The drek was no drek.

We meet tomorrow, Mal and me. Mainbrain the data.

Sick news. The taste's gone sour.

0.04

12.10pm

I let Malik in through the gate. That's OK so long as it's one at a time. Two visitors counts as mass assembly. One's just a social.

Dad's on us before the gate closes, iron spike in hand.

- Out! he says.

Malik stands still. Dad steps closer and lifts the spike.

- I'm not here to see you, Malik tells him - I'm here for Bender.

The name throws Dad. It's not how he knows me. He gets his focus though. Looks quickly up at Karen's room to check she's not there, flirting, like he thinks she's doing all the time. Then he opens the gate and levels the spike as a barrier that he holds in both hands to push us out on the street.

- I know what you're doing, you little brown wanker, he tells Malik - Checking the layout. You're the scout. First the scout, then the gang. I've been young. I've been horny. I'm no fool. You're after my daughter. Give me time. I'll finish my defenses. No brats will get past me then. Now get out. Both of you. We don't need friends in this house, Steven. It's not a place for friends. If you come back, come back on your own.

- Your Dad's a drek, Malik says - I smelt it on him.

- He drinks, I admit - But he stays home.

- He steps out on the street and he's a drek. He does that, Bender, and we get him. I promise.

- Thanks, Mal, I say.

Your best mate offers to slice your Dad, you've got to thank him. It's a big deal.

He's got the stats on yesterday's case on printout in the back pocket of his shorts. We drop over the garden wall of a burnout from last summer, and make a cushion of brown weeds. Malik sits cross legged and spreads the stats out on his thighs. It's hard to concentrate on the paper. My eyes wander. Dark hair slicks his legs. His skin's from Asia, he says. It's some genetic throwback makes his skin so brown. I like it.

- She must be busting to get out of there, your sister, Malik says - Does he feel her up, that creep of a Dad of yours? Does he stick her one himself? Makes you sick just thinking of it. You should break her loose, Bender. Bring her out on the street. We could all go running. Far away.

- All?

- You, me and the sister.

Dad's sick, but he's not dumb. He smelt Malik right. He was casing our house. Sniffing round Karen.

Malik can have her. I don't mind. I'm not jealous. So long as he has me too.

- So what about the stats? I ask.

Malik snaps his attention back to em.

The facts: Yesterday's hit. The drek who begged for it on the reckie.

Name – Jan Stovok

A Polak or something. I didn't know you got blond Polaks.

Occupation – genebank profiler

Some job. Reading genetic samples. Picking who gets into the gene pool. Guess he'd profiled himself. Ruled himself out of the future.

Age – 25

So well past it.

Blood sample – alcohol count 0%

- It's a mess, Malik says - We sliced a wrong one. He didn't have a drop of licker in him.

- Your mess. You're the prime examiner. You broke the bottles.

- Mess is mess, Bender. We all share in this. You and him? You eyed each other. I saw you. He looked at you, you looked back. You must have seen something.

I see what Malik's getting at and go on conscious flashback. Shit.

The glow. Jan Stovok had an off-white glow. It haloed his whole body.

- You screwup, Bender. You saw it. You saw the glow and never let on. You say I'm prime examiner? What about you? You're the fucking official empath.

- I was checking the physical.

- Screw you. You had the hots. Eye contact, and you gave up control. He wanted to be meat. He made you see him as meat.

- You checked this out?

- Look at the bottom of the stats. His dosage is down there. He was no drek. He's never been a drek. He was on quals. Just like you. Just like me. We sliced him, Bender. Sliced one of our own.

- Did the bodysquad get him?

- We went back. When the results came through. When you were tucked up in bed. Jan Stovok's in the communal dump. He won't be missed. Not for a day or so. We've got his card. His computer clearance code's in there somewhere. Hand it to your brother. See what he can run on it.

- Paul's not into quals.

- Your little brother's got his own highs. Natural neural connections. You've seen blue light zipping from his brain, you said. That's what we need. I'm not saying you can trust him. Just use him.

- When?

- Now.

- You've talked this through? This is a mob rule?

Malik grabs hold of my forearm, I grab hold of his. That's democracy. That's how we show it. It's been talked through. This is a mob rule.

- This is a good place, I say, changing the subject, nodding at the garden - How about a qualrun here sometime, just you and me?

Malik smiles. His eyes glitter, his teeth shine. - Great, he says — Let's do it.

The fucker. He winds me round him with promises like this, every time. I'm happy as I jump the wall. I swear it.

I'm near home before I see I'm taken for a sucker. Malik's not into me like I'm into him. I don't have to be an empath to know that.

10.20pm

Paul's still running Jan Stovok's card. He's goggled up and giggling. That computer flashes mindcontrol or something. He'll be plugged in for hours. We won't get a sane sound out of him till daylight.

What a twisted bustup of a day.

0.05

6.50am

Paul's asleep ... I got up as he came to bed.

I've been to the reckie. Picked up the dirt where Jan Stovok bled. The dust where he died was red. Red from wine, and red from his blood. I stripped down and rubbed the dust over my body. All over. I snorted it. Poked it into my ears. Dusted my hair. Stuffed it into the crack of my ass.

Grit for the day. A way of getting real.

No-one knows I work like this. It's an empath thing I guess. When others fight, what I do looks like standing still, but it takes it out of me. It drains me. Coming to the death scene after, getting naked and rubbing myself in the blood of battle, it's charged me again. Like if the moon's shining I lay down flat on the earth and stare up into it. That charges me too.

There's no handbook for empaths. You just do what seems right.

11.23am

It's girl hour on the computer. Karen's going live with other locked up lastgaspers. Paul hangs out by the back wall, eyes closed, counting down the seconds till Karen's hour is up. Countdown started at 3,600, the moment he was prised away from the keyboard. It'll stop at zero, when girlchat's over and his fingers scrabble back into control. His brain's on automatic clock. He's got second-counting down to precise science.

- Get a life, I tell him.

He hears it. He takes it in. He keeps his eyes shut but answers back.

- Karen's on girlchat. You're fucking off to group session. You both live for time with others like you're nothing on your own. And that's too fucking right. You are nothing on your own. Fuck off and play.

He talks but his brain's still counting. He hasn't missed a beat. His brain's a freakshow. His mouth's on automatic crap. His face is as slack as oatmeal.

- Go fuck yourself, I say.

It's not clever but it's clever enough for Paul. I leave him to his own company. It's what he deserves.

8pm

The buzz is we're all excited.

Some of us are excited so we're all excited. It's a group thing. I popped a qual to feel it.

So how's it feel?

I'm coming down now. My brain's kicking in. So the feeling's got two sides.

Side 1.

The high. So fucking great.

Group tremors get to me. This new excitement, it's not a cut to the chase excitement. It's hope and greed and lust. It's coming up for air in the sewer and spotting the sky. It's thinking age won't come before triumph. It's running somewhere other than circles. There's shit to look forward to so it's living for now but life's crap, so it's sensing there's a moment better than now and it's coming. Eyes open, cogs stir, cocks stir, we grin, it's fucking great.

Side 2.

Coming down.

There's running and fucking and jerking-off and quals. Qual moments like dancing and group tremors. On the highs you forget the downings. The highs lose gloss on the downings. Highs are highs, downings are everything.

10.53pm

Paul lies on top of the bed, playing with himself. He doesn't come. Just arches his back and brings himself to the point of coming again and again.

He's got this thing about wasting seed. Thinks if he builds himself up like this and holds back, he'll have a great store of quality come when statesquad calls. He'll fill a tube right up on first pull and be the wonder of the reprobank.

- What's going on in your brain, dickhead? I ask him – When you close your eyes do you get zapped with streams of numbers? Do your fantasies come in binary code? Is that how it is, nursing hardons for clones they'll never release from a lab?

He opens his eyes, then closes em and starts pulling on himself again.

- You wait, Paul, I tell him – It's not long now. Turn sixteen, they'll shut down your education, you'll be running teensquad like the rest of us.

- No ... fucking ... way, he says.

He misjudges and come shoots up his chest to splatter white gunk on his chin.

- You've seen my scores, he says when he's recovered a bit, talking to the ceiling – Fuck with the system, the system fucks with you. You and your teensquad, you're all fucked. Do you think they need you to chase down dreks? Do you think statesquad couldn't clean every drek out of society in a morning if they wanted? Teensquad's not a job. It's not a role. It's a channel for the aggression of fuckbrains like you. It keeps you dumbucks busy till they're ready for the cull. They keep teensquads going till they choose to wipe em out. That's your future, that's your present, that's your history. Extinction. Me, I'm digital boy. The system transmits my profile as its model. They'll use me, Steven. They have to. See this?

He wipes the edge of his hand along his chest and up to his chin, gathering up his come, and holds it out toward me.

- Scores count. I'm up in the nineties. Hitting perfection for a model citizen. All of that perfection, every scrap of it, is encoded in my sperm. And I'm only fifteen. You wait till I'm sixteen. The legal age of harvesting. I get to sixteen, then you'll see. They'll fill freezers with my spunk. I'll have enough spawn to populate whole cities.

- No chance, I tell him — If they know you that well, their profile's that deep, then they know your flaw. Your genetic flaw.

I've got him now. He wipes his hand dry on the bed and sits up to look at me.

- It's a fatal gene, I explain - You caught it from Dad. Reproduce. Reproduce. Reprofuckinjuice. You've got the breeding gene. That crazy fix on living through offspring instead of through yourself. You'll die of it, Paul. It'll be the end of you.

- It's called being straight, he shoots back — It's called family life.

I laugh. Not for long. Laughter never lasts long. Just a few snorts to show him what a prick he is.

He sighs and lies back again, talking on to the ceiling.

- You won't understand. You can't. You're the tag end of a different species. You, your teensquadders, everyone older than you, you're heading for extinction. You failed. You came to an end. You came at the very end. Karen pops out from Mom's womb as a girl, and the whole universe turns itself inside out. You pop out minutes later as a boy, but those minutes include before and after, you're two twins with an age in between you. No girl's been born since Karen. Only boys have been born since you. Parents got selective. New boys are terminated when they're first scanned. There's no point adding to the problem. Mom and Dad scored high though. I got through. I'm an exception. I'm new wave. I come along in a time of new beginnings.

It's worse than I thought.

- They've got you, I tell him — You've been cruising the message boards. Picking up all their master race shit.

- It's not shit. It's obvious. Earth can't sustain us all. We've got to be selective. We've got to breed the finest from the few. That's my job. I was born to be a breeder. One of the few.

- You know that thing I do? I tell him – When I look into the future and get it right? You know I've never done it for you till now?

I've got him again. He sits up.

- I've never done it, I tell him - coz you've not got one. I've tried. I look into that space where your future should be. It's blank. A total blank. You've not got one, Paul. There's no future for you. This is it. This moment is it. That wank you've just had? It's probably the highlight of your whole fucking life.

- You mean that? he asks.

- I wasn't going to tell you. It seems wrong though, holding it back.

- I've wondered, he says – Wondered till now what side of the divide you were on. Were you the last of those that could have been a girl, or the first of us who had to be boys. Now I know. You can't see it. You really can't. You're blind to the new future.

- You're an atav, I tell him – Your brain's caught in some history program. Future? Wait till you join a teensquad. You'll get it then. On teensquad we're not stuck on breeding. We're a team. We don't need more like us. We're good as we are. When we're gone, we're gone.

Paul looks at me.

It's not compassion. Not even gloating. His eyes dilate. He's taking me in, looking for failings, finding his next step.

The last boy standing. That's what he wants to be. He'll take it that far if he has to.

Lights out.

The downing of another day.

0.06

10am

Once a month. It's worse than her period.

Karen's Day Out.

Dad's been outside since sunrise. He's gone haywire. It used to be enough to stand on his ladder and peer over the fence till her bus was out of sight. Not now. He's been sawing all morning. Soon he'll be hammering. Some new structure's set to rise out of his dust garden.

Mom's singing. It's like she gets to stick her own beak out between the bars on Karen's day out. She flutters her stubby wings, clocks the sky, and opens her throat.

We put up with it. Singing stops her eating for a while.

She makes the songs up as she goes along. These songs aren't German like she used to sing. Some people sang to make people laugh, she says. Joke songs. She leaks tears when she sings though coz people don't laugh any more. She says she sings coz someone has to. The show's not over till the fat lady sings.

> I'm married to a fascist
> My kids have gone berserk
> Being a Mom this day and age
> Is a funny kind of work

The melody's bouncy. It's hard to tell her mood from her face coz you can't read the emotions of a balloon, but I'd guess she's bitter. The song's got more bite than smile.

> It used to be a love thing
> All gooey eyed and sweet
> But far from mother's milk my babes
> Sucked toxins from the teat

Now no-one changes diapers
We live in our own shit
Survival of the meanest
Is the new holy writ

- What'll I wear? Karen asks.

Asking Mom, who's so big she wears drapes. Mom's good though. Her eyes are sharp. The thread quivers between the fat of her fingers but she always slips it through the needle. Then she flattens the fabric under her palms and shifts it round the machine. She doesn't measure. She doesn't draw. She just cuts and sews. It's like the size and shape of Karen is locked inside her head somewhere. Paul and Dad and me could go naked for all she cares. She only makes clothes for Karen. It's all that interests her.

This outfit she's made is simple. Mom's taken two different strips of government issue material, some lightweight synthetic mix, one strip olive green and the other orange. She's cut em into four triangles, two of each color. The orange ones hang front and back from Karen's waist, pointing down. The two olive triangles are attached by points to an orange choker round her neck, her shoulders bare but with one triangle broadening out across her back and the other across her breasts, their remaining points sewn together at her sides.

The outfit suits her. It frees her legs to stride out, and lets air pass around her midriff. I see her modeling it for herself. I'm meant to see. She's left her bedroom door open, knowing she's safe indoors from Dad for a while so long as she can hear him banging around in the garden. She strikes poses in the mirror, clasping her hands behind her head and arching back her body so that her new top rides up a little and exposes the lower rim of the globes of her breasts.

- Why do you bother? It's just girls you're meeting. Why get dressed up for that?

She turns to face me, stares, straightens her top out by flattening her hands across her breasts, but she doesn't answer.

- It's sad. You get all dressed up. You go out. You girls look at each other. Then you all come home again.

- You're sad, she says.

Wit fails her sometimes. Her days out don't do her any good. They give her something to hope for then phut, it's gone. She knows it and it makes her vulnerable. She goes on the defensive. Oh well. She's not at her sharpest but at least I've got her talking.

- What have you got planned? I ask her.

- What's it to you?

- You're going swimming.

- How did you know that?

- In a pool. A blue swimming pool with pink inflatable animals bobbing around on its surface. Some of you will be naked, others in T-shirts.

- You don't know that. You can't see into my future.

- You'll splash and be silly for twenty minutes. For the next fifteen minutes you'll gather in rows in the shallow end and follow an aquarobics program on vidscreen. Then for ninety minutes you have free choice. You can swim lengths, drink soda and chat under the shade of four artificial trees, or sunbathe. After that you'll get on the bus and come home.

- You can't know that. Only us girls know that.

- You get three options for your days out. One is a hike up and down the same hill. Another is team games on a field. The third is swimming. You have to do each of em at least once a year. You've hiked your hill, and you've played your games. Now you girls have the vote, you'll choose swimming. It's always the same.

- You don't know that.

- It'll all be confirmed tomorrow. Cameras are fitted to the sides of the vidscreen at teensquad. The day after the girls' day out, your nude aquarobics sessions are broadcast. We use em as a team-building exercise. We watch and we laugh and we jerk off.

- That's a lie, Steven.

- You know it's not. Why else would the state go to the trouble and expense of herding you together and getting you naked? They sell rights to their nude bathing films all around the world. They trade em for tropical fruits.

- It's a lie, Steven. We're not going swimming. We never go swimming.

- But you told me…

- I lied.

The horn of a bus blared from outside.

- Do you think I'd tell you what we girls do, what we girls talk about? Do you think your tiny prick-focused brain could even begin to think wide enough to imagine your way into a girl's being? Out of my way, pussy breath. I've got to go. We girls have got a revolution to plan.

I guess I was wrong. Karen never was the vulnerable type.

The windows on the bus are all blackened. Women with automatics take up six of the double seats inside, they say. The bus is flanked by eight riders, all of em soldiers, young males hidden under polaroid visors. They're trigger happy, they say. They shoot to kill. For each death on the road, the riders are granted girl privileges. So they say.

That's a shitline. No-one believes it.

No-one's ever fucked with a girlbus either. Some things, like white hot steel and nuclear fallout, you just know not to touch.

- So long, Dad says. He's up his ladder near the fence, set far enough back from the path so Karen isn't tempted to kick it as she passes. He's building a scaffold but it's not firm enough to stand on yet. He speaks soft and stares down. He likes looking at Karen from unconventional angles, hoping for an extra glimpse of flesh.

This new top must disappoint him. It offers no cleavage.

Karen doesn't look at him. A sigh hisses past her teeth, and she smashes the bolts on the front gate with the heel of her hand to free em.

I follow Karen to the girlbus door. I'm meant to be her escort, it's a legal thing when a girl has to step onto a street, but she prefers to use me as her wake. The bus door wheezes open. A whiff like lavender growing through tar steams out, the latest girlscent. Then the door sucks Karen inside and the bus eases off.

Dad's head's looking out from over the fence. He watches the girlbus till it's out of sight. His forehead crinkles up.

- It's a violation, he says - Taking a girl from her home like that. Tempting her with things beyond her grasp.

I know Karen. She's my twin. Day by day we put up with the bastard. Getting out of Dad's grasp once a month, that's what she lives for.

It's something.

Not enough, but it's something.

6.05pm

Karen's come back on schedule.

Dad grabs her as I follow her through the gate. He holds on to her right arm, his fingers digging into the bare flesh, and scans her with his eyes. Checking for damaged goods.

She flushes as red as her hair.

- Mom, she yells.

Mom's not fast, but she swells out the door like a gathering storm and Dad backs off. Karen folds herself into the flesh of Mom's sides.

- I'll put food on the step, Mom says to Dad and me — You can stick in the garden till the sun's down. It's our day. It's the girls' day, the women's day. The house is ours. Stay out.

Paul's inside. Goggles on, phones clamped round his head, he's in another world. He's not worth bothering about. They leave him there, romping the corridors of genebank.

They think him innocent.

He's as innocent as the fetus antichrist floating in a womb.

I lift planks up to Dad. He reaches down, his new scaffold's that high already.

- You run the streets, he explains when I ask what he's up to — Don't think no-one sees. I've got my eye on you, Steven. You and that scum you call mates.

- You can't see round corners, I tell him.

- That gang of yours, you're all pups, he says — You run about the streets, pissing and yapping. You think it's fun, but it's mindless. Soon you'll be dogs. Young dogs sniffing out the scent of bitch on heat. I'm an old dog. I know where you'll all be running to then. Don't think I don't know it. And I'll be ready. I'll be ready for you.

He looks up at Karen's window, checking her out. She's not there so he reaches down for another plank. He's building high so as to see over the loops of razor wire that decorate the top of his fence. Kids have treehouses. Dad's grown up. He's building himself a control tower.

Great. Home's a concentration camp. Dad's the madman at the gates.

One more day in the construction of hell.

0.07

9.48am

The family that eats together, stays together, Mom says.

It sounds like a curse. It's enough to set us all fasting.

She sings Jesus wants me for a sunbeam while whisking up stacks of pancakes. It's her Sunday tradition. The pancakes are like leather. It's as close as we come to eating meat in the house.

Dad's chosen the topic for the day's forced conversation. Every scientist in every country all over the world is working out why no more female animals are born. It's all that science does, and they're getting nowhere. Dad's decided to do em all a favor. He reckons we can crack the problem over a family breakfast.

- It's the heat, Dad says, sitting down at the kitchen table.

He jumps round newstext on TV when he's not building his defenses or running his futures, and reads the daily science forecasts. He plays his pet theory.

- Global warming. It's the heat that does it. Every damn fool knows that. Alligator eggs don't start off sexed. They heat up, they turn male. They cool down, they turn female. It's the same with the goddam world.

He's got two fridges and a freezer stacked in the cellar, and enough fuel to run a generator through the electric lapses over nine months. He plans to isolate Karen in a chillroom once her eggs are fertilized and then keep her that way. At least that's my guess of his plans when I warp through the slush in that fucked-up mind of his.

- It's the spermcount, Karen counters. She doesn't want to be chilled. She's passing the buck. It's a girlpower thing, saying girls have got the power even though they're obsolete, and men are fuckups even though they swarm the planet. The logic's warped but she's got a point – Men's spermcount's low. They don't pump it out like they used to. The game's all over before the sperm even reaches the egg.

- You never had an egg, Paul, Mom says. Her newstext settings only deliver food items — Common as muck in boxes of twelve they used to be. I made pancakes so light you could chew em with your tongue. They've cloned some hens, they say. Not breeders, but layers. You'll get to eat an egg before I die, Paul. That's my hope. I'm going to start saving.

Paul takes his turn. No-one gets to leave the Sunday table till we've all said something.

- A boy I'm schooled with, we share the same surftime, his Dad saw a pike, he says.

- He still goes fishing? Dad asks.

- He sits by the river where he used to fish. Next time though he's taking his tackle. That pike'll need a few tricks to see the week out. Everyone's onto it now.

- It's a rumor, Dad says - That pike story comes up in my chatrooms every other month.

- You know the thing about rumors? Karen says — They can be true. It's not just low spermcounts. Men's erectile potential is down. I read a survey. It seems images that got men going now leave em flaccid.

- You're obsessed, I tell her — All you can think about is dick.

- Look who's talking, she answers back — If I choose to get pregnant, I'll leave it to science. At least their inserts don't go limp.

We chew on the pancakes while everyone waits. It's my turn to say something constructive. Slagging off Karen won't do. This ordeal won't end till I've said something related to Dad's chosen topic.

- I saw a sparrow yesterday, I lie.

Sparrows are childhood memories.

- Liar, Karen says — That's a lie. It doesn't count. Tell us something real. Tell us why your shoes were covered in blood when you got back yesterday.

- I heard it singing. In a garden. I climbed onto a wall and there it was. In a tree.

- Liar, Karen says - Birds sing before mating. There's nothing to mate with.

- Not so, Paul says.

I look at him. He's not helping me out. Not consciously. He just loves showing off, knowing more than we do.

- Sparrows can live forty-five years. It's not seventeen years since the last female birds were born, so go figure. Owls, they live eighty years.

I've said my piece. No need to add that every bird got blasted out of the sky years ago. Paul's a cipher. He'll never get a grip on the ways of the world.

- He sees the meanest sparrow fall, Mom adds — Jesus does.

That's the Sunday moment we've been waiting for.

Leaving halfeaten pancakes on our plates, we push back our chairs and stand up.

Mom stays sitting, tears running down her cheeks. The cheeks are smiling somewhere deep beneath their discs of fat. I bet they are. She looks forward to these Sunday mornings. They're what get her through the week.

Dad goes down his cellar. Mom won't have him crashing round the garden on Sunday mornings, building his traps and his barricades. On a Sunday he can leave our defenses to the Lord.

He shuts the cellar door to mute his sawing and his hammering. Officially he's at work when he's down there, but that just means looking up occasionally and triggering a few moves on a keyboard. He's got his own screen scrolling numbers all the time. From being a lumber man he switched to trading virtual wood. It's called trading in futures. Trading in futures is like dinosaurs trading in evolution. We've got no futures but people still pay for em. People as dinobrained as Dad. They trade saplings before they sprout. They trade acorns and fir cones in bulk. They trade forests as they die, so they can harvest the prime moment between death and rotting.

Dad says he's good at it because he knows trees.

He doesn't know trees. He knows killing trees.

He says it's the same thing. He's making a killing. Where do I think our family credits come from? Do the scum I run around with eat the quality we do? You don't get brand names on food cans for nothing. You don't even get labels. He's tracking a consignment of corned beef as we speak. It's just about the last supply of edible meatstuff in the public domain. It'll cost him an acre of Brazil if he gets it, and he's talking a can not a carton.

He can stuff his corned beef. I'd sooner chew bark than be grateful.

8.30pm

Sundays are a day of breast. That's a joke. Jokes made people laugh when people still laughed. We don't laugh now but we snort sometimes.

They say dreks hang out in churchyards on Sundays. They lean themselves against gravestones and drink and drink till they pass out in the shadow of stone. We're on different details so we don't seek em out. Slicing dreks belongs to weekdays. Sundays are for personal community service. On Sundays we round up women.

That's the joke. The day of breast joke. It's the day we round up women,

Rounding up women is hard work. We use a special reinforced cart. Fold down steps lead up to a platform surrounded by iron bars. The cart has solid rubber wheels. Families call in when one of their women goes missing and we wheel our cart to the neighborhood. It's semi-official business. It keeps us busy. Every teensquad has an undertow community quota to fulfill.

- She's big, they say in the official reports they log when one goes missing – A big woman. Vast. Legs like trees. Face like a beachball. Answers to the name of Mom.

One description fits all.

In their own homes these women make some kind of sense. Out on the streets all they want to do is talk. They stare and they talk. Their brains migrate to some distant past when bodies were normal and life went on.

– Up you go, we tell em, and steer em into the carts.

They stare through the bars and often sing as we steer em through the streets, not made-up songs like Mom's but songs they used to dance to when they were young enough and slight enough to see their feet. One of us guides the front and at least three of us push from the rear.

Malik conducts the inquo as we move. He puts obvious questions, ones such women are used to. Address? How many kids? What ages and sexes? Who's at home?

He taps the answers into his pad. If answers match a map comes up, the woman's house marked in red. Click on it and the family details come up on screen. We arrive, let her out the cart, see how she gains entry to her home, log that in, and off we go.

We had lousy luck today. We found us a whalewoman wrapped in light blue sheets. She gave her address in a high girlie voice. Malik tapped it in, and did a search. He had to flip back decades. The street she says she lives in burnt down thirty years ago.

She's a regress.

It meant the long haul to the pound. It's five years since dogs were there and they've put beds in the cages to make it homely. I doubt the blue sheet woman is reclaimable. No credible family would certify her useful. She'll be hauled off to the stacks inside a week.

We get a merit blip for the find. It brings our teensquad up to 28th in the city league. None of us gives a shit.

At the end of the details we drop the uniforms to the floor, get into our own kit, and go home.

That's it. The seventh day of my first week as scribe. I'll sleep, wake up, and it's Monday again.

What a crap prospect.

0.08

7.17am

Spent the night on qual.

The usual effects.

I've been watching Paul a while, blue light fizzing from his head. My heart opened toward the little freak. Sleep flutters his lips, and now I'm in the downing. The sun beats at the window to start another heatblast day. Love will never touch Paul. It'll burn up in his atmosphere.

On qual you don't love for return. You love for love's sake. That's the difference between qual and non-qual.

A frenzy of dots, all different colors, like a cosmos of stars, filled the room in the night. I watched em shift in and out of shapes. Then they licked into flames, blue with orange flashes. People ran through em. Not silhouettes coz it was all 3D, these were more like ghosts waiting for substance. They ran through the flames and I watched them ignite. Their screams were notes of beautiful music.

It'll happen. Not long now. The day's so close I can almost smell it. The fire that's coming will end my world.

8.40pm

The downing ended. I got of sick of watching Paul sleep. I crossed the room, grabbed hold of his pudgy white shoulder, and shook him awake.

- You've had Jan Stovok's genebank card too long, I told him – The undertow needs feedback. We're getting bored with waiting. Give em something back or they'll chop you in.

The freak blinked up at me and took notice. I was talking computers. It's the one thing that gets him going. He put on his shorts, wandered downstairs, and plugged himself in. He was ready for us by noon. Teensquad got cancelled so I fetched him. We convened as undertow and sat in a circle in the dust of a cleared house with Paul at the center. He spouted, we listened.

- I'll talk frank, he starts off – I'm not one of you, never will be, never want to be. You all get by on state qual handouts. You think it makes you elite.

- Qual gives hope, Runt says. Sandyhaired Runt, he's our teensquad's smallest and quickest. He parrots statesquad slogans like dogma. We listen to him when we're starting to doubt.

- Qual is medicine, Paul tells us – You get it on prescription coz we know you're sick.

Paul's not one for false endearments. The group stirs. They don't have to put up with shit like that. They'll silence him. They'll slice his tongue first then cut up the rest of his body while he squirms.

- Thanks for this, he says, and tosses Jan Stovok's card onto the ground – I used it to key myself in with full access. Stovok worked homebase. So long as his brain turns up onscreen every day his body won't be missed. I've routed myself through his terminal. I am Stovok's brain.

Malik flicks his knife.

- Brains don't work without a body, he says.

- Stovok was good, Paul goes on - His brain's got lots of responsibilities. One of em is assembling statesquad's hitlist every day. Now I'm keyed in as Stovok's brain, the fun of that hitlist falls to me. It's finalized at noon. You're all on tomorrow's list. You'll be collected and no doubt eliminated by 2 tomorrow unless I get back to revise it. It's the cull for you lot.

Paul's the image of Dad now I look at him. The blond hair's gone grey in Dad but it sticks out in the same places. They've both got the same high cheeks, long jaw and sunken eyes. Dad wears retro steel specs, Paul's had laser correction, but the pupils have the same intense blue-green bulge. Paul's as close to my looks as an alien.

- So you'd best listen and let me walk, Paul adds – Tomorrow's list won't change till I find good reason to change it. Stovok took qual.

- You know that? Malik asks, and flashes a look at me.

- It's your fault that I know it, Malik, Paul tells him - Don't blame Steven. For prime examiner of your teensquad you're far too free with texting. I've read every message you've sent these past weeks. Stovok took one dose of qual. His first and his last. His eyes would have given him away on his next sign-on. He's been eliminating qual squads one by one. You think you rise to 28th in the league just by merit blips? Squads above and below you are gone. Wiped out. I guess Stovok stepped from his screen to take a look from the inside for once. He wanted to be a fucking empath, just like Steven. Guess it got to him. One qual trip like that, you're fused. Individuality's gone. Plug yourself back into the mainframe, you carry the qual virus with you. You caught him on a downing. You gave him the only way out he had. The next day's hitlist for statesquad was programmed. You were it. All of you. Jan Stovok wasn't going alone. He was taking his new qual buddies with him.

- But we're here, Runt says.

- I made it. Got through with twenty minutes to spare. Won you a reprieve. That's the best I can do without a reason. Names on that list get bedded deeper in the system than I can reach. I can't pull qualheads off it without good cause. I've checked your gene data. Stovok was right. You're worthless. The future needs nothing from you. You should all be zeroed. Any ideas? Any thoughts on how to save yourselves?

Undertow once had an idea that Paul was bright. We gave him the card so he could work wonders for us. I watch that old idea start to shift. Thanks for the warning, the shift says. Since you've sent death coming you can show us the way. You can die. Let's slice the freak and split. Let's go outlaw.

Give a thought like that one more minute to develop, and it expresses itself. Paul will get to watch his tongue flap on the ground.

- The gene data, I say — You have access to our gene data. So change it.

Malik, the other part of mainbrain, catches on.

- You can do that? he asks.

- Ask empath here, Paul says.

I read his eyes.

- He can do it, I say — But he's got terms.

- He lives, Malik says, fingering his knife - That's the deal. He changes our data, we don't slice him.

- A little gratitude, Paul suggests - You gave me the card. You want something out of it for yourselves? Here's what you're getting. You're getting your lives. When you sign on at your terminal, when the monitor scans you, your location won't be beamed straight to statesquad's elimination troop. Your food rations, your qual rations, they'll keep on coming. OK, I agree, your lives aren't worth much but they're all I've got to give. I'm giving you your lives. Be thankful for small mercies.

- How do we know? Malik asks - You do nothing, then we're all taken. What have you got to lose?

- I'm doing you a favor. A favor this big deserves one in return. You owe me one. That's all I've got to lose. The big favor you all owe me some day.

He walks away. No-one stops him. We each take a half dose of qual.

Not enough for a high.

Just enough to ease the urge to slice the freak.

10.38pm

Paul's reading this. (Fuck you Paul!)

He says wherever I hide it he'll find it. I won't hide this bit.

This is the flaw in Paul. He can't just know stuff. He has to tell you what stuff he knows.

It's a tactic, he says. Tell the enemy their own secrets and they have to start again. Their capacity's limited. Keep on doing it, keep on telling em their own secrets, and the enemy runs out of ideas.

Soon they're running on empty. You're cruising where you want, no problem.

I don't get him. I don't get YOU Paul! You're so bright yet you're so dim. You're a cold star. YOUR ideas aren't worth a toss. OUR ideas keep you alive. Take em away and you're dead.

For all your ideas, one idea saved you today. My idea. The idea to keep you alive to change the genebank data. That idea.

We're the force in the world, Paul. Don't prig yourself. Ideas don't stay brilliant when your brain pulps the dirt.

0.09

I'm speaking this to card and that's how it stays. No downloads to screen from now on. Paul's in bed across the room, his eyes closed like he's sleeping, listening. This is the big fuck you, Paul. No text, Paul. Just voiceprints on card. I'm making records, Paul. The record of our lives. A record you'll never break into. A record you'll never change.

This is a favor, little bro. You flash round the console till everything's hacked, nothing's secret, nothing's secure. This is a taste of how the rest of us live. Your life's stored away somewhere. Your life as I tell it. On card. Here in my pocket. You've no access. No control.

Sweat it, Paul.

Sweat it.

The wooden hatch that opens onto the attic's gone. Karen's door's open. She sees me standing on the landing, looking up, and calls me in.

- Is that creepy or what? she asks.

We stand at the window. Dad's outside twenty feet away, at the same height as us. He's finished his scaffold by the gate and built a box on top of it. Four thin posts at its corners hold the hatch door over his head for shade. He's holding binoculars to his face and looking down the street.

- You see I've moved my bed?

Karen likes to lie in bed and look up at the sky. Now the bed's set along the outer wall, so her feet are under the window.

- I opened my eyes this morning and there's Dad, staring back, perving at me through his binos. What do you reckon, Steven? Is this as good as it gets? A girl gets to lie in bed and be her father's jerkoff material?

- Dad's just sick, I tell her.

- You're sick. Mom's sick. Paul's sick. The whole fucking planet's sick. Sick's not so special. Dad's beyond sick. He's to sick what malaria is to a mosquito. Sick's just his vector. He uses it to get around, then lays his poison inside you. He's a one-man plague. A fly that spews on you before chewing you up. A viral overload. He comes upstairs to the bathroom, his breath slinks under the door and feels me up. I can't breathe when he's near. He snatches all the air and makes it foul, leaves me choking. See this?

She lifts her pillow. A paper knife is under it, with a thin brass blade and a serpent's head made of ebony for a handle.

- It's Dad's. Some relic. I got it from his desk. If he ever comes in and lays a finger on me, it's going through his heart.

I don't know what to say. You should get out more? Go make yourself some friends? Find yourself something to do? None of those old things work anymore.

- Why wait? I say — Knife him if you want to. Forget about his heart. Go for his throat. How good's the knife? You want me to sharpen it for you?

- Where's that get me?

- You're studying medicine. You've got to get beyond the computer course some day. Dad can be your first cadaver. He's got those fridges in the cellar. We'll turn em on, make the place down there into a mortuary. Take out his eyes first. We'll pop em on stalks and poke em at the screen for his biofeedback time. That way his supplies keep coming while you cut up his body. See that trench?

I nod outside. A spade's leaning against a fence near where a short line of Dad's latest defense project is dug into the earth. He means the trench to spread right round the garden, but the few feet he's dug are already big enough to serve our plans.

- Bit by bit, as you grow tired of him, as his lungs and his kidneys and his heart and his balls start to rot, we'll bury him out there. Dad thinks he's digging a trench? He's digging his own grave.

We laugh.

Not enough for him to hear.

He spins round though. Adjusts his binos so he's staring straight into our faces. Lowers em so we see his eyes.

It's like a chill fills the room. We both shiver.

- Fucking Dad, Karen says.

She scuttles into the corner of the bed where cushions are stacked high, pulls in her knees and hugs em.

She'll be back in the bathroom soon. She'll turn on the spigot till the water sputters brown, then sit in the inch of it in the bottom of the tub and scrub and scrub herself. Dad's stare does that. He strips you naked then ferrets through the guts and bones. It soils you, having a man like that look you over.

I look around her room. It's good what she's done. No chair, just these cushions on the bed. No furniture, just clothes hung on lines of string stretched along one wall. She's taken paints to the other clear wall and made a picture of it. Blue sky with white clouds is at the back, and a pale orange sun with yellow rays. Then come a series of low hills, green all the way up. In front of em are flowers, tiny at the back but the ones at the front as tall as me. You have to look through em, like looking out through a forest. One tree stands on the left, another on the right. Their leaves are different shapes but their branches join to frame the whole picture in an arch, and in the middle the leaves are mixed.

Karen's dreams aren't like this. Her dreams aren't soft landscapes of rivers and sunshine and green hills. Her dreams are nightmares. I hear her tossing and moaning in the night. She's painted a picture of the dream she wants to have.

- It won't be long, I tell her – You'll get away.

She looks at me. She's Dad's daughter alright. Her looks can burn as much as his do.

- How? she asks – Paul's way? My IQ goes so strato they take me in for their breeding program?

- It's one way. Cut down on the girlchat, plug in for more stat sessions, your scores would shoot up.

- Like you? Paul's checked your stats record. You were stellar. Then you fell. A researcher's been assigned to your apathy count, he tells me. They're about to brand you a niyo. Someone whose not giving a fuck is so total it's dangerous. You know that?

It's news to me.

- What's to believe in? I ask her — We're all dying out. If now's no good, fuck the future.

- Paul said you were plotting. Flames and chaos and the end, he said. He read it in your journal.

- Not plotting. I just see it. See it coming.

Karen's holds her stare.

- If this big moment comes don't you dare leave me behind, she says — You do that and I'll get you. I swear I'll come and I'll get you. That's when you'll know the end has really come.

Paul comes off the motherboard for us to sign in. It's Family Biofeedback time. First though he makes me look at the screen. It shows a page of data.

- I don't do data, I tell him.

- It's you, he answers — This is your genemap.

- You've changed the data?

- No need. So far as I can see, you're near perfect. I've just scanned the essentials. Disease immunity, right handedness, clear color perception, they're all here.

- The others? The rest of the undertow? You've altered their genemaps?

- Don't know that I can. Don't know that I want to.

- So I'm saved? Is that what you're saying? The others are still on the statesquad list for today?

- You think I still get around on that dead guy's card? He signed in at 2pm daily. How am I going to eyeball my way onto his system? The moment the screen doesn't flash his eyes on his biofeedback appointment, the system goes alert. I'd be locoed in an instant. System shutdown and statesquad at the gate.

- So there's no hitlist?

- Today? Who knows. I've no access. The morning I had access, you were on that day's list. It went by teensquad so I saved you all. Put another teensquad in your place.

- Why?

- The truth? Ignorance. I don't know what happens after statesquad swoops. Are you eliminated? Put into service? Your own gene data's so good maybe they just harvest you in some way. One thing I know. No-one who's chosen for the breeding program has a sibling who's disappeared. My scores are good. Family data might not boost me much, but it doesn't drag me down. I'm going to make it. I'm about to make it. So long as your disappearance doesn't impact my score.

- So it's your self-preservation that keeps me alive?

- You're an empath. You think you know about people and you don't even know the golden rule of politics.

- Which is?

- Self-preservation.

Karen hooks the repospecs behind her ears, sets em on the bridge of her nose, and stares dry-eyed at the screen. As statesquad's eagle symbol swells to fill the screen you're supposed to stare into its eyes, but that's just a control thing. Stare at the wall and the repospecs would still go about their business, reaping info from your pupils and sucking it back through the wires.

Karen turns her body away even while her head is still. She hates being catalogued.

Mom's eyes stream tears when her turn comes. She appreciates attention even from a machine. The eagle blinks slowly to show her session's over and she wipes the tears from her cheeks with the flesh of her fingers.

Dad comes in from his lookout post, takes off his own specs to make room for the repo ones, glares the necessary second after login, and paces out again.

My turn.

The screen flashes goggles-alert on login. I put the goggles on instead of the specs and try and think blank while the machine strobes me. The pulses feel a bit like qual, white light that collects in my head till it's all there is.

Paul snaps the goggles from my head as the signal fades.

- Great, he says – I've got a headfuck for a brother. So warped he registers for mindwipe.

He puts on the visor and reconnects. His program scrolls across the screen and his pupils dilate. He's pushing up his score. Thinks he's earning his way out of here. He'll stay logged on till we drag him off to feed him.

I get the qual, but Paul's the one who's hooked.

Air crosses the landing. I feel it on my skin. I get up to check it out.

Karen's door's open. Her window's open too, and she's standing in front of it. Her back's to me and she's looking out.

- It's Dad and me, she explains - We're psyching each other.

It's more than just Dad and her. I come up behind her and look out. The undertow's on the far side of the street. They're just standing, one line of em, and looking up.

They're studying Karen.

It's the best they've ever seen her.

She does nothing special, just stands there in her lilac halter and silver shorts, but her top holds the weight of her breasts and her arms are so white they're naked. I get to see her as the others do, just for this moment. We run so much, stripped down in the sun, the flesh we get to see is brown. White flesh like this is when shorts are hooked down. It's a come-on.

She's not posing. She's just standing, naked white arms and hands by her side. She's not even looking at the gang.

Her stare is fixed on Dad.

He's on lookout. His head turns through half degrees, like a surveillance camera. He's scanning the line, taking in every detail of every boy.

I know his game. He'll play em back, every image he's trapped in this sunlight, as he works the wood and metal in the cellar. He calls it picturing the enemy.

His head continues its sweep. He stops when he connects with Karen's stare.

She does well to keep standing. Dad's stares are killers. She holds the stare till he breaks it. Dad climbs down the ladder, then Karen turns her attention to the undertow.

Each of em shifts. I watch em shuffle and try to stand taller.

We hear Dad coming. He slams the front door and runs up the stairs. I step to one side but Karen doesn't move. Dad crosses the room in two strides. Taking hold of her right shoulder he shoves.

Karen doesn't fall. She springs her legs somehow, and leaps. Her feet land on her bed. The cushions muffle the blow of her body against the wall.

Dad points at the door.

- Out! he says to me – Carry a message to that scum of yours. Tell em next time they line up for me, I'll pick em off one by one.

- Steven stays, Karen says – No-one lays a hand on me, Dad. No-one. Steven stays till you're out my door. I'm not getting locked in with a perv.

Dad stops still. He's not good with words till he's had a chance to build up steam. Now Karen's gone for the insult he's out of his depth. He'll have to get physical.

Karen's crouched near the end of her bed. The fingers of her right hand are under her pillow. I know what's there.

- Mom! I yell.

A yell as loud as that, Mom's on her way.

- You're right, I tell Dad – Karen's out of control. Leave her be. Mom'll sort her. I'll go, Dad. I'll follow you downstairs. I'll clear the street like you want. I'll tell em what you said.

Mom was in her room. Coming up the stairs she'd have been ten minutes. Coming from her room she just had to roll off the bed and follow the momentum. She's squeezing through the door as I finish speaking.

- Who wants me? she asks.

I point to Karen. Dad has to move to one side to give Mom a direct path.

- My baby? Mom says. She holds out her arms and heads for Karen's bed.

The room's crowded.

Dad leaves. I follow and shut the door. Dad pauses at the top of the stairs.

- That scum? he says — Tell em nothing. I don't need you running messages for me. Run with scum and you fall with scum. Is that clear, Steven?

He takes off his specs. They magnify his eyes so as he takes em off his eyes go smaller but the effect is worse without em. Like that tunnel you see through the wrong end of binos. You get to glimpse inside him, and see through to the dark bubbles of his thoughts.

He steps into his and Mom's room and slams the door.

- You're the scum! I shout against the door.

It's a stupid shout. It's pathetic. I know that much. Stupid to show he's hurt me. Still, I'm young. The world's fucked. Clever's got us nowhere so why not give stupid a run.

I join the undertow outside.

- Sorry we just turned up, with no warning, Malik explains - We had to cut you out of textloop. We didn't want Paul crunching the info.

Runt comes running. It takes a minute, then he's got the breath to talk.

- Seems safe, he says - I did the rounds of four houses. No sign of statesquad.

- Looks like you've still got a brother, Malik says – If one of us goes, Bender, if just one of us gets taken, then Paul's meat. Tell him that will you?

We drift off together, down to the end of the street.

That's new. We never drift. We always move in one body. Something's snapped. We don't hold together like we used to.

- Paul's winning, I tell Malik – That talk of statesquad coming for us? It convinced us. We're targets. Look at us. Forget statesquad. If a teensquad finds us like this … if a drekgang finds us … they'll rip us. Runt squawked his news back there and the fire went out. No-one wanted to be safe.

- We wanted to gut Paul, Malik says – The prick.

I start running. Just slow. Malik keeps pace.

- I see it, Mal. Paul, statesquad, flames, the end, I see it all. It's set. You've changed. You're all targets now. The power's leaked out of you.

- What's all this you stuff? It's us, Bender. Not you. Don't say you. It's us.

- You cut me out of textloop.

- We had to. This once. Paul's intercepting your text.

- I don't blame you. I'm just saying. You cut me out. It changes things.

I loosen up. Take longer strides. We've got thirty minutes till teensquad. I've got to run things out of my system before I submit to probe.

Malik shuts up. He keeps pace.

This'll do. Mainbrain on the run.

The undertow's behind us. They're running, but it's not like it was. We're not one body.

They're more like a tail.

0.10

Mom never came in to pull on my tits this morning.

Can't say I miss it.

I get Dad instead. He sits on the bed and strokes a hand round my face.

- Smooth, he says — You've got cheeks as smooth as your ass. Know what I should do? Know what a good father should do? Slash em. Your face and your ass. I should slash em both.

He's got my attention. Not for the words, not for the stink of drink on his breath, I'd have squirmed away from both. But the blade of a cutthroat is poised just below my left eye.

He thinks it through.

- Bender? That what they call you? Bend for em do you, Steven? You've got a girl's face. Girl's eyes. Girlie ways. I watch you move. It's taunting, Steven. You slink about like you're asking for it. I should slash you. Add a few rolls of scar tissue to those cheeks. Your ass too. Even that scum you hang with would think twice about poling you then. It's not cruel Steven. It's kind. Like an oldtime surgeon. Cutting the flesh to save the life.

I watch his eyes. They're close. I see the blood vessels like veins in granite. I keep my own eyes steady so that narrow spot in the center of his can stab home. It's a trick. Dad's proud of how much he can hurt with his eyes. Let him stare without flaring back. Make moon eyes to his sun, so he burns you up. He likes that. Let him win with his eyes.

It hurts inside but there's no blood.

His eyes go milky. They break from mine and glance to the side. He's searching up a memory.

- This razor? he says — It passes down from father to son. Oldest son.

As he says the last bit he looks across to where Paul lies in the other bed. I can't look myself, the razor's got me pinned, but I know little bro's enjoying the show.

- It was my father's. And his. And his. And his.

He pulls the blade from my face and stands up. I sit up and lean against the wall. It's not good to lie down in front of Dad too long. He gets ideas enough without that.

- You like it? he says, and snaps the blade back into its handle.

The blade's silver and smells like he's just polished it. The handle's ivory turned yellow. He lets it drop on the bed.

- It's your life, he says – You make that clear enough. Why should I save you? Cut your own cheeks.

- You're just giving him that? Paul asks from across the room.

- You want it?

- Why not? I'll get on the program. If I don't breed daughters I'll get sons. Steve's the end of the line, Dad. I'm the beginning. Give the razor to me. I'll pass it on.

Dad stares at him till he shuts up. He's having a good morning with his eyes.

- Bring the razor downstairs, he tells me – Show your mother. She'll be pleased. She was worried we had nothing to give you.

- She's downstairs already?

- She got up in the night. She's been making you a picnic. A family picnic for you and Karen. That's why I came up. To call you down.

He makes to leave the room but stops by the door.

- By the way, he says – Happy birthday.

A sheet of blue plastic covers the patch of dead garden outside the back door. Wedges of tomato inside thick slices of bread make up the plate of sandwiches. Five plastic tumblers are full of lemonade. A cake is in the middle. It's round and much of its top has collapsed into a hole. White icing is running down the sides and onto the plate. Seventeen tiny candles are stuck in round the edge.

The others are in place. Dad on the left, Paul on the right, and Mom facing the kitchen door. She's lowered herself to a cushion, her legs stuck out in front.

Karen and me wait inside till the candles are lit, then Mom calls. This is our big entrance. We're the birthday twins.

Mom claps in delight when we come through the door. Her spongy hands don't make much sound. She's wearing her favorite drapes, white cotton splashed with orange poppies, her toenails a matching shade. Karen must have painted em. Mom's worked hard. The scraps on the table are a feast. Her family's all around her on a special day. For Mom, this is as good as life gets. Her eyeliner streaks tears of joy.

It's a toss-up between heartbreaking and pitiful.

- Happy Birthday To You! Mom sings.

The others open their mouths but no sound comes out. Mom carries on to the end. She's heavy but her voice is light. She's never minded singing on her own. It must be a wonder that a bit of her, that voice of hers, can still float so easily.

We kneel down. I blow out the left side of the candles, Karen the right. Some sugar icing blows off the cake and onto the blue plastic. That's OK. There's more left. The icing's as thick as my thumb.

A knife waits on the edge of the cake plate.

- Cut and make a wish, Mom says – Don't tell us. Keep it secret so it'll come true.

Karen and me share a grip on the knife. It slips through the icing then I press down hard to cut through the cake to the plate.

- Make this my last birthday picnic ever, I wish.

We leave the knife in the cake. No-one wants to eat a slice. We each pick up a sandwich to keep our mouths busy.

- Look! Paul says.

Bread and tomato skin foam out of his mouth but no-one complains. We look to where he's pointing. We don't look in the sky much as a rule. The sky is a smudge of blue and grey burnt by the sun that starts at dawn and ends at dusk with only insects to fly across it. It's not much to look at.

This is different.

- A whirlwind? Dad says.

It has that shape, a long cone with twists, but the point of it is dark and high above the earth like a copter. The darkness of the tip fades through grey and brown as its tail broadens.

- It's electric? Dad says – An electric storm?

He says that coz the thing hums, more low than high. It's not a clean note, more like lots of sounds glued together.

Paul glugs.

He likes to have the answer to things. He's beaten us to it again. The explanation of the whirlwind in the sky is coming out of his mouth. The mouth's still full and open. Pulped bread and tomato lies in a mound on his tongue, and it's moving. The white and the red of the food show through a shifting wash of black.

His mouth is filled with flies.

Outriders.

We've seen em onscreen. Outriders come first, landing on anything with life in it. Then the screen goes dark. The swarm arrives. It encrusts the camera lens on landing, and everything else.

I look down.

The birthday cake isn't white any more. It's black. Flies have even filled the hole, mounting each other to give the cake an even top.

The hum is loud now. I look up. The sky is gone. The cone is passing overhead, its tail dropping like exhaust.

- Inside! Dad yells.

He's long legged. In three strides he's at the back door. It swings open and slams closed. His face peers out through the glass, waving at us to hurry, then fades to nothing as more of the swarm drops in.

Paul is choking. He grabs hold of my leg, crawling toward the house, and passes out of sight in the insect fog. I hear him knock. The door opens, then slams closed again.

Karen's not running. She's kneeling in front of Mom.

I open my mouth to shout at em both, get em moving. Flies stream in and coat the roof of my mouth. I feel em crawl down my throat.

No shouting.

Karen's sweeping Mom's face with her hands. There's no point. Mom's not looking. Her eyes are closed. Karen's must be too. I watch for a moment. It's like skimming your hand through water. The insects flow over Karen's skin, coating the hand and fingers, and cover Mom's face again the instant the sweeping's past.

Insects march across my eyeballs.

I screw my own eyes shut.

They're in my nose. One breath and they stuff my nostrils.

I grab Karen. Grope for Mom's right arm and direct Karen to it. Karen's smart. She catches on. I grab Mom's left arm and we pull.

It's like the insects are behind her, giving her flight. One tug and Mom rises on her straight legs and is on her feet. We move with her. I tread through the cake as we race on. Insects squelch and crunch under my bare feet. We collide with the door. It opens and we squeeze Mom through, then follow.

Dad slams it after us.

- Idiots, he says. He's slashing at the air with a towel – You were too slow. You've brought em in with you.

Karen grabs the towel from him, wipes her own head clear so she can see, then starts clearing Mom. She presses hard so some insects squash against Mom's skin and hair. Others fly and crawl away.

Mom wipes her hands clean against each other, then reaches up a finger to pick her nose. It comes out of the nostril black.

Karen gives in. She stares at Mom's finger then lets her hand drop to her sides. She stands still and cries. Mom opens her arms, steps forward, and hugs her daughter close.

The bodies of the two women tremble together.

I think we all feel cold.

0.11

Dad points Mom's face at the screen and clicks through the family album.

- Look! You're smiling! he says – That was a happy day!

I take a look.

- You think Mom's cracked? I ask him.

- Shut it, Steven. We're looking for happy times, your Mom and me. That's got nothing to do with you.

- Great, Dad, I tell him – The first happy time you come up with is a lie. That's not a picture of Mom. It's Karen.

- What's that? Dad asks, and touches the screen.

It's part of the background to the picture.

- The sea.

- You ever been to the sea?

- Course not. They wired it off years ago. That doesn't mean I don't know what it looks like.

- You know so much. You tell me this is a picture of Karen. So tell me how come she's standing on a beach? Out in the open? Full grown? In a bikini? How long would a girl last in the open dressed like that? She wouldn't be smiling. She wouldn't be innocent. She'd be stripped and raped and left as a carcass on the sand.

- It's digitally remastered, I try - Karen's head on a pin-up's body transposed to some beach setting.

Dad smirks.

I hate that.

When he knows he's right, 100% right, he won't even argue. Just smirks.

- Imagine that, Alison, he says to Mom - Your own son mistakes you for his sister. You see it? That same red hair. Same cheekbones. Same teeth. You're trim but not skinny, the pair of you. Same full breasts. Amazing how those tiny green straps held em in place. It's you, love. Take a look. This is you. My flaming beauty.

Mom doesn't look. She's facing the right way but she takes nothing in. Dad watches as her top lip trembles though. He's stirred her. Something's happening.

Her mouth opens.

Then a song comes out. It's a different tune to normal. It's got highs and lows and pauses and it's not bouncy. More like one of those German songs she used to sing.

> Angels have wings
> And so do flies
> They pour in through my nose
> And out through my eyes

- Stop it, Alison, Dad says – Talk sense.

> God's in the details
> The little one said
> As roaches and dragonflies
> Streamed from her head

- I'll call em, Dad threatens – Call the authorities and certify.

> With bugs up my nostrils
> And ants for a brain
> I feel great comfort
> I am quite sane

- Snap out of it, Alison. We've cleaned up. The swarm's gone. You weren't the only one, you know. We all got mobbed. You got first shot of the bathwater. Karen scrubbed you. You're clean. They're gone. No more insects, Alison. No more insect songs, OK? It's over.

My bones creak like crickets
I've got praying mantis knees
My hair grows in thickets
That hum with wild bees

Mom's alert now. Her eyes start moving about the room, looking into the high corners. She hears her own voice. Now she wants sight of it.

Butterflies mate
Inside my throat
I open my mouth
And out they float

Dad's eyes water. He lifts his specs and wipes em with his hand. That's it. Mom's wrung a drop of emotion out of him. Now he's dry as bone. He puts on the headset, flicks down the mike, and types in the security number.

- Statesquad, he says, when the system answers. He gives Mom's details.
Name.
Address.
Age.
Number
- No longer certifiable for family use, he says.
The screen goes blank. Mom sings another verse.

At night my belly
Becomes a moon
It attracts the moths
They'll fill me soon

On the screen an eagle takes flight from a mountaintop. It's the symbol of statesquad. Their response follows. It's no debate. Dad's certified her as useless, so statesquad's obliged to take her in. They've sent a collection time and list of legal terms that form the access agreement. Dad codes in his acceptance without reading the details.

- It's for the best, Dad says, and strokes Mom's head - I'll tell Karen to pack your things. We've got till tomorrow to have you ready.

So this is Mom's last day at home. Give it two shakes, the day'll turn into a family occasion.

I head out the door.

I should name em. All the bits of us that make teensquad run.

There are 24 of us. Malik, Runt and me, the three I've named already, plus 21.

Mug, face squashed since birth, so no-one knows he's smiling.

Flint, solid and flashy, first to strike.

Scud, not subtle but effective. Deploying him's like flinging a hammer.

Ozie, short for ozone, as round as a boy can get on veggies, farts are his biggest weapon.

Skink. A slight thing, stands still, studies, blinks slow then darts.

Furbo, olive skin and dark eyes. A schemer.

Skel, grey eyes on a stick, skin on bone. He rattles in the wind.

Ant, wire haired, black, pinched waist, big head, just like an ant. Knock him down, he won't stay down.

Soo, good old Soo. He's got a chiselhead, 200 solid pounds, no fat, muscle for brain.

Kes, beaked nose, flopping fringe, flaps his arms to show he's keen, runs and dives at the smell of blood.

Mulch. His jaw droops, his mouth gapes, his bug eyes look small even when they stare. He hangs out in the middle of whatever's going on.

Pint's the same size as Runt but only half the speed on a short dash.

Jok. Black hair, blue eyes, high cheeks, wide shoulders. He's a poser, or maybe just good to look at.

Roach's eyes look two ways at once. His legs bend at angles when he runs.

Toast goes pink and sweats at runspeed. The skin flakes when he stops and dries out. He rasps it loose with his hand, and goes white again.

Melba's blond. If you want a kid sister, he's as close as you'll get. His voice won't break and his sweat smells sweet. The air's cool when you run behind him.

Zeb just is. His head nods or shakes, both of em slow, but he never speaks. His head's shaved. You can watch the pulse beat in his thick brow.

Saf knows nothing or everything, fuck knows which. He's browner than Malik, close to real dark, runs with long strides and talks in long words.

Parch is bloodless. His eyes are bruised, his skin is white, his body's stooped, his elbows are knots. He could run through walls and not slow down.

Rasp can lick his nose with his tongue. That's his best feature. His ginger hair grows in tufts. His nose runs as well as he does.

Dome's head is shaved and shiny, his cheeks are fat with smiles. He's our secret weapon. There's nothing upsets people like a smiler does.

That's my teensquad.

I get to teensquad depot early, check available quadrants onscreen, and click on the farthest. That quadrant shows the perimeter roads of Cromozone. It's available for duty. I punch in our code to accept the quadrant for our teensquad, then wait for the others to turn up.

- We've got to shake loose, I tell em as they come in. Cromozone and its perimeter flashes onscreen. They don't know I selected it. It doesn't matter. All duties are the same. — We get to kick town dust and hit the country a bit.

The others nod, strip down from their clads, and pull on the uniforms. Yesterday's swarm got to each of us in some way. We need action. We need a good run.

- Tell me about running, I say to Malik, coz it's clear we're all eager for it — When we've not been running, I feel lousy. When I feel lousy, running helps. Is running like a cure for life? An antidote?

- It's a condition, he answers — Like living and dying.

He's right. The first strides, the first blocks, and I feel it. We're coming back to health. Coming back into the ultimate. Coming back into condition.

That's the way with running. Forget it and the whole world falls apart. Run and you're back online.

Teensquad has maxims. They're not rules. They're just things we've noticed between us.

One squad, twenty-four breaths.

We're on our own. That's the meaning of that maxim number one. We're on our own but that's no small thing. Twenty-four breaths is a turbo charge.

Don't dumb down, wise up.

We cover all the bases. When it's time to strike, don't analyze. Strike. When it's time to analyze, don't slash out, think it through. Every individual's got weaknesses. Together we have no weaknesses. Quick, bright, paranoid, reckless, dumb, sazzy, heavy, brutal, gentle, kind, savage, charming, demented, they're all qualities. We've got em all. When each one of us takes over at the right time, that's wising up.

One breaks, all break.

We've got to act together. Teensquad is like one body. If your foot starts doing its own thing, going its own way, it doesn't matter how good the rest of you feels, you're fucked.

Same formation, different shapes.

We run like a river in a dry land. We adapt to what we meet, we cut new channels, but we stay a river. We shift our shape but we stay together.

Direction gets you there.

Direction's the key, not the destination. If we keep moving, if we run as one steady and surging body, who gives a fuck where we end up. We're *it*. We're supreme.

More hate, less speed.

Life's crap. The planet's fucked. People are sick. That all goes when we're running. Let hate in and strength leaks out. Life's crap, we're great. We've got to love what we are. Running on love makes us deadly.

Deal with what's in front of you.

The seas are winning. They're rising. They're chewing the edges off land and swallowing em down. They don't think about it. They just go on and on. Waves roll across oceans. The best waves die with a crash on the land. As they die, they win. That's the best we can be. A wave powering toward a crash.

They're good maxims. We fixed em on qual.

Off qual, maxims like that, they fuck your head in. There's no sense in em. I've just tried to explain em. It's made my head hurt.

On qual, they light up the world.

We wait as we run. Then it comes. It's a group thing. One moment it's effort, our bodies thumping down heavy on empty streets. Then the switch happens. Zing. The change. We're not *on* the street. We *are* the street. Zing, just that switch, and an animal's born. Twenty-three times bigger than any one of us, this animal's made up of every one of us. Inside a power like that, we surge. It's a qual thing without qual. It's running. The trip of animal running.

Soo's thick skull, Malik's dark golden thighs, Roach's roving eyes, Dome's smiles, Rasp's tongue, my brain, every bit of each of us is part of one beast.

It's a roar.

Dad says not everything's bad. Not everything's worse. Big-bellied planes don't shake the house like they did. One passed overhead as they tugged me out of Mom's womb. It's one of his favorite stories. He tells it like a sick joke.

It's the boy, Alison, that's what I said, he says, and goes on — Then I shouted it coz the plane overhead was so loud. IT'S THE BOY! Karen was lying stunned and bloody in the corner, she got to be beautiful but you wouldn't have guessed it then, and your Mom managed a laugh so loud you could hear it as the plane came in to land. We'd had the scan so we knew you were a boy and we were so pig ignorant that made us happy. Imagine that. We were happy to have you. Happy you made it through safe.

He laughs his inward laugh, sucking the air in like he's choking.

No-one laughed for Paul. Mom roared as loud as an airplane but that was with pain and the skies were empty by then. Planes were one of the first things they stopped. They carried viruses. They poisoned the air. And nowhere was worth flying to. Everywhere was fucked.

Dad still calls Cromozone by its old name when he's lickered up. Heathrow, he calls it. It was an airport. The biggest in the world.

Heathrow. They think they mean something when they say it. They think they're conjuring something up into existence just by using the name. They're not. They're lying. The meaning's dead. All their words, all their memories, are lies. All their meaning is dead.

Cromozone wasn't there when planes flew. The towers are too big. You didn't build big towers on airports. Now we don't need airports. We need Cromozone.

The Towers are black. Three of em stand in the empty land inside the ring of fence. They're big but their shadows are bigger. The shadows move around and nearly touch the town but not quite. Things that big, as big as the Towers, they pull you in like a planet. At night, when the electric's off, I lie in bed and hear the place humming. I ran out there one night, on my own. The place is white like the moon in its halogen glow.

That's where we're running.

The motto over teensquad depot's door says SAVING STREETS FOR THE NEW WORLD ORDER.

We're sixteen, seventeen. We're the new world. It's our order. Nothing worth having is kept behind a fence. We're it. We're now.

I think that sometimes.

I think it now, as I speak this.

On teensquad I forget it. My brain's on limb control. I'm thinking with Mulch's lungs, Saf's liver, Pint's guts. We're one heart racing. Everything we want is through that fence. We're here to keep it safe.

Dust is the future. It's lying to be kicked. We take it in turns to run at the front. From up there our soles are the first to spit the dust. For forty paces we stare into burnt sky. The dust is on the ground and not in the air, our lungs are clear. Then two from the back peel round the sides and take their place at the front.

The pace is steady, and teensquad is trained up to it. No-one's too slow to spurt from back to front and lead the way for a time. Slipping back through the running body of teensquad is running to the sound of tread. Sun leaks through to light the runner in front but nothing else is seen. You're held and running inside teensquad's dustbody, running inside the skin of a cloud, coasting inside run's thunder.

Roads from the city are great places for dust, thick coats of it blowing off fields. I'm at the rear, Malik at my side, seven runbeats short of sliding round the side and to the front.

- Twelve.

The shout goes up from the front and starts its step back toward us, a pace at a time.

- Eleven.

- Ten.

We slow by fractions at each shout, shortening the pace.

- Two, the pair in front of us shouts out.

- One, shout Malik and me with the next step.

And we stop.

The dust drops around us. Sweat starts to streak our bodies clean. A view appears. Malik moves left, I move right, till teensquad's stretched as one line along an asphalt road. Dust is thinner here. This is the perimeter track round Cromozone. The fence of the complex is in front of us.

The outer fence is studded with camera posts. Motors whir as the cameras scan us. Beyond that fence is dust as neat and crazed as any gardening by Dad. Two rows of tank traps throw crisp shadows from their concrete spurs. Razor wire is coiled between each trap, and the dust around and between em lies smooth and even. No-one rakes here. Gardens like this are kept smooth by blowers. Dad would wet himself for a smooth dust garden as fine as this. Smooth dust gardens are mined just a fingernail's depth beneath the surface. A rabbit's paw would set em off if rabbits still existed. Now the only thing that lives here is insects. A scorpion squats on the dust just outside the tank trap's shadow. It's a piece of overkill thrown into the mix by nature. No-one's going to tread as far as its sting.

Cameras keep on whirring and teensquad catches breath. We start to hear sounds beyond the camera motors. Big ones first. Technosheds hulk near the center of the complex and solarpumps thrash and echo from powerhuts to their sides. I trace a different sound that's closer. It's the buzz of an AC that sticks through the wall of the security hut just beyond the secondary fence. It drops moisture that splashes on dust, magicking up a patch of mud where two pumpkins swell.

Drip. Drip. Drip.

The sound of water on dust tunes us in. We hear smaller sounds behind em, distant and thin.

A squawk. A squeal. A grunt.

We played a game in undertow once. We read out the words

for the sounds that animals used to make, then tried to make em ourselves. First we tried for a grunt, then we tried for a squeal, then we mixed our grunt and our squeal to make a squawk.

It was just playing, just guessing. Nothing squawks now. Well Runt maybe but no real animal. That's what we thought, only now we hear a grunt, a squeal, then a squawk.

- Animals, Malik says from the far left – You hear em, Bender? You see em? It's the animals they speak of. They're cloning em.

I look around the fence for electric speakers but don't find em. The sounds come from further off. The technosheds have blank walls with no windows, but the nearest one has skylights with solar flaps drawn high to catch the sun. Wind plays sound through dead trees but no dead trees stand here. The air is still. The sounds we hear are floating out from inside the technoshed.

- A cow, I tell the rest of teensquad. One of my jobs as empath and mainbrain and now scribe is putting stuff into words that don't make sense without em. Teensquad's ears are keen for the news. I talk in my normal voice and we all draw an image in our minds, a picture that matches the word and sound of cow as close as we can get.

I carry on, naming sounds.

- A calf. They've cloned a calf. And chicken. That was a chicken. A pig. Piglets. And that one? That sound there? It's a lamb.

I don't see em. I don't see animals. I see the future when it hits me but I don't see through walls. Instead I conjure pictures from scraps of sound that float across the dust, and fill em out as words. I make up a story. Teensquad's stopped, we're breathless, we need a story. A story's something to run for.

- The stories are true. They've cloned em. Cloned animals. They've opened the skylights to show the animals the sun. The sun naturalizes em, it gives em a sense of day and night. Cromozone is conditioning its clones for release. Out here we're doing the business for em. Our teensquad's running the world clean. Clean enough for clone release.

We listen harder.

- Hear that?

Fuck knows what's really going on inside the sheds. New machines I'll never see grind different noises I'll never make out. Inside the sheds is their world, the world of Cromozone. This is our world, the world of the streets. We kick dust into the shape of clouds. That's what we have to work on. We make up the rest as we go along.

- A song, I say. I'm making it up, I don't hear a song, but lying's alright when you mean it as a treat – Do you hear it now? Do you hear who's singing it? Five little girls are singing a song. La la la la la la la. They've done it. Cromozone's cloned us some little singing girls.

I close my eyes to concentrate and hum the girls' tune. Others along the line pick it up from my voice, their eyes closed and pictures forming. I lead the hum through a final verse and then we go silent. We've each formed a picture of girls in our head and now I guess we're watching what they do.

My own girls look like infant Karens and stand there doing nothing. I've not got much imagination when it comes to girls. Girls aren't my fantasy. I open my eyes and look right.

Furbo's into it. His favorite street-talk tells of girlcloning in Cromozone. Street-talk calls Cromozone the cloning ground for all species on Earth. Everything female will stem from here, and from that we'll all be reborn. Furbo's brain is running hot. It flashes him his dreamgirls, strips em to bare flesh and makes em stretch while his tongue licks the dryness from his lips.

- You hear that? Dome asks. He's near shouting with excitement. His question chases out all pictures and sounds from teensquad heads. The others open their eyes.

- It's fish, Dome says – I hear em. I hear fish. They're cloning fish.

Water drips from the AC onto the pumpkins. The drip's affected

Dome's brain, leading it from water to river to fish. We laugh. The laugh shakes our bodies loose. That's enough of standing. We're ready to run again.

- Perimeter duty, Malik says – Teensquad divides. We go two ways, one left, one right. We'll circle the compound and reunite here for homerun.

One strategy on qual is to surround any strangeness and feel our way inside it. Malik's idea's a good one. It's fitting qual strategy to our running. We'll divide in two but we'll still be one body running. By circling Cromozone, we can come to know it.

It's so good an idea we've no need to discuss it. We head off. Malik leads left, I lead right. The teensquad whole is now two halves. Two halves running as one.

Each of the technosheds is thirty strides wide, and I guess ten times that long. None have windows but solar skylights reach up from pitched roofs. Twenty technosheds form spokes in one vast wheel that fills the compound. Some stories tell of these sheds acting as vents for multilevels of subterranean activity, while the hub of the complex provides an aerial platform. That hub consists of three buildings, each with three sides, each of em 23 storeys high. These are the Towers. The Stacks. The Towers are the parts that go up while the Stacks go underground.

These Stacks'll be Mom's home from tomorrow.

I doubt Mom'll get a window. They say new arrivals are lodged in vaults. Women are hoisted up to viewing floors for a glimpse of the sky once a day. It helps keeps em natural, clocking the sun like that. To turn full natural and breed girls again, women have got to stay on a natural track. That's what they say.

Mom'll come and be a vegetable here.

You don't get more natural than a vegetable.

I hear the thud of Malik's half of teensquad hitting the asphalt. Their tread's in exact timing with our own. Two halves, one whole.

We keep to fence-side, Malik's half takes dust side, and we pass. We're halfway round and keep on running. This outer road's like a racetrack with nothing to give pause.

Few tracks cross the dust of Cromozone. Heat's driven the main passage of traffic into ventilated shafts below ground. This outer asphalt track of our patrol is matched by a rail on the inner boundary. A black-screened squadcar distorts us in reflection as it passes then comes to a halt at the base of a sentry point. Eight towers mark the perimeter, eight sets of faces look out from behind the reflective glass of the capsules that crown each one. That's as close as Cromozone comes to showing us a human side. Any relief details that have arrived in the squadcar wait till we've run past before showing themselves.

Cromozone's strange. We surround it to know it. As mainbrain and empath I look for the words as my legs stretch round its perimeter. Cromozone's creeping up on me. I'm coming to know it like I come to know a lie. They sell Cromozone as hope. Hope's a lie. Hope's a jerkoff. Here's what Cromohope is. It's like spunk jerked off in a dark room. One of a billion sperm lights up. It wags its tail and jets after life. It's on the high road to big time. Watch me now, the jerked sperm squeals. The future's here and it's mine.

Then the spunk lands on a towel. It lands on dust. It dries to crust.

That's how Cromozone feels inside. Cromozone's not about hope. It's a billion billion to one chance of hope. We won't survive on hope like that.

We don't do hope. We run.

We keep on running. We keep steady, no slacking. The tread of the teensquad's counter-circles is still in time when we meet at the junction of our road. We merge two abreast, kicking up the thicker dust, counting to forty in our share of the lead till two run in from the rear and Malik and me drop back to run inside teensquad's dustbody. The cloud we kick up smothers Cromozone behind us. I snort at the dust and breathe easier.

- You got any qual? I ask Malik, as we slip uniforms to the floor.

- You want to do our qualrun? he asks back.

Sweat coats him. He smells good. Halfway rancid halfway sweet. His black hair's slick against his skull. The light in the depot's old neon, left over from when it was a dried food store, as flat and dull as light gets, but even that drops shadows over his muscles and bones. Malik naked. I see him like this, and life looks good for a minute. It's got potential.

A qualrun starts on streets, then zeroes in on skin. I want to zero in on Malik's skin.

- Tomorrow, I say – I get my own tabs tomorrow. We can do our qualrun tomorrow night. I'll be ready tomorrow, Mal. I'll need you then. Tonight I just need two tabs. Home use.

He tilts his head. It's a question.

- Cromozone, I tell him – We explored it today. Mom's off there tomorrow. I'll explore her as she goes. If she takes a tab and I take a tab, we'll be sharing one mind. As she goes inside, we go inside. Deep inside Cromozone.

He pulls on his shorts, reaches into the back pocket, and brings out two tabs. They lay on his palm, then he closes em into a fist.

- I'll keep em, he says – We'll drop em at nine. See you in the garden of that burnout near you.

I tilt my head. It's a question, the way he's just taught me.

- Inside Cromozone. Inside your Mom. That's not deep, Bender, he says - That's a black hole. You need practice to run out of a hole like that.

He leans forward and licks his tongue across my throat, collecting the taste of me. It's the way best friends say goodbye.

I lick him back.

His salt on my tongue.

I won't eat. Not till the qual.

My hunger tastes too good.

0.12

It's hard to keep this in order.

I'll go back to last night and tell it as it happens.

9pm

I jumped the wall into the burnout's garden and met Malik.

His Dad's a doctor. Mal's picked up the doctor's bedside manner.

- Qualrun, he says – It's a bond. We don't run. Qual does the running. You get that?

I nod. It's that bedside manner thing he puts on. Those long lashes, those brown eyes fixed on mine, the voice gone soft and smooth. He can play doctor all he likes, I'll play patient.

- So no hiding, he says – Qual can't take us where we don't want to go. We don't run if we resist. We'll just go round and round. Just like every fucking day, Bender. Round and round and round and round. Qual's our way out of the everyday. That what you want?

I nod again.

- Me too, he says – The two of us, Bender, we can make this great. You know how?

I don't bother to think. The patient role's fine by me. I shake my head.

- Solo qualruns? he says – We do em. They're fun, but they're fantasy. Mass qualruns, it's tribal dancing, you get excited, you jump up and down, you think you're ripping through to something new, the dance ends, and where are you? Nowhere. Round and round and round and round. Two of us running though, two like us, that's what qual was made for. We can't spin off into fantasy. We've got to check in. Check the other one's coming with us. Check he's not got somewhere better to go. We're checking, adjusting, all the time. Neither of us goes where he would have gone alone. We both get to go somewhere new. You see that?

- We take it in turns to lead, I say.

He pushes his hands back through his hair and shakes his head.

It seems I'm wrong.

- It's more side by side, I try again – Joined at the hip. Two pairs of legs but only one way to go. It's qual that leads us, qual decides. No-one leads, no-one follows. It's wild, we share it. It's a thrill, we share it. Black white light dark fast slow loud quiet we share it. Shitscared or heavens open we share it.

- That's it! Mal joins in – Qual opens us up, opens us right up so we've nothing left to hide. That's everything we can be, everywhere we can go. That's our potential, Bender. Put yours and mine together, that's wild. You see how wild that is? We've got some real running to do to explore all of that.

The doctor patient game's been dropped. We're both just grinning.

He takes out the tabs and hands one over. We open our mouths. He places his tab on my tongue. I place mine on his. We sit a moment, then both stand up. Already we're working together without words. We climb the wall and drop down into the street.

It's the best way to start a qualrun. You run with the body till the qualrun turns inside.

We run blocks side by side, stride for stride till that first tremble of perception near the roof of the skull. Qual is sneaking into effect.

We climb back over the wall and lie still.

Pattern on entry ... the cosmos arranged as points of light. Red green orange purple blue against black sky. Join up the dots for a picture of existence.

Then whoosh. Every point bursts and scatters into a cosmos of further points. And again. And again. All lights fuse into one dazzle of silver light that flies against us.

We hear its rush.

It's not the roar of wind. It's the emptying of vacuum.

I see nothing of Mal, just light to both sides, but I turn my head and we're there. Not our bodies but the spangle of two shadows. I feel him turn in step with me and we pounce, leap with hands held high to dive upon the shadows. They tail behind us as we stream into silence, riding as one with the speed of light, floating as wide as space.

No bodies now, just a memory of bodies. A memory of Mal and me stretching limbs around the block, lungs breathing in rhythm, looking ahead with two pairs of eyes. We float as space with the memory of body, our four eyes set to see all things at once.

One way jungle. We fly as a swarm through a swelter of leaves.

One way sea. It scatters as bubbles as we race beneath the surface.

One way city. Our passing sends trash spiraling round highrises.

One way … Sound returns as the distant beat of a vast drum. All ways are this way now, the swallowing of light in a crimson black, space confined by a narrow tube that jets us round smooth corners.

Pulsing.

Pulsing.

- Bender

He speaks it soft and the name's like a breeze, coating my body as it shapes me.

I move a finger. It meets a hair growing on Malik's wrist. The hair's as wide as a trunk. I stroke the width and height of its bark, smooth as blood, then travel down to where it plunges its roots into the earth of his skin.

- Bender. End it Bender. Come back. Come back now.

He strokes his hands through my hair, across my face, down my body, bringing me back.

- You scared me, he says.

Night's passed. Mal's on his back, looking up to where daylight smudges the sky.

My head is on his chest, my ear pressed to the flesh above his heart. The heart pumps steady. I feel the tremble of his voice as he speaks.

- What do they give you, Bender? It's not qual. Qual like I know it's what I gave you just now. You went wild on it, like a little kid. That was your first time. You've never been in qualspace before. You were out there. Way out there. Way out of control. I couldn't break it. Snap. Flash. You kept to no line. You were all places at once. Then you got stuck. Dark, warm, wet. Where was that?

- Blood, I tell him — We were one cell two cells who knows same thing. We were what blood feels as it shifts round the bloodstream.

- What bloodstream? he asks.

It's a no sense question. Like asking which Bender am I.

- There's only one, I tell him.

I move my head so it's flat on his stomach, and look up at the sky. I love the soft round of his stomach. Colors are seeping in with the daylight now. The full drab display of daytime.

- I've got to go, I say — They'll be preparing Mom for the off.

- You think you'll miss her? he asks.

- Like pickled onions miss vinegar. We'll bump against each other more when she's gone. Bruise more easily.

- You don't have to stay, he says — Leave. Bring Karen. Bring her here. Run off.

- Go outlaw? I ask.

- Not outlaw, he says — Outlaw's their word. Leave their system, fuck their words.

- Who needs Karen? I ask.

- The system'll get her if we don't, Mal says.

- It's welcome, I say.

I sit up. There's no point staying for talk about Karen.

- You got a qual for Mom? I ask.

- You still want to do that? Your Mom goes into orbit like you, she'll blot out the sun.

I hold out my hand. He sits up and hands me a tab.

- It's my last, he says — You get yours this morning. Bring em straight round when your Mom's gone. I'll be here.

- You want another qualrun? Straight off?

- It won't happen, he says — Whatever they give you it's not qual. You don't handle it, Bender. It smashes you. If I hadn't pulled you back you'd still be out there. No, they're giving you something special. Something different. I want to try it.

His skin's the same oriental brown as ever but the sheen's gone out of it. He looks pale beneath.

- I'll bring you food, I say.

- No need. Just a tab. Wake me when you get here.

He lies on his side and curls himself ready for sleep. I lick my tongue across his throat in goodbye.

Mom's lodged on the sofa when I get home. Karen's worked on her already, brushed her hair and tied it back in a red ribbon. Mom's eyes are open and they blink, as she sweats. Those are the signs of life in the woman.

Dad shouts at me when I step into the room.

- Been peddling your ass? he says — Your mother's last night in the family home and you spend it fagging around those streets of yours. She's been here all night. Sitting up. Waiting. Worrying herself sick. Did you give her a thought? Just one thought of your mother while you were parting those cheeks of yours? Like hell you did. Come to bed, Alison, I told her, he's not worth it. Would she budge? Would she hell. Look at her. See what you've done, Steven.

He stares right into Mom's eyes.

- Look Alison, he says, pointing a finger across the room at me — He's home. You can snap out of it now.

Karen comes through from the kitchen with a plateful of toast.

- Dad's lying, she says — Mom's not waiting for you Steven. No-one is. None of us gives a shit what you get up to. It's you she hates, Dad. It's you who's throwing her out of home. Isn't that right, Mom? You didn't go to bed because you can't bear to spend another minute with this creep of a husband of yours?

She leans forward and looks close into Mom's eyes the way Dad's just done.

- That's right, Karen says – I can read Mom through her eyes like a book. She despises you for what you've done to her.

- Keep on like this, Karen, Dad says - and I'll have statesquad haul you both off in the same van.

He steps close so Karen flinches, but all he does is swipe two slices of toast from her plate.

Paul breaks away from his monitor in the corner for a slice of his own and takes it back to his console.

I take some too. Mom says it's not the same without the proper butter you got from cows but the smell of toast like the smell of fried onions is one thing can't have changed much.

Dad swallows his mouthful before speaking – he's got a hangup about manners. He waves his remaining toast at a picture of Mom in a frame above the fireplace. He must have put it up in the night. It's a printout of the one by the sea, the one where she looks like Karen.

- Funny thing, he says – when your mother was young she ate like a horse and looked like that. A great body. Not skinny but firm. Now she scarce eats a thing. It's like every breath she takes just gathers inside her and balloons her up.

He turns to Mom.

- Perhaps they'll deflate you, love, he says – Deflate you and send you back home.

No-one thinks to offer her toast. Eyes open, mouth shut, she sits and waits.

Three of us chewing, Mom staring.

It's a shame there's no photo. We'll never do better for a family show of togetherness.

Mom's allowed to take one bag with her. One small bag, personal items, no change of clothes. They have her size and will drape her with something new.

Karen's done the packing. She opens the bag so we can check it out.

A mirror and brush, both made out of pale yellow plastic, shaped like seashells.

A white mug from six years ago, with a picture of us three kids in fuzzy dots on its side.

A jar of odd buttons.

A small biscuit tin with a bird's nest inside.

Five pale lengths of ribbon, yellow blue pink lilac green, plus a white and a red one.

A dog-eared paperback called Women Might Fly.

A small china dish with a pattern of red roses.

A silver brooch of a flying seagull.

A pair of wraparound sunglasses.

A plastic bottle of rosewater.

A framed picture of dried flowers.

A hologram globe of tropical fish.

- We're sending your mother to be cared for, Dad says – not tossing out the garbage. You've packed nothing but crap.

- It's all the things she cares for, Karen flashes back – The sum of her twenty years living with you. That's why it's crap. Crap's what you've been good for.

Dad picks up the case. I think he's going to fling it, but he just flaps the top shut and zips it tight.

- I've given her memories, he says – Some to be proud of. What about you, my girl? What memories of you will make your mother happy?

He says it as a challenge, then turns his head to include Paul and me.

- She's given you life. All three of you. What have you given her in return? You might start thinking of that now it's too late. Start thinking whether you made your mother's life lighter or heavier.

Karen goes off to the kitchen. Paul taps away at his console. I leave the house. We've all learned life's better when we don't take Dad's suggestions.

I've got time to run to teensquad depot for my qual supply.

I can send Mom out on a surf of memories if that's what she's looking for.

My qual and Malik's look the same, transparent capsules with powder inside. Even so I decide to give Malik's version of qual to Mom. I know it works.

I'm just in time. 11.20. They're due to collect her at 11.51. You don't keep statesquad waiting. It's time to get Mom to her feet and roll her down the front path.

Karen's crying. Not the loud sobbing stuff she also does well. This is just tears and a screwed up face.

- Paul! Dad shouts - Leave that damn computer alone for a moment and come and say goodbye to your mother.

- Bye Mom, Paul calls across. He's on a roll. It takes sustained bursts of computer drive to reach the highest percentage points. He's deep inside the system and on track.

Dad wants him to do well. He doesn't insist.

- You, Steven, he says instead – You can spare ten minutes for your mother's farewell, or is your streetscum waiting outside?

- I ran to get back, I tell him – I'm sweaty. Just let me get a towel and dry myself off.

I run up, wipe myself down with a few strokes, and grab a clean towel off the bathroom shelf for Mom. It's the one idea I've had of slipping the qual into Mom under the beam of Dad's eyes.

- What you doing? Dad asks.

- Mom was sweating too. I'm drying her.

- You may as well mop up a tide. She'll sweat buckets before we get her to the gate. Bring the towel with you.

The qual's still in my hand. I meant to press it between Mom's lips while padding her mouth dry. I slip it into the back pocket of my shorts as Dad grabs hold of Mom's left hand.

- Take her other hand Steven, he says — Karen, you carry that case and fetch an umbrella. Keep her in shade as much as you can while we're outside.

We lean back to lever Mom out of her chair. Her stare's still vacant, her mind's not in it, but her body remembers the routine. She rides on the momentum of that first movement, her legs pumping away. It's just a matter of steering her. We let go of her hands and group behind her. Dad reaches round me as we hold Mom beneath the armpits and head for the door.

It's sad seeing Mom's arms when her drapes fall off. They're like a map of the moon, craters of brown and yellow marked by bruises. Her arms scrape the doorframe as we leave the front room. The front door's wider but it's still a squeeze. It's got to be this way. Mom's lost the knack of walking sideways.

Mom used to garden. Green just happened in those days, she said. Now stepping stones lead the way over baked earth. Some she lands on, some she doesn't, it doesn't matter. We keep her moving forward.

- Rest here, Dad says, when we get to the gate — We'll hear em. No point waiting out on the street.

Mom stands still. She's steady that way. It's only movement that gets to her. Dad snatches the towel from my shoulder and starts dabbing Mom dry.

- I can do that, I tell him.

- You can take the umbrella from your sister so she can give your mother a hug.

Qual in my pocket, I stand there giving shade.

This is lousy. I don't know why it means so much, Mom taking qual. Maybe it's everyone's secret wish. Your Mom gets to know and accept all your secrets without you having to tell em. Qual can open her in that way. It's my parting gift. She can float out of her body and see us for what we are. Qual separates love from the effort involved. Maybe she'll see that we love her. It'll make it easier to love us back. Maybe she can see me, see all of me, see deep inside, see what I do and what I want, see all that and forgive. Maybe.

- You'll be fine Mom, Karen's telling her – The Towers and the Stacks come up on girltalk. Some girls have visited. It's a co-op, they say. Run by women for women. You'll do better. Better than staying in this hole. You wait and see.

She pecks the discs of fat that are Mom's cheeks, wraps her arms around her, and hugs. It's like the tree-hugging people used to do. That kind of hopeful. That kind of unresponsive.

Dad takes hold of Karen's shoulders and peels her away. It's his turn.

- Goodbye, love, he says.

Mom's eyes stay vacant even with Dad staring straight into em. He takes her head in his hands and presses it against his own. Their mouths connect. We have to stand to the side while his tongue works to prize open her lips and dip in between her teeth. This is Dad's way of showing love.

The truck pulls up outside. Its engine's silent but we hear its tires crunching the surface of the road. A door slams, another slides open. Dad lets go of his kiss and stands back.

My one chance. I put down the umbrella and slip the qual out of my pocket and between my teeth. I don't speak. You can't say goodbye with your teeth clamped. Dad's opened Mom's mouth for me. I follow through, stick my mouth to hers, and blow.

It works. The qual capsule shoots down her throat. She splutters a bit but she doesn't cough it up.

- You're sick, Dad shouts. He pulls me off so hard I fall back, grabbing the towel from his shoulder before I hit the dirt.

The qual won't take effect for a bit, but the spluttering sees Mom stir.

- Air, she says.

- Breathe, she says - Let me breathe.

She reaches out, pulls the gate open, and bulges through it.

The statesquad official penscans the tag on Mom's necklace as she stands on the hoist. A wave of cool air passes out of the truck's body and touches our skin as we watch. The scan matches official data and triggers the hoist to rise. It reaches its level, Mom steps forward, and the doors wheeze shut. A faint burr and the electric engine connects. Wheels turn and the van grows smaller, then turns right.

- Her case, Karen says, and holds it up – She's left her case. She needs her things.

She doesn't shout. There's no point. The street's empty. The truck's gone.

That's OK. We've got nothing that Mom really needs.

- You see, Dad says – We did right. See how she livened up at the prospect of a little trip?

I walk off.

Dad shouts after me but it's only insults.

It's OK. It can't hurt now. We don't live at the same place any more. Mom's gone. Home's gone. It's just a shell of a house now. Just another scene.

- She gone then? Malik asks.

He's in the same patch of garden we lay in last night. He never looks for shade. He's in his beige muscle shirt and satin shimmy shorts, lying in full sun.

- I gave her your qual, I tell him – It'll be kicking in about now.

- You brought yours?

I hold em out. We put one on each other's tongue.

- Mind if we just lie here, I say – And not run? This is Mom's towel. It's still damp with her sweat. They'll be wheeling her into Cromozone about now. Finding her a slot in the stacks. It'll help us follow, having something of hers to hold onto. That OK?

- We'll lay it over our eyes, Mal says —It'll make it dark enough to see, but the sun's still there. I love that. I love it when the heat melts your body so there's nothing but the trip.

I lie down next to him. The towel's dark blue. It's scented with the perfume Mom uses to top the stink of sweat. Looking up through it the view is part black and part bright, like looking up into a sky of exploding stars. I feel for Mal's hand and lay my own on top of his fingers.

At the touch of his skin my qual takes hold.

The journey's starting.

Mal, Mom and me. This is it.

Some trips aren't easy. You head down this corridor, more like a tube, and something catches hold. The smell of Mom on her towel. A fly landing on my knee. The stone in the ground beneath my left shoulder. The feel of Mal's hand, the feeling stretching till I've imagined the feel of all of him. These things catch hold and you're lost.

Mom's there though. The trace of her is faint but I strain to get nearer. It gets stronger. I stay with it.

It's there. She's there.

From steady I shift to the speed of rush and the light goes rosy. It's not free-fall for something's underneath me, it's more like surfing the inside of a sunrise cloud.

Some heatspot kicks in around my chest and flushes through me. The towel's done it. I've connected. I'm inside the experience of Mom somehow. It's like she's unfolding herself in light from her navel, her body generating ripples of liquid flesh that turn to vapor, opening a whirlpool with her as its center and base.

- Gentle I say, for Malik gets it too. Gets this eruption of soft strong energy that's bursting out of Mom. His hand is on top of mine. He's lifted my shirt and licks his tongue around my left nipple.

Mom's sweat runs from her towel now. It coats my face and I lick in the taste of it. It's salty but thick and creams my throat.

- Good, Malik says — Stay with it.

I arch my back as he slips the shorts down my legs and off my feet. He strokes from my chest down to my toes like he's shaping me out of all the pink light. Air touches where his hands have passed. My body forms itself from the passage of his touch. He takes hold of my ankles and lifts em into the air, hooking my legs over his shoulders.

I open my mouth and some words call out. I don't know what. Mal's reaching inside me now so I'm not just surface. With one finger then two he's starting to moisten, to shape my insides.

I'm singing now. Shouting and singing all at once, one of Mom's songs streaming through but the words all lost in the tune.

He holds his hand across my mouth. It seals the song inside of me as he finds its rhythm. I throw the towel to one side and stare up. His eyes are closed. I watch the rise and fall of his stomach and chest. His mouth stretches and opens. He holds still but I feel the pulse of his dick inside me, the warm spurts of his come.

I lower my legs but reach round to his buttocks to hold him in place. His head hangs over my shoulder. I match my breathing to his, breathing in as he breathes out.

He rolls to the side. I use Mom's towel to clean him off.

- You alright? Malik asks.

I just look at him. I don't speak.

- You done that before? he asks.

I shake my head.

- What is that stuff they give you?

- Qual.

- No way, he says – I know qual. They're slipping you something different. You don't mind? You don't mind that we fucked?

- I wanted it, I tell him.

- So you said. Fuck me, you said. You kept on saying it. Fuck me fuck me fuck me Mal. I put my hand over your mouth to shut you up. What's that voice you were using, Bender? It was like some woman's. Your mouth but some woman's voice. Karen's was it? What's that drug do to you? It's not qual. They're fucking with you, Bender. What's this non-qual do? Turn you into your sister?

- What's it do for you? I ask him.

- Colors, he says – I just got colors. Orange, yellow, flashes of white, that sort of thing. And hot. Hot inside. Then you started calling. What's it like? Did it hurt?

I smile.

- I've never done it like that, he says – Not with a mate. Not face to face.

- You like it? I ask.

He pulls up his shorts.

- That sister of yours, he says – That Karen. You reckon it's safe, her being around your Dad now your Mom's gone?

- What do you reckon? I ask him.

- You could ask her, he says – We can run off. Tell her that. Tell her we three can run off together and look after her.

- I'll tell her, I say.

- You coming? he asks.

He's up now, ready to take the wall and run off.

- In a bit. I'll lie here a bit then come.

- Yeah he says, and grins – You've got to come too. You've got to jerk off.

He puts a hand on the wall.

- See you, he says, looking back.

Then he's gone.

Dad hands me a spade when I walk through the gate.

- Here, he says — Your Mom's gone. It must break your heart. Use this to work off your grief.

I throw the spade to the ground.

- Suit yourself, Dad says — The house is locked. The locks are changed. I've been digging since you ran off. Finish the trench, you get a key.

- That's hours.

- Could be, he says — Could be days the way you get stuck into things.

- I've got to eat.

- You know where the kitchen is, he says — You'll find the back door's got a lock on it too. That's a separate key.

- What about Paul? Why isn't he digging?

- Paul's got his education. You threw yours away.

- What's the point? What's the point in your stupid fucking trench?

- You finish it, you get back indoors. That's the only point you need.

He climbs back up to his control tower. There's no way I'm digging with him watching over me.

I move round the back of the house, into the shadow, and start channeling through the dust.

0.13

I walk in on Karen. It's a deal we've got, part of the twin thing. I walk in on her anytime I want, she yells at me to get the hell out.

She's busy. Her visor's on so she doesn't see me, just the 3D image they're beaming to her. Her right hand's working the thinnest of tubes against the air.

I wait till she's finished. She takes the visor off and sees I'm there.

- Fuckers, she says.

I'm safe. She's got someone else to be angry at. Her eyes are red. Sweat and tears have mixed to wet her face.

- I'm seventeen, she says – Only just seventeen. This is meant to be my history of medicine module. Medicine for beginners. So what do they have me do? Perform a virtual operation. What I've seen, Steven ... what they've just made me do ...

She gags before she can say more and runs off to throw up in the bog.

I put her visor over my head and flick the control to review.

It's a bloodbath.

The scene's in close-up from how Karen left it. It's hard to make out through the gore. One part is an adult belly sliced open. The other part is a baby, its head dropped into the adult's open wound.

I move my hands into the frame and waggle the fingers about but nothing shows up. Just the same bloody image of mother and child.

I flick on the audio.

The voice is male. Old male. Maybe a surgeon old enough to have worked with knives.

- Expertise aggregate, 16%, he announces – reduced to zero on this second fatality.

I look around the chamber. The belly and baby are brightly lit. Beyond em everything is a blur. The whole scene's running in reverse but it's as still as death.

Then it quivers a bit, going freezeframe.

- Point of death for parent, the voice announces.

The scene rolls on, going back in time toward the source of the massacre. In a moment, the picture changes. It's subtle. I don't see much of a change, but blood is flying. A few drops take flight from the belly and vanish into the wound. Then a few more. The action speeds up till the blood is gushing back into the body.

- Point of death for baby, the voice says.

The baby twitches. A foot moves. And an arm. Soon it's writhing as blood flows over its skin. The body flips over and I see its face, twisted and scaly like a bad glue job.

Karen won't be long. I flick to hi-speed reverse to see as much as I can.

What seems like guts are stuffed into the wound along with the blood. Enough blood's flown up from the surface to show white patches on the belly's flesh. The baby's tucked in with the rest of the organs. The flesh is made clean. The wound is sealed tight. There's just the belly now, breathing sharply. A shiny belly, skin stretched tight over its mound.

The mother's alive and intact again. I look down. She's got to have a cunt somewhere inside the blur. Surely that's got to be part of a birthing.

Karen yanks the visor off my head.

The picture goes.

- Great work, I tell her — We need a doctor like you in teensquad. You could operate on the dreks. Seems like you manage to kill every time.

She checks the controls. Sees I've been through review.

- You look like shit, I tell her.

- That's just the first operation of the day, she says — I spew up my guts, things get easier.

- What are you trying to do?

- Step 1, sex the baby. If it's a boy, step 2: keep the parent alive. If it's a girl, step 2: keep the baby alive. Step 3: keep both alive. I've not got past step 1 yet.

- You've done this before?

- For days now. Again and again. It's my project. I have to stick with it till I get it right.

- So you kill em every time?

- I'm getting better. They last longer.

- Maybe you're just getting slower. The voice gave you 16%. Zeroing when they died.

- Wow, she says, but it's a yawn more than a cheer – I've never beaten 13 before.

- You might do better if you chuck the lasers. Births are meant to be natural.

- A friend's got natural childbirth. She texted me on day 1. Told me she'd passed. She had nothing to do but watch more or less. Another friend got skin grafts. She unsealed the packet, kept it the right temperature, toned it for color, and rolled it on the wound. Pass. Day 1. What do they give me? An ectopic pregnancy. Normally that means a fetus getting stuck in the fallopian tubes but they don't even give me that. An embryo bypasses the uterus, gets lodged in the abdomen, latches onto some organ like a bowel to get its blood supply, so you have to cut the flesh and reach into the stomach and pull the baby out.

- That's so hard to do?

- You don't want the mother to hemorrhage, sure it's hard.

- Why start you on the difficult stuff then?

She slides her hands back into her fiberoptic gloves and picks up her knife.

- Maybe coz there's more to life than running the streets. Maybe coz time's running out and they want to put my natural genius to good use. Maybe coz no-one's an expert in everything and they need an expert in this. So maybe if I stop gabbing with streetscum like you I can practice and get it right.

She drops the visor back over her head.

It hides her bagged and bloodshot eyes and her skin that's parched of sunlight. It makes her look like an ant.

It's an improvement.

- You off out? Dad asks.

He tries to talk in a cheery voice now Mom's gone. It comes from Section 4 from the take an interest in your children website that's mandatory for stay-at-home fathers. It's scary when he starts using the stuff instead of sneering at it.

- That's good, he says. He sets down the ladder he's carrying from round the back – There's worse things for teenagers to do than keep order on the streets.

- What are they? I ask him – You know me Dad. I'm always on the lookout for something worse. Ever eager to live down to your expectations.

The cheeriness goes from his voice. That's good. It's best he sounds like the mean and scheming bastard he is. It keeps me on my guard.

- I've got mixed emotions, he says – I'm proud of my country, shamed of my son. Shamed that you have a clever way with words yet nothing at all to say with em. Proud that my country's found the best use for you. Teensquad keeps you running and keeps your mouth shut. I've registered my support. Dialed through a request to have teensquad sweep my neighborhood this afternoon. Should do you some good. I've heard that proof of community interaction earns merit points. Are you going to thank me, son?

- Better than that.

He stares at me. I open the front gate, ready to run off.

- I'll give you advice, I tell him – If teensquad's coming

down this street, stay indoors. We're proud of our country. It doesn't permit dreks like you out on the street.

I bang shut the gate and run. Dad doesn't shout. He moves quickly though. I look back from the end of the street and he's already on his lookout platform, staring out.

- What's the game, Bender? Runt asks.

He's up with me at the front. Short legs but great stamina balances him out. He's a good pacesetter for the group.

- Dreks are getting harder to find, I guess. Splitting us up this way, we cover the same ground in an hour as we did in four.

The assignment was onscreen when I got to the depot. Our area was divided into quadrants. Split into groups of six, our teensquad was given an hour to cover em all.

- What then? Runt asks — Do we leave the area if everything's OK? Do we get to circuit Cromozone again?

- You like that?

- They'll let em out one day, won't they, Bender? All those girls and birds and animals they're growing out there in their sheds. We're in the same business, Cromozone and us. They clone stuff. We keep the streets clean, keep the world safe for when they open their gates. Sure I like going up there. It lets em know we're ready. We've got the world in shape for whenever they come out and join us.

- You're a good kid, Runt, I tell him.

His cheeks dimple. He's the happiest person I know. Or he's the happy person I know outside of Dome, who knows nothing but happy so he's probably not happy at all, coz happiness is something better than what you're used to. Something like that. I'm not that good on happiness.

- Those guards and defenses at Cromozone, I ask Runt — What do you think they're doing? Stopping people going in, or stopping em coming out?

He thinks it through for a few paces.

- Who's to stop? he asks — We go up there, we run a circuit, we run away. They don't have to stop us.

- Other people might want to get in.

- Sure. Like in a zoo. They let you in for an hour or two and you go round and look at the creatures. You don't break into a cage though. Those guards are manning the cage.

- So they're stopping things coming out.

- Maybe freaks. Maybe they're stopping the freaks. Cloning's tricky. They can't get it right every time. Maybe misclones turn out freaks. Is that what we're training for, Bender? When we've dealt with the dreks, they can trust us to deal with misclones that slip through.

- Misclones that want to run free aren't the freaks, I tell him - The freaks are the ones that stand guard.

Like Dad in his watchtower.

- I could do it though, Runt says - I could stand guard. Does that make me a freak?

- Keep running, I tell him - Running like this, it clears things. It makes you see right. You see as far as you can run. Up in a tower you run nowhere. You see nothing. Never trust a guard, Runt. Never trust anyone who's stopped themselves. That's all they know. Stopping.

We report back. Our four groups have covered all the quadrants. The streets are clean of dreks. None to see, none to chase, none to wipe out. Job done.

A message onscreen asks us to move to headsets. State issued for wireless reception, the aerial arcs out from the earcups to clasp the set to the head. It's an offence to travel without one, but they're so lightweight it doesn't matter.

The state uses a woman's voice for its announcements. It's warm, slow, and a bit husky.

- Congratulations, she says — We thank you for your success in building a better world. A better world for us all. Please watch the screen.

Colors ripple from the edges of the vidscreen to a dark point at its center, then start to form into images.

- The future, young man, the voice announces – You're watching the future of our human race.

We don't laugh. Music comes through the phones as a pulsing bass line, and we just watch.

Watch sunlight catch the gloss on Dome's scalp and glint from the smile of his teeth.

Watch Roach's eyes bulge as his body strains.

Watch sweat fly from Soo's head.

Watch the pump action of Skink's elbows.

Watch Jok stare direct to camera.

Watch Skel sway in the slipstream of the boy who runs before him.

The lens draws close on each of us. It watches us draw near then speed away. We're in teensquad gear, running in full and steady flow. I come into focus, approach, and pass on. Even at speed the definition's good. I make out the cuts in my scalp from shaving my head.

The film's recent. We're running on paved road, open dirt at our far side. The focus is on individuals. Some run left to right, others right to left. Then I get it. Get the angle. The shots are from the security cameras in Cromozone's perimeter fence. They've assembled a film from when teensquad split into two and ran its circuit.

The film shifts. It's a group shot of us running in pack, the 24 of us racing toward Cromozone out of our own dustcloud.

A halfbeat is added to the soundtrack, a higher note between the pulses. The video morphs. There's no cut, no obvious break. Just a gradual melting of the bone structure of each of us, of our frames, our postures, our hair.

Furbo goes past. His eyelashes grow. His cheekbones move higher. His soft goatee grows back into his skin. Without a stumble, without missing a beat, he turns himself into an olive-skinned girl.

Kes is running. His elbows out to his sides, head thrust forward, his nose grows trim as he presses it into the wind. His hair rises into golden spikes. His lips swell. The straps shorten on his singlet to hold his budding breasts in place.

I look around. No-one's laughing. They know it will happen to each of us. Our teensquad, in full spate, is turning into girls.

I'm next.

My hair grows back. It's my old red color but longer than I had it, long locks that fly back in the wind of my running. My own straps shorten, my own breasts swell. My neck turns more slender, my throat smoother. Small tics shift across my face, and each is an adjustment. I can't watch and say what I was like before. I just see what I've become.

I'm Karen. Karen running.

- Steven, the woman's voice says through my headset — We call you by name as we call to your nature. As a twin you know what the others cannot know. Teensquads run for a purpose. Your running means nothing till Karen runs free. Run for yourself and you're running away. You must run till all others can run.

I watch the image of Karen. Of me as Karen.

Her mouth bends up. She's smiling. Her mouth opens. She's laughing.

Words spill out. I don't catch their sense for they come from many voices. Many women's voices. Thousands of women's voices. Their high notes blend together like an insect drone and rise higher. Higher. Its pitch climbs to the edge of my range of hearing.

- You OK, Bender?

Malik crouches in front of me. I'm on my knees. He's taken the headphones from my head and puts one cup to his ear, then snatches it away again.

- Man, he says — That's some fault, Bender. Hey, listen to this everybody.

Pint's closest. He holds the headset to his ear then snatches it away.

- It's a whistle, Malik says – A high-pitched dog whistle. They're calling Bender home.

Everyone laughs. It seems Malik's told a joke.

- We've been reassigned, he explains – We've succeeded. The streets are clear of dreks. They've given us a new job. Look.

He points up at the screen. A flashing red arrow points to the center of a map that switches to close-up. It takes a moment, then I recognize it. I read the street name HALEWOOD. My street. See number 17 in the middle of the screen. Recognize its shape.

- That's my house.

- It's more than that, Malik explains – It's the center of a new model community. That film, morphing us into girls, it shows what we're running for. We're running so one day girls get to run free. Drekfree streets are safe for girls. The first two families with daughters under 21 are ready to relocate. They'll be your neighbors. One family in 15, one in 19. We're assigned to go in, clean up both houses, splash some paint around, make the places decent.

- We're not painters. We're runners.

- It's just two houses. It won't take long. We'll be back on the streets again.

I don't believe it. I close my eyes. Keep em closed till I feel the cool of Mal's hand pressed against my forehead.

- What's up, Bender? You're burning.

I open my eyes. It's hard to see. The depot's dull in its neon lighting, no match for the flames that were licking round inside my skull. I cough, clearing my lungs of the sense of smoke.

- You seeing something? Mal asks.

My mouth's dry. I lick my tongue around it so I can speak.

- Eyes, I tell him – A pair of fixed eyes, spitting flame.

- Weird, he says.

- Not weird, I tell him – Just Dad. He's reeling us in.

Soo does the picking. He's not designed for mental calculation. His decisions are as random as tossing a coin. When Soo does the picking, no-one gets to complain.

I'm in the first group, assigned to house number 19, to the right of my own home. The second group gets to clear out 15. Soo makes his choice while we're standing on the street between the two houses. So as we're standing and waiting we're on the street outside number 17. Right outside my house.

The first time we hear Dad is when he speaks. People must have hated Dad as a kid for him to learn to sneak round like that, without a sound. No-one would welcome him, seeing him coming. Sneaking without a sound is the way he gets close. He speaks to me.

- When you've thrown out their garbage next door, you can come back and clear your own room.

He's in his tower, gripping the outer railing, staring down. We all look up.

- Watch the birdie, he says. Mom calls him a relic, the way he speaks sometimes, linking words together that if they used to make sense don't do so now - Say cheese.

It's clear what he means despite what he says. He points at a camera that's fixed to one of the poles that hold up the roof of his control tower. The camera's angled down to where we stand in the street, and hums as it pans between us.

He puts a cap on his head. It's light green with a dark green peak and the eagle logo of statesquad.

- We're a zone of extra protection now, boys, he tells us – You should have seen em when they came to fit the camera. Officials stood in this tower and widescanned the whole layout of my defenses. They were impressed. They especially liked the concept of my trenches. I can see my layout here forming a whole new home defense model. They gave me this cap. It's like a medal. A medal of honor. They respect me. They've asked me to oversee your work and report back. I've started. I'm filming. I'm watching. And I've found nothing good to say about you so far.

Metal scrapes against brick behind him. He turns round, and we all step back so we can see over the fence.

It's Karen. Her head comes into view, then her body, climbing a ladder up the outside of the house toward her window. The window's closed, and she's carrying a bucket.

- See, Dad says — You scum laze around while we're at work. Keeping up standards. While you stand there chatting like old women, my girl's busy keeping the place in order.

Karen's dressed like she's stepped straight off her treadmill, lycra shorts glued to the curves of her backside, sweat coating the whites of her legs. She's wearing one of my T-shirts, loose and white, but tied in a knot to bare her midriff. Her hair's tied too, a tight orange plait hanging down her back. Putting the bucket on her window ledge she stretches up to wash the glass with a cloth. The water runs down her arm to soak her body. She just carries on, cleaning the higher panes and not the lower so the water keeps running down her.

- Great ass Karen, Furbo shouts up. He's good at appreciation.

She brings out a squeegee and scrapes the top of her window dry. More water runs down her arms.

- Full infrared capacity, Dad calls down — That's what this camera's got. It's state of the art. The night won't hide you. Any of you scum come crawling round here after dark, this camera will catch your every move.

- So far we've got to know two big cunts in your family, Furbo shouts up to Karen at the window — One's your Dad. The other's your brother Paul. What about you, Karen? Have you got a cunt you can show us?

- You're the first, Dad shouts, his finger quivering as he points it at Furbo. His voice is hoarse, rage squeezing out the triumph — You're logged, kid. The camera's got you. Your time's up. You're dead.

We ignore him. Karen's got our attention. She turns round. The wet shirt clings to her skin. The dark pink of her nipples shines through, as broad as targets. She pauses and smiles out at the street, then finds handholds for herself. It's hard going down a ladder backwards. Her legs part as she stretches down the rungs.

She gets more attention than I'll ever get.

- Clamp em, Dad tells us – Clamp those thoughts inside your dirty little minds. My daughter, she's a national treasure. She's not for the likes of you.

- Who says? Furbo shouts back – You and whose frigging militia?

- You, Dad yells back to remind him – You're first!

He points down at Furbo like his finger has the power to shoot laser. His stare is made of cold stone, but his anger's too much for his voice. It breaks to a squeak, like a twelve year old kid. Everyone laughs.

Everyone but me.

I know Dad. He's a black streak. Make light of him, you get scorched.

Two houses at once felt wrong. We came together at number 19. We'll finish that then move on to 15.

The workday's finished. Teensquad's split up and goes home. Dad's developing the trench I finished for him. I ignore him and head straight upstairs to lie on my bed. Crashes come from the front of the house. I go through to Karen's room to take a look down into the garden. A wooden chair flies over the fence. A leg breaks off as it lands but Dad won't sweat over that. He's not into sitting. Furniture's lumber. He tacks it on to his defenses or stacks it in a corner of the garden.

A table comes over. Crash. A wooden base for a lamp. A roll of chicken wire. Stuff teensquad cleared out next door, things we viewed as trash, Dad's busy collecting.

- That window cleaning stunt, I ask Karen – Was that your idea or Dad's?

She's posturing on the floor, one foot gripped behind her back. She calls it yoga.

- You think I do what that creep wants? she says, and switches foot.

- He set the ladder up for you. I saw him.

- So?

- He's using you, I tell her.

- I want to do something, I do it. I don't want to do it, he can go stuff himself. No-one uses me Steven.

- You're bait, I tell her – This house is a trap. He's building a trap. He's showing you off as the bait.

- Are you going to get me out of here? she asks.

I just look at her. She lets go of her foot and sits up.

- See, she says, like she's won a point – You say he's building a trap. And you're not going to get me out. So who is?

She goes over to her treadmill, turns it on, and starts running.

- If I've got to be bait to get out of here, then I'll be great bait, she says.

Dad's got carried away. Next door's front door slides up over the fence then tips down on our side.

Suits me. Get all the lumber you want, Dad. Fire's coming your way. You may as well fuel it.

0.14

Karen's shout wakes me. It seems I've slept in. Paul's bed's empty and Dad's sawing in the garden. I slip on my shorts and go to her room.

Whatever excited her seems to have passed. She's staring down the snout of her visor, her hands flashing around in her fiberoptic gloves. Her fingers squeeze invisible things into place. It's feverish work for a few minutes.

- Shit, she says. Her shoulders sag, she takes off the visor and turns to find me watching. I expect her to frown, to stare me out, to yell. Instead she's smiling.

- Look at this, she says.

I fit the visor over my head. She presses replay and I see a white creature squirming in blood.

- I did it, Karen says — It's alive.

- What is it? I ask.

- A baby. I pulled it out of the stomach and kept it alive.

The sound's turned off but the baby's mouth is open and wailing. Its legs and arms jerk on its blood soaked mat.

- It's a girl, Karen says — I've just delivered a baby girl.

I remember the drill from the old surgeon's voice. Step 1, if it's a boy, keep the parent alive. Step 2, if it's a girl, keep the baby alive. I reach up to the controls and click the scene forward. The wound in the adult belly gapes open, but the scene is still. The belly doesn't move with breath. Blood doesn't pump. Small white clamps are fixed to tubes and what I guess is the placenta is stuffed inside the corpse. I take off the visor.

- So you killed her, I say.

- No, I told you. She's alive.

- The mother. You killed the mother.

Karen snatches the visor back to view what I've been seeing.

- You don't get it, she says — OK, the mother died, but look at her. It's carnage inside that body. I'm a beginner. I'm on my own. I doubt a team of top surgeons could save her. But I pulled a baby out of that mess and kept it alive. It's a miracle.

She shifts the scene backwards till she's staring again at the squalling mess. I know she's got the baby in her sights coz her cheeks tighten back into a smile.

- What do you see in babies? I ask her – It looks like a maggot to me. A maggot fattened on its mother's blood. You know what you've done? Saved the parasite and killed the host.

- OK, she says – Get out.

- You going to moon over that baby all day? I ask her.

She turns her ant head toward me.

- Mom did what she could, she says – She sprogged me and you and Paul but she never got over it. I'll never do that. I'm not emotional over babies, Steven. I'm clinical.

- You're not natural, I tell her, but she doesn't listen.

The planet's screwed, the future's now, and Karen's stuck on hope and science. Her ant head's poised before its vision and her hands are adjusting the nanocamera. She's giving birth again.

Paul's at the console in the front room. His lime green muscle shirt is dark green on his sides where sweat's poured down from his armpits. The screen's streaming a sequence of zeroes and ones as he stares into it through the goggles. A counter in the bottom right blinks as it tallies his score. It's a game of instinct I've never cared to handle. The streaming figures are a program, and the eye dilations adjust it. Paul can't know what he's doing at that speed. He just does it.

A message in flashing red type tracks across the top of the screen. It's a command to call in for a message. It's in my name. I reach over Paul's shoulder and tap my ID and password into the keyboard.

- Fuckhead, Paul says. He stares unblinking into the screen as his stream of numbers disappears and my message comes up.

Steven Sickel. Deliver the suitcase of Alison Sickel's personal effects to Cromozone front gate by 10.00. Report operation code SG17. Key password for mission acceptance.

Paul feeds my password in for me, then rattles off another chain of commands. My statesquad message shifts into scrolls of code, white figures on a blue screen. Paul grins.

- Bye bye big bro, he says.

- What's up? I ask him.

- I sourced your message, he says — Tagged in your operation code. That crap about Mom's personal effects? It's a shitline.

- How do you know?

- Nothing so simple comes up so complex. Look at it.

He scrolls down. The white figures on blue run for page after page.

- You know what it means? I ask him.

- Not the specifics, he says — I need to access the program for that. It means one thing though. Statesquad's got your number.

- More, I say — Find out more. Access the program. Find out the details.

He flashes round the keyboard. The series of zeroes and ones returns. His eyes start to dilate. The tally in the bottom right corner mounts again. He's back to his game.

- Paul, I say, shaking his shoulders.

He sets his game on pause, pushes my hands away, and stares up at me through his goggles.

- You're my brother, he says — Not my rat. Go run your own maze.

Dad's laid the hatchet to next-door's chair. Its legs, back and seat are splinters. Dad's setting em in a line across the garden, crawling in the dust and laying the blond wood scraps down like he's a craftsman. He tries to refocus when I come outdoors but the process is slow. He's looking for stuff he can use. He blinks at the suitcase in my hand.

- What's that? he says.

- You remember Mom? She used to live here?

- Don't get fresh, Steven, he says — Your mother packed that case for our honeymoon. It's seen better days. What you doing with it?

- It's her things. She forgot em. I got a message to deliver em to Cromozone this morning.

- A real message? Not just one of those flash fantasies you get in that screwed up brain of yours?

He's staring at me. I stare back.

- You're planning this, aren't you? I say — This fire.

- Ha, he says — What fire? You won't catch me out with trick questions like that, my boy. I know what you've been seeing. I know what you've been writing. Paul's told me. You see me going up in flames. You see your old Dad burning. You think you see the future Steven but you see nothing. The future's what you make it. I'm prepared. You and that scum gang of yours, you'll find I'm prepared. You won't catch me when the time comes. It's my time, Steven. My time that's coming.

The front door opens and Karen comes out.

- So it's true, she says, seeing the case — Paul says you've been called to see Mom.

- Not to see her. To deliver her things. I'm late. I've got to be there by ten.

I've got time enough. I just don't want to hang around. I want to be gone.

Karen holds out a silver chain. A small enamel dove hangs from it. The dove's white, and it's got a green-leafed twig in its beak.

- Give Mom this will you? she says.

The chain's short and thin.

- You should keep it, I tell her — Mom'll never fit this round her neck.

- For fuck sake, Steven, she says — You've got Mom's things.

You're about to run off on your own while I'm locked in here. You can't take me, so take this. Take the fucking dove. Mom gave it me. I love it. It's my favorite thing. I want it out of here. So take it, Steven. Just take it.

She presses the bird and chain into my hand.

- You'll see your mother? Dad asks.

- I'm just delivering the case, I tell him.

- You see her, he says — You tell her from me, I'm on course, you tell her. We might have lost, her and me, but it doesn't end there. You tell her nothing ends while I'm alive. We might have lost, but no-one else'll win. No little pricks'll inherit this earth, you tell her. Not while I'm alive. You tell her that, Steven. Let her rest easy.

Dad's madness sucks up all the air. I go out through the gate and don't look back.

It's not easy running with a suitcase, but it's easier than walking. Easier than staying home.

I put the case down at the edge of town and rest a moment. I'm panting, but at least I'm breathing.

One thing I've never been. I've never been lonely.

Till now. That's what this is, I think. If lonely's feeling small that's what this is. My heels spit up dust but no cloud. Teensquad running is something. It's power. Going solo is puny. I turn and my dust trail is already settled, flat and lost on the road. The town's a smudge behind haze.

Cromozone is close. It fills the horizon. I'll already be logged on Cromozone's screens as a dot on the approach road. I feel small.

It feels lonely.

1.00

They took this voicecard from me. Took everything. Fuck em.

Was I in there one day? Two days? Three? Fuck knows.

It's morning. I'm out. I'm running.

I'm in a forest. It's still standing. No-one really wants the lumber I guess. Who needs wood? Who needs to make things? Who needs to burn up heat in this weather? The trees have no leaves but the deadwood gives shade.

I've moved twice. Crawled away from my own vomit twice. Their drugs make me throw up. Or knowing what they've done makes me sick to die. I bet that's it. My body's trying to chuck up what they've done. I've checked myself. There's no new cuts, no lesions. A couple of tiny pinpricks, one on my stomach and one on my side. That's it.

Maybe they're lying. You can't change a body with a pin.

Fucking insects. Mozzies. I've just smashed one on my scalp. It's body stuck to my skin with my blood. I scratched it off and now my head's bleeding. I've opened up a wound. Blood's running round my ear.

What is it they've done? They fixed my head, they said. What was it? What've they done?

- Go back.

- Who's that? Who said that?

- Go back to when you entered Cromozone. Step by step. Remember. Step by step. That's how to do it.

- Who the fuck are you? What kind of voice is that?

- What do you think, Steven? Think. Think for yourself.

- Deep like a man's, soft like a woman's. Are you some woman or what?

- I'm a voice. Your voice. Assigned to you.

- Where the fuck are you?

- You're running, Steven. I hear the twigs breaking underfoot. You're barefoot. I feel your pain. It hurts. Stop. Stop yourself.

- Can you see me?

- No. We see nothing. We track you but we can't see you. Our choice.

- You hear me but can't see me?

- We hear you. When you want us to.

- Where the fuck are you?

- Don't shout, Steven. There's no need.

- You're fucking shouting. Shut up. Shut up.

- There. Is that better?

- What have you done?

- Adjusted the volume. Is that fine now? … Steven? Talk to me, Steven.

- You're in my head. That's right isn't it? You're a voice inside my head. Fuck. What am I on?

- Don't worry Steven.

- Shut up. Shut the fuck up. I don't want this. Voices inside my head. I don't want this. How long? How long before the stuff wears off? How long before they go away?

- It's no drug, Steven. It's not madness. It's a receiver. An implant. We've fitted a receiver inside your head. Call us. We're here whenever you need us.

- Call you?

- Whenever you need us. Your voicecard's a transmitter. It beams your voice to us, and receives an imprint of our conversations. Press playback to review what we've said. This is enough for now, Steven. We're stopping transmission. Go back. Retrace your steps from when you entered Cromozone. You'll understand everything in time. We'll be listening. We can help. Steven. Steven! Stop it! Stop it!

- I'm sorry Steven. We don't like to do that. We transmitted a high frequency to paralyze your nervous system for a moment. What were you doing? We caught sensation from your fingernails. You're opening wounds. Digging out the receiver. Don't think of it, Steven. The receiver's linked to your brain. Damage would be irreversible. You won't be worth our saving. Here. This tone will soothe you... Relax, Steven. Relax. Understand what's happening. You'll live with it. You'll learn to live with it.

- You slept. That's good Steven. We didn't want to wake you. This is being imprinted direct to your voicecard. We want you to understand something. You are not alone, but this does not mean you are not independent. It's vital to us that you are free, Steven. Use this voicecard when you need someone to listen, when you need understanding. Unless you use this voicecard we will hear nothing. We will only transmit to your head when neurotransmitters alert us that your body is in danger. Without your questions we have no answers for you. Aside from your use of this card you will not notice our existence. Your life is your own, Steven. It is not ours. We only hope you use it well.

- Go back, Steven. Back to your first steps in Cromozone. You'll understand. Piece by piece you'll understand. You need to understand.

Thanks for the knife, you fuckers. You think you get to read everything I write? Not so easy. I've carved you a message in the trees. A secret message. It says everything I think about you and what you've done. It's sliced into the bark. Download that if you can.

You think I talk my secrets into voicecard? Fuck you. This is no secret. It's just my life. Just a story. A short fucking story. No-one steals days out of my story. I'm getting em back. Getting em back so I can use em. You think you know my future? You think you've implanted it? Stupid fuckers. You're dying. You're passouts. I'm not your future. The young are not your future. There is no fucking future.

We're now.

You stupid fucking breeders. Don't you get it? It's over. Now's now and then it's gone and then that's it.

This is it.

They gave me a chicken. They called it chicken but it was fucking big. More like a hen. Pimples in the skin where feathers should have been, legs and wings tucked close to its body, head chopped off. It's a special project, they said. I'm the first man in ten years to get to eat chicken in the outside world. The first man to eat a chicken that didn't crawl out of an egg. Eat it, they said – It's cooked. It'll make you strong.

It made me throw up.

We made a chicken, they boasted, like I cared – From out of nothing we made a bird. Think what we can do with you. You can trust us.

The bird was one special project, and I'm another. I asked the bird what it knew about trust. Dead, headless and cooked it couldn't say much. Study a corpse and the findings aren't good. Run while you can the corpse said, while you've still got feet and your legs aren't pinned to your sides. Running's good. Trust in that.

I scooped a hole in the earth and wiped the vomit into it. Added the chicken's flesh and bones and covered it up. That's the best I could do for a grave for the bird.

I think it's all gone. Think its meat's all out of me.

Anything else they've stuck inside me, that's coming out too. If it kills me to do it, then it kills me. At least I'll die natural.

What's so fucking natural?

I can't tell my story any more. It's his story. Steven's story, Bender's story. I'm not me I'm some weird fucked over alien thing they've twisted out of shape. Steven went in to Cromozone but he never came out. Something else came out. It's not Steven and it's not me. I'm not this, I'm not me, I'm Steven, I was Steven. I've got to get back. I've got to tell it as it is, as it was. As it fucking is.

Steven was sixteen turned seventeen. He was a runner. He was me. He ran with his Mom's blue case in hand. He kicked up dust and left the town behind him.

I know what he was like. I was inside him then. Not some fucking freakish shouting implant. Me and only me.

This is his story. Steven's story.

1.01

The next machine that gives me orders, I'll call it Dad.

- Do this, do that, do it this way or that, do it now, it'll say.

- Fuck off Dad, I'll tell it.

I'll turn and run, I'll lie on my back, I'll do whatever the fuck I want to do but I won't do what it says.

- Stand on the yellow cross, the machine said.

- Fuck off Dad, Steven should have said.

Me and Steven share the same Dad. Dad's a bastard. The machine was an ugly speaker on top of a thin pole so it even looked a bit like Dad. It didn't listen, just gave orders, just like Dad.

Steven looked down at the asphalt that covered the dust in front of Cromozone's main gate. The yellow cross was a step away from the brick wall of Cromozone's reception point. Steven wore his whiteflash black trackers, the same I'm wearing now. Vent holes round the base, a suction system in the sole to pump out sweat, great for steady spurts into long distance. Shoes like that, they run you way off-camera. You don't turn seventeen and do what a squeezebrain like Dad tells you. You don't wear whiteflash trackers and stand em on a cross in front of a wall.

But that's what Steven did.

Perhaps some high pitch tone comes out of those speakers, some brain numbing silent squeal that turns you into a stupid fuck. Perhaps that's why he stared into the visor on the wall as the screen came back and the lens came out. It focused on his sightwaves and stalked up to his right eye. You use your eyes for seeing Steven, you assbrain. Screw your eye shut and you had a chance.

Instead you stood, you young prick, stiff as death, staring into the black as the lens eyeballed you.

Sorry to be pissed at you. You had a lot in you. I was hoping for more, that's all. I'll let it go.

Just like you did.

A barrier of steel bars rose behind you and to your sides, a cage with the dull-bright sky of dust-and-sun for a ceiling. The cage reached full height and locked into place. No retreat from that point. None of the friends who hadn't come with you and couldn't give a damn, none of teensquad's prime and distant assault and support team, not a single fucker could drag you back or stand by your side.

Seconds passed. Heat gathered. No wind blew. Sweat streamed down Steven's arm and collected where his hand clutched the handle of his Mom's scabby suitcase. He was little boy fucking lost.

Stupid fucker. I've no patience with him.

The brick wall of the entry point surrounded a black plate steel door. That black plate door breathed open at the top and slid down. It stopped level with the dust of the ground.

Beyond it was a steel box. The cool of chilled metal breezed out and touched your skin. You stepped forward. You stepped inside. You let the elevator suck you in.

They had you then Steven. They had us.

Two steps inside the box you faced a steel wall and turned around. The plate door was already rising from the floor. Outside was patterned by the steel bars of the cage. Your last sight of Steven's world was the smudge of sky, squeezed to nothing as the door drew closed at the top and sealed you in.

You thought it was an elevator and looked for the control buttons, like you'd been in an elevator loads of times before, like statesquad was always whisking you up and down to important meetings. The box was dayglo lit by lights paneled in the ceiling. The walls were burnished steel. You saw no buttons. You saw no glidepads to run your hands across. You had no control.

The light was tinged red from behind you. You turned and found a message projected in thin red letters against the wall.

PRESENT PACKAGE OPCODE SG17/5HP3

The code was statespeak for Mom's blue suitcase. A slice of wall drew back, twice the width and height of the case. You looked inside. Beyond the steel of your box's wall, beyond a layer of brick, was a small steel container. You reached the suitcase up and slid it forward. The hatch closed. Fair enough, you thought. They've got to play safe. They've got to screen the case before they let you walk it to your Mom.

Dumb fuck. Statesquad doesn't operate to let dipstick sons deliver crap to mummy's arms. Did they bother to even open the case, do you think, or did they incinerate it there and then? You carried a suitcase, Steven. But you were the delivery.

Nothing clicked. Nothing shuddered. Nothing on the outside registered the elevator dropping down the shaft. Just the feel of your heart squeezing itself up through your throat.

The elevator stopped and the door slid back. Steven stepped out.

Stupid fuck.

He'd seen nothing. He could have waited. Waited till they ejected him and sucked in someone else.

Why go back? Why remember all this?

Memory's crap. Follow the memory step by step every fuck of the way and where's it get me? Sitting here in the woods, talking to voicecard, Steven gone so I'll never get him back. Memory screws me to a lie.

Their lie.

I've got to change it. I can't tell this story and end up here.

Steven stepped from the elevator and a message flashed on the opposite wall.

DECONTAMINATION ZONE.

The elevator doors closed. They vanished. You turned and found flat panels behind you, in front, to the sides. Lights were embedded in the ceiling, behind Perspex panels. The floor was cement. It was light blue but not sky blue. Blue like grey is blue. You were stuck in a blue grey box.

First things first, you looked for the lens. You sad fuck. Here

125

in the woods I know better but I did the same when I was you. Looked for the camera. Life's snapped off when no-one's watching. Doing nothing's something when it's watched. Stare at a lens and you're staring some fuckhead in the face. With a camera to stare at you could have stuck it out.

Instead you had the screen. Decontamination Zone flashed across it, red letters on blue.

The first word, the first lie.

Don't change the lies. Don't make up new ones. Lies altered Steven and turned him into you. Find the lies that hurt him. Work em out.

With nothing to stare at Steven stared at the screen. Decontamination Zone. So what was contaminated Steven? Not you. Don't forget that. You're clean. Whatever they did to you, you started clean.

The screen's a lie.

They don't want to decontaminate you. There's nothing to decontaminate. It's the opposite.

Contamination's coming.

- Decontamination Zone. Remove all clothing before proceeding.

Steven looked for the voice. It repeated itself. He traced the sound to perforations in the ceiling beside the light panel. The voice was deep like a man's and soft like a woman's.

- Remove your clothes, Steven. Leave them on the floor. They will be cleaned and returned to you. You're about to enter Cromozone at hygiene clearance level nine. A new outfit is through the door. Remove your clothes.

Steven looked around for the door. The room was sealed.

- Decontamination Zone. Remove all clothing before proceeding.

It was a recording. The line ran into itself as it kept repeating.

- Decontamination Zone. Remove all clothing before proceeding decontamination Zone. Remove all clothing before proceeding decontamination …

He stuck it for a few minutes, then pulled his shirt over his head. Pushed off his whiteflashes. Pushed down his shorts and stepped out of em. He might as well have peeled off his skin.

The recording stopped. A paneled wall slid open, just wide enough to enter sideways.

- Step through the door, Steven, and into the shower, the voice lied.

Fuck that voice. It can't speak without lying. I hate that voice.

You skinny freak, Steven. More muscle, more flab, less lean, you wouldn't have got through the gap. Your stomach pressed against the panel even so. That poor stomach.

So what happened?

Here's where I begin to lose it.

You had to snatch your body through as the panels closed. No way back and no way out.

It was dark. Black. You were in a cubicle, its walls shaped like the closeness of a coffin. No way to move your arms, shuffle your feet, flex your knees. All you could do was spring up on your toes and you did. You sprung. No scope for liftoff, your head never touched a ceiling, but you lifted yourself as hot water pooled around your ankles. It whipped around like you were a spindle, your toes jammed in a plughole, round and round the water rising, jetting round your kneecaps, pushing against your balls, racing round your chest and splashing over your shoulders. You'd be spinning if the walls didn't hold you in place, falling if your knees had room to buckle.

Two minutes to drowning. Your life didn't flash before you. Your life? A lightning jag of boredom. Fuck that. Fuck memories. Now's all there is. All there'll ever be.

Now was a scream.

You opened your mouth. Water went in, sticky water with a

film to it that coated your tongue, a hot jet pumping all around your head, a stream slashing down on your scalp, but no scream came out. It was inside your head, high pitched like all your senses scattering, a blade of noise that scoured your skull and left it white like light.

The water stopped. It must have done. It licked back down round your body and out through the floor. Jets of hot air blew the water from your skin. Lights came on, a door opened, and you stood there. Not still. Shaking. You stood shaking and crying as hands pulled you out. Gloved hands that smelt of gel.

The voice was there.

- You're alright, Steven. You're alright.

All that voice does is lie. The lights were bright. You saw nothing but light as they lay you on a trolley. Your limbs were shaking as they strapped em down. A needle pricked your arm. Panic slid away like blood down a drain. You were empty. You were gone.

So much for you, Steven.

- I'm a doctor. Dr Lester Drake. You call me Lester.

He leaned over the body that used to be Steven. They'd done their stuff with it. Fuck knows what it is now. It's me. It's Bender. I'll call the body Bender.

Bender twisted to the side to get away. He twisted to the side but his body held still.

- You ever been in a car, Steven? You know about safety belts? That's what these straps are. They're not constraints. You're wearing them for your own safety. Any sudden movement like the one you just made, and they tighten. They bind your upper arms and thighs to the bed. We don't want you falling. We don't want you running. Not till you know where you are. Stay still for a minute, Steven. Loosen your muscles. Then the straps will relax. I'll be able to release you.

It was something like that that he said. Pretty much like that.

People fill me with their voices till they're bursting out my mouth. I sound like em sometimes but I'm not being em. I'm just letting em out, letting em loose, letting em escape. Lester Drake filled me with his I-know-better docshit. His words are stuck inside me. He thinks I needed what he said, he thinks his words explain me, but that's shit. They just foul me up. I've got to let em out.

Bender closed his eyes.

- Have you got any questions, Steven?

No questions. Bender was looking for the moment he was in before waking. That moment was a place of calm, of dappled light, of soft green and reflecting water.

He searched and caught some sense of it. His muscles eased. The straps relaxed their grip.

- You're free now, Steven. I've released you.

Bender knew better. The middle-aged black man with the buzz cut, heavy muscles beneath the clinging white of his doctor's kit, dark brown eyes that sucked you in, was lying. He was spouting docshit. Free for Bender wasn't opening his eyes, sitting up, taking part. Free wasn't stepping from an elevator into a decontamination zone into a bath chamber into straps. Bender was free to lie still without constraints and close his eyes. That was the only freedom going.

He took it.

- I'll leave you, Steven. Sit up when you're ready. Take your time. You'll feel unsteady at first.

A door breathed open then closed. Bender presumed he was alone. He moved his hands to his chest and slid em down his body. He felt the outline of his shape, felt the dips around his bones, but the skin wasn't his own.

It was time to open his eyes.

The skin he was feeling was a bodysuit in black. The bodysuit was sleeveless, cut in a vee around his neck and shaped round his body and thighs to end as shorts below his kneecaps.

Bender felt the line between clothing and flesh and felt no join. He sat up and looked at his feet. They felt naked. He flexed his toes. Nothing pressed against em but it looked like he wore shoes, black shoes that were hooked around his heels and molded over the arches.

He rubbed his hands over his face. The door sucked open and Doc Drake walked back in.

- Looking for stubble? the doctor asked.

Steven would have bumfluff, not stubble, but yes doc, yes.

- You're testing how long you've been here by your growth of beard? Right on, Steven. You're a bright kid. We shaved you. Shaved you while you were sleeping. We've sealed the hairs away if you want to inspect them. Try feeling your head though.

Bender touched his fingers to his scalp.

- Your hair's growing back. Just a touch. Just enough to take away the gloss. You've been here three days.

- That's docshit. I'm not hungry. After three days I'd be starving.

- Your body ate what we fed it. You've been functioning in the physical world. Your mind was elsewhere, disassociated from your body. That's all.

Bender slid from the bed and stood up. He looked down at the ground. It was plastic but veined like marble. That's what his eyes told him.

His feet said something different. He was standing on sponge.

- We've been busy, Steven. Those shoes are a new device. Their soles communicate with the mainframe computer. Your body's been programmed. We've watched you closely over these past months. We know you. You're a runner. You're other things too, but you're a runner. A good one, but not faultless. You use your height to lean in against the angle of your instep. Those shoes are remolding your feet. They adjust your physique with every step. In your world you were good enough, Steven, but what a lousy world that was. Things have changed. You've got to be the best.

Bender tried his new feet out, step by step to the window. You see views like that when you die if you're lucky. Just flying in dreams you don't see so far. Out running, everything's dust. Now he was high in a Cromozone Tower. The land was brown from up there, but he could kid himself. He could say it was green. Blades of grass, scraps of weed, leaves on twisted hedges, it was all just enough to make a pattern. Things still lived out there.

Then the edge of the city scraped the life away and the green was gone. Dust smudged the city sky. Bender's eyes went blank while he saw the future. It filled his head so he could see nothing else.

The city would burn. He watched it happen. He heard flames shoot high and fire crackle. The city went dead and turned to dust.

He closed his eyelids then opened em again.

The flames had gone. The city stood.

- Are you for real, doc? Are you a proper doctor? I wasn't sick when I got here. You've done something to me. I know it. What is it? What have you done?

- You'll learn, Steven. In good time. Soon. Before we let you go.

- Just tell me.

- I can't. Telling's no good.

- Fuck what's good. Fuck you.

Doc Drake's body was old but strong. Maybe in its forties. The neck looked creased and older than that. The eyes were worse. Extra dark in the center with a glint in the whites. People get that look when they think they know better.

- Do you ever listen to your Dad, Steven? Do you let him tell you things?

Bender shuddered. The doc was talking about Steven's Dad, not his. Bender had no Dad. A lifetime's conditioning takes a while to shake but he'd do it as quick as he could. For now, Steven's Dad was what the word Dad meant. It meant the same sick fuck of a man as ever.

- Of course you don't. Why believe your Dad? Why believe me? Why believe anyone? The whole planet's cheating on you. That's how much you know and you're not wrong. No-one can tell you anything because you know all there is. You know that it's all change. That things will die before you'll get to describe them. I'll not tell you anything, Steven. I'll show you instead. Show you everything I have to show you. Hide nothing. You can see everything for yourself. Then you can make up your own story.

- What have you done to me? Tell me that.

- I'm a doctor. Bodies fall apart. I'm trained to keep them together as long as I can. The day you were born changed my life. No more girls came after you, Steven. Baby after baby followed you into the world, every one of them a boy. Imagine it. In seventy years a few geriatrics will stumble over the wreckage of Earth, then phut. We'll be extinct as a natural born species. It's a fact, Steven. What would you do if you were me? Would you keep the old bodies going till they die, or help the young ones? Change the young ones? Give them hope?

This doc was good. Steven's Dad had skills but no charm. Doc Drake's words oozed round Bender's brain and slicked inside him. When I speak em now it's like vomiting poison.

- This doc is Steven's Dad, Bender told himself - Dad plus charm. See through it. He's only Steven's Dad.

- That outfit suits you, the doc said.

He held out a hand. He was showing off the manicure on its long nail. Then he sliced it down the center of Bender's chest.

Bender stared down at himself. The nail had cut him. He felt it, but the pain faded even as he reached up to finger the black material of his bodysuit. He could find no slit.

- You see, Steven?

Doc Drake looked from Bender's chest to his own raised finger. His eyes bulged in a comic show of surprise.

- You've never been safer than you are in our hands. A fingernail's as lethal as it gets round here. Not deadly but you'd think it would scratch. Check your skin and you won't find a blemish. The material of this slinksuit was developed for condoms. Maximum protection with maximum sensitivity. It lets your skin breathe like it's naked. It keeps your balls pouched from slapping about when you're running. It restricts no other movement. These new shoes of yours, this slinksuit? You'll amaze yourself, Steven. It's like running in a permanent slipstream. You won't believe it. You won't believe any of the things we can do for you, Steven. The greatest brains and the most powerful computers are focused on you right now. You can't understand what we're doing. Even I gasp in wonder at times. The best you can do is run with it.

The doc pressed the flat of his hand against a panel beside the door. The door breathed open.

- Come on, Steven. Let's see those shoes in action. Let's go and explore the new world.

Bender got as far as the door and looked out into the corridor.

- Mom? he said.

Be kind to him. Say all mothers look the same. Inflate a body to three times its size, wrap its head in a ball of fat, and you have to get subtle about distinguishing features. You have to start counting warts or something to tell one fleshblob from another. Mom, you have to say, I love you for your warts and the difference they make. You have to come up with something as rich and moving as that.

Bender saw a fleshblob on a slipcart far off down a corridor. He watched this blob draw near and thought he might be saved.

That's sick of course.

Nothing out there saves you, Bender. Nothing's worth saving.

It's now Bender. Everything's now.

What's not now is nothing.

The fleshblob drew nearer. Call it instinct but before she passed, before he smelled her, he knew this woman wasn't his mom. With one hand she worked the controls of the slipcart, the flesh of her palm pushing against a lever. Her other hand pressed a large plastic jar into the folds between her breasts.

- Come on, the doc said – We'll follow her.

Bender stepped from the doorway of his room. All he can do is take steps, I guess.

The black shoes felt good. The slinksuit felt good. The fleshblob drove her slipcart fast but keeping up was effortless. Bender left the doc in his wake. He felt like his old self. Whatever they had done to him wasn't that bad.

That's what he thought.

What's left to trust when your own thoughts lie?

The fleshblob turned her slipcart to face a door. The door had two panels, one at eye-level for women seated on slipcarts, the other at standing eye-level. The fleshblob stared her sightwaves at the lower panel and the doors slid open. Doc Drake caught up as Bender waited, and told Bender to stare into the upper panel.

- Don't worry, he said – You've got full clearance for the day. We've nothing to hide, Steven. We want you to see everything. We want you to understand.

Bender stared. The door drew back to let him in. Doc Drake followed and started to explain. More words of poison to vomit out.

- The creature in the woman's plastic jar is a girl. It's a fetus in fact but we speak of them as girls. This woman's brought it from the maternity section. Look around you. They're all girls here. Every one of them.

The walls were lined with metal shelves, and the metal shelves with plastic jars. Each jar contained a pickled fetus. Bender looked at one up close. It curled against itself inside the jar. Its head was big, its limbs tiny, its eyes shut. At least the thing couldn't see.

The blob of the woman inserted the fetus into an orange fiberglass cylinder, then turned away. Her job was done. Tears made her cheeks glow in the halogen light.

- No male hands ever touch girl fetuses. It's a council directive. You'll see the point in time. This fetus now goes through a comprehensive screening process. It won't come up with anything new, but we have to try. It's strict policy. No life must go to waste.

Doc Drake opened the door and waited for Bender to step into the corridor. Bender stayed put.

- Go ahead, Steven.
- Which way?
- Turn left.

Bender left the chamber and turned right.

The shoe molds triggered his feet muscles to adapt to his lengthening stride. His soles flexed to spring him forward. Between steps he was airborne. His body was light as he ran.

- Steven.

The doc called but didn't shout. Bender turned down a side corridor. A picture of a staircase was stenciled on the second door down. He stepped through it and ran up two flights. Up there he stepped through a door, and waited.

One minute, maybe two, and the door opened.

- Impressive, Steven, the doc said.

He held a screen in the palm of his hand.

- The green light is you in your current location. Your turn of speed was admirable. You took the stairs five at a time. Your pulse accelerated slightly but has already returned to normal. You're a lovely specimen. In fine condition. We're lucky to have you. I'll flick the screen to a smaller scale. There you go ...

He handed the screen to Bender. It showed a floorplan.

- Make your choice. The green dot is you. Turn left and you pass through admin. Right and you're in the early stage ward. That's the more interesting choice of the two, wouldn't you say?

Bender glanced at the map. The doctor's right hand gripped the nape of his neck. Bender walked the way he was pushed.

- It did me good to see you run, Steven. No-one runs in this place. Your body will make a remarkable impression on the ward. I'm glad you chose this route. It'll be fun.

If that was fun, then running barefoot over glass is fun. Stuffing wasps up your nose is fun. Lying comatose in some fucked-up institution while some crazed doctor slavers over your body like meat's back in vogue, that's fun too. That's what fun means in Cromozone.

Cells with plate glass walls lined one side of a corridor. Each cell contained a woman. Not mothers or fleshblobs but young women.

- This a prison? Bender asked.

The doc laughed. The women turned their heads his way for a moment, then snapped straight back to face Bender. The nearest pressed against her glass screen as she stared.

She was young, young enough to be lean, but her stomach bulged in its white cotton smock. Her hair was black and pulled back behind her ears. She tilted her head to one side. She smiled as Bender watched her.

- These are our paying guests, Steven. They have external windows with panoramic views. They see the sun rise in the east. At night they see the moon and stars. We play them birdsong. Glass walls give a sense of community and a screen against alien bacteria. Vidscreens play footage of the pre-male era. It's the full dynamic of the natural world. And now they can see you. A lean, fit, young white Caucasian in a slinksuit. You're a hormone pump, Steven. You see this one with her palms pressed against the glass? Her belly's swollen but the pregnancy's false. Her embryo is formed but it's kept in a separate unit. Impregnation happens tomorrow. Having you fuck her would be more natural of course but it's the last thing she needs. You'd make a male embryo. These young women want to hold a baby girl in their wombs. They'll naturally abort, but they'll keep on trying. If they knew what we were doing with you, Steven. If only they knew. You'd die of their envy.

- If they knew what? What the fuck are you doing with me?

- All in good time. We've got no secrets. You'll learn the story as we go along. First the story, then the happy ending. Let's show you the basement. We house volunteers rather than paying guests down there. The elevator's back this way.

Every man is Dad. Bender had to remember that. He had to do the opposite of what he was told. It wouldn't make him safe. But it would land him in his own kind of trouble. He could live with his own kind of trouble. It's other people's trouble that fucks you up.

The women in their cells turned their heads as Bender passed. The first door to his right was another staircase. Fuck the doc and his elevators and his plans. Bender pushed open the door and ran.

He didn't count the floors. Why count when you're going nowhere? The new shoes gripped the cement. He twisted his body round sharp corners. Level after level, down and down and down and down till the stairs ran out. He was on level ground.

He turned sharp round and up again. Three steps at a time, then two, then a rapid run up single steps. Bender's breath grew short, his heart hurt. Up up up up.

The stairs ran out on a small cement strip in front of a door. Bender came to a stop but his head still span. He leaned on the door for balance. Through the door a motor buzzed. A sensor was reading the print from his thumb. He lifted his head and another motor hummed. A scanner located his sightwaves.

The door opened under the pressure of his weight. He stumbled through. The door closed.

The door was double sheathed. The mechanisms and sensors were sealed inside it. It had no handle. Rubber flaps sealed the edges.

No light. Only black.

The door held firm. Bender worked his hands and fingers around its edges but couldn't break its seal.

Black. He was trapped in black.

His breath was tight, caught in a knot deep within his throat. He screwed his eyes shut. He and Karen had played this game as kids, closing themselves into the loft and cellar, holding their eyes shut till their eyeballs ached. When they opened their eyes the darkness was smudged with shapes and you could see enough to move within a shadow world. Bender opened his eyes now.

Nothing. No shape, no outline. Only black.

And a sound.

It was faint, but constant. The pulsing of water down a pipe maybe, echoing inside the walls. Bender edged toward it, sliding his feet along the ground. His right foot tucked beneath a rubber flap. He pushed forward with his hands, reached and parted a curtain of rubber, and stepped through to the other side.

Black, still black, but the sound was louder, one beat on a skin drum then a second. Its note kept fading and the first beat returning, ba-bum, ba-bum. The beats filled the room from above and below and from the sides. Bender ran his hands along the floor, looking for speakers. Nothing. Just a polished surface.

Reaching to feel the way ahead, his fingers touched a different surface and burrowed into its sides. The material was soft, like wet brushed cotton. It moved like waves of water.

He tried to climb and cross it, to roll his body to its other side. Aim a fish across an ocean, you've got as much chance. The surface eased his knees against his chest, pulled his arms around his knees, smoothed his spine into a curve, and tucked his chin against his breastbone.

He was tired. It was black. The space was warm. Why move?

Ba-bum, ba-bum.

The sound was a heartbeat. Colors flowed like a dream. He was rosy with comfort.

- Steven

A whisper inside his head.

- Steven

He kicked in spasm.

- Steven

Mom? Mom's voice?

He uncurled his fists and stretched his fingers. A hand clamped hold of his. A large hand. The hand turned Bender's own upside down then pressed something inside it.

- A visor. Put it on, Steven. Look around.

Hands supported Bender's back as he sat up. He put the visor over his head. His eyes were open. He saw a white that was as brilliant as silver but no colors. Perspex tanks lined the walls of the room. Inside each tank was a translucent pod. Thin tubes squirmed between the pods and the wall.

- This is the womb room.

Bender turned his head and saw the doc, his eyes wrapped by a strip visor like Bender's own.

- You've heard street-talk of artificial wombs and female hatcheries? Here's the reality. Each of those tanks contains a fetus. Male, female, it doesn't matter. We keep a fetus alive until it dies. In remote secure storage we've got freezers full of fertilized eggs, but science will die before we know what to do with them. It's something to try, it keeps us busy, but it's not the future.

Ba-bum, ba-bum. The heartbeat still filled the room but it didn't drown out the docshit.

- Listen, Steven. Understand. Mothers were miscarrying while you were in the womb. Your sister Karen, your twin Karen, was the last baby girl brought to term by nature. At present female wombs reject female fetuses. The cause may be chemical, it may be psychological, it may be environmental, no-one knows. Natural wombs reject females. Women's bodies refuse to bear their own kind into this world. We're world leaders in cloning techniques here. We've managed five generations of cloned mice. I could show you the end result. It would make you weep. Genetic flaws multiply exponentially with each generation. We're scientists, Steven. We don't create life. We parody it.

Ba-bum, ba-bum, ba-bum

- You know that sound, Steven?

Ba-bum, ba-bum

- It's a heartbeat. A mother's heartbeat.

Ba-bum, ba-bum

- Your mother's heartbeat. Do you want to meet her?

The visor was lifted from Bender's head and he was blind again. Hands gripped him under the arms. They pulled as he kicked. Rubber curtains flapped around him and light flared, so bright he didn't dare open his eyes against it. He stopped his kicking and let himself be dragged.

- Your mother, Steven. Your mother.

His head was pressed into the softness of cushions. Ba-bum, ba-bum, the heartbeat sounded in his ear. He opened his eyes into a rosy glow. Reaching to push himself back so he could see, his hands pressed into soft cushions. They were white cushions flecked with pink and scored by the blue and purple of veins. Flesh cushions. A pair of arms.

- Mom?

Her body was draped in soft white cotton till the flesh resumed at her neck. Bender looked up beyond the folds of the neck, over the swells of her cheeks, in search of her eyes. The swelling had pressed at the flesh of her eyelids and sealed em shut.

The woman's mouth opened.

- Maaa-aaa, she said.

It was a bleat. A sing-song bleat, in some thin echo of his Mom's voice.

Bender stared at his Mom. His Mom directed her sealed eyes at the wide wall of window and the burning of the sky.

- You fed her qual before she got here, the doc said – Where did you get it?

Bender glanced at the doctor then back up at his Mom.

Mom.

Death's easy. Death's the end. I get death. Snap, you break a spine. Death. This I don't get. Even thinking about it now I don't get it.

Burn Mom, you get ashes. Bury her, put her in the ground and cover her up, you've built a hill. You can scatter ashes. You can squat on a hill. What do you do with this? What do you do with a woman dressed in a white sleeveless tent, tubes coming out of its base to feed into bottles, cables looping out of its neckline? Wires stream from suction pads glued round her head. She's tethered to machines. What do you do with a thing like that? Call it Mom? Press its lips back over its gums and brush its teeth?

- She's smiling, the doc noted – You notice that? She's always smiling.

Push Mom's cheeks high, hold em in place, I guess you could shape a smile out of her mouth. Pry her eyes open and you can watch her cry. Jolt volts up her spine and you can make her shiver. Push her hard and maybe she'll fall over. Stop her heart and you can have her die. She reacts but doesn't act. She's like an iceberg. It takes global meltdown to shift her. She accumulates or she melts.

- What have you done to her? Bender asked.

Bender had a Mom. I had a Mom. This wasn't our Mom.

- She was on the edge when she logged in for her last biofeedback from home, the doc said – When your father certified her. Then something extra happened. Something tipped her over. She could crash or she could fly. Look at her. She's lucky. She's flying. You gave her qual. A high pure dose. That wasn't your dose, Steven. You've never been issued that grade of qual. Where did you get it?

Bender stared at the doc. He watched the man's mouth move, and heard words coming out, but still it made no sense.

141

- I'm not Steven.

The doc stared him out, waiting for more.

- Steven was a kid in a house with a Mom. You've fucked him over. He's gone. He's history. I'm Bender. That's not my Mom. That's nobody's Mom. I've got no Mom.

- Steven had a Mom. He gave her qual. Not his qual. Not Steven's own. Steven was an empath. Like his Mom. You don't give an empath high grade qual. With qual like that an empath starts absorbing the whole fucked world. It's like pouring hot lead into a crystal glass, giving high grade qual to an empath. You just don't do it.

- What are you on about? Qual's qual.

- Qual's a streetname. The capsules aren't called qual. Qual's the name you give to the high. We've got a saying here in Cromozone. Different highs for different guys. Each day you sign on, the optical scans beam the biofeedback direct to our laboratories. Those on qual rations have their dose adjusted accordingly. We have an overwhelmingly young male population deprived of legitimate sexual focus. We adapt brain chemistry at the local, individual level to facilitate some harmony at the societal level. You've got a gland in your brain, Bender. A pituitary gland. We've all got one. It pumps out tiny doses of dimethyl tryptamine. DMT. You've heard of toads, squat little reptiles? Blow them up to the size of a hot air balloon and they look something like Steven's Mom here. I can show you some toads later if you like. We've cloned a few trays-full in one of the sheds. Their systems get soaked with DMT. They're hallucinating all the time, only for them it's standard. Human brains pump quantities of serotonin, toads pump equivalent quantities of DMT. Inject serotonin into toads and they wouldn't squat. They'd hop cartwheels, they'd flip into orbit. We're all on mindbending trips, Bender. All of us, all the time. It's just a question of what you get used to. Are you any good at history?

- History's fucked.

- I'm talking recent history here. The history of Steven. You remember how he used to get flashes of the future?

- How'd you know that?

- We're experts on Steven here, Bender. He and his twin sister Karen are the most logged humans in the history of the human race. Those flashes of the future that Steven had? Brain chemistry. As simple as that. Little tripwires in the neural network that screw up the standard sequencing perception. Steven had something of the toad in him. His pituitary gland produced irregularly high quantities of DMT. Any slight artificial increase could give an immediate sense of wellbeing. Steven was a special case in hard times. We treated him gently.

- He never got high grade qual?

- Not from Statesquad. Mix a cocktail of DMT, harmoline and dopamine, you don't give it to an empath. That stuff's for leaders. Kids with the strength and ability to match their own smug idea of themselves. Kids with talent and self-confidence who only lack a vision.

- Malik?

- He a friend of yours?

- I'm Bender. Bender's got no friends.

- He could do with one. Someone to share his vision. You've got vision. High grade qual gives vision to those who lack it and need it.

- So what was in Steven's capsules?

- Not a lot. A little DMT boost. Enough to make the capsules feel worth taking. Enough to give a qual high. Plus some hormones.

- Hormones?

- Look at your mother, Bender.

- Bender's got no mother.

- Look at your mother!

A shout. A shout that echoed round the walls of Bender's skull. An echo that flew higher and higher in pitch then was gone.

Ba-bum. Ba-bum.

A heartbeat stirred in Bender's head. Not from outside. The heartbeat started soft and low. His head stayed still but the sound increased. Notch by notch. Someone was turning up the volume. Fuckers. Heartbeats don't do that. They don't increase in volume. You're playing with me. Playing with Bender's head. Am I deaf? Is that it? Did you probe inside Steven's eardrums and snap some cord to make Bender? Does any sound come in to him from outside anymore? Is everything he hears some recording?

Bender lifted his head. Quickly. One moment his head was pressed against flesh, the next it had pulled back a distance.

Ba-bum Ba-bum.

The same old heartbeat, the same fucking volume. Not possible.

Then snap. The heartbeat stopped.

They turned the sound off. Too late. You think Bender didn't notice? Course he noticed. Now he's remembered.

Bender looked up into the face of the mound of woman they called Steven's Mom. It wasn't Steven's Mom. Steven's Mom lived in Steven's house. She didn't exist out of context. She'd become something else. They'd pulled this woman's feet to stick out in front of her along the floor and propped her back against cushions. Bender had been laid across her body, his head on her chest. Her hands had been placed around his shaved head. They were clammy. Sweat ran from the hands and down his cheeks. The woman's head was tilted down at him. Tears bulged behind the sealed lids.

You think I'm going to get weepy over my mother? You're fucked.

Mothers mean nothing to Bender. Bender has no Mom.

He pushed himself back. The doctor was gone. The room was empty but for the woman. He stood up and tried the door. It had no handle. The indicator light stayed red as he pressed his thumb against the scanner.

- Relax, Steven.

Bender looked round the room for speakers. He saw none. Of course he fucking saw none. Voices don't need speakers. They play inside his head.

- Go to the window, Steven, and look back.

What sort of voice was that? Man, woman, freak, voicebox?

- I'm not Steven.

- Bender. Go to the window, Bender, and look back.

He did it. I don't blame him. Bender and me, we're just about on the same side. Just about the same person whatever that is. He turned his back on the window and looked above the head of the hulk who used to be Steven's Mom. The wall behind her took on a glow. Images formed as light spread across it. The whole thing was a vidwall.

- Do you see us, Bender?

Not every boy needs a mother. Bender knew that. No boy needs four of em, but four Moms stared back from the vidwall. It had to be a vidwall. The Moms were projections. Only projections flare as big as that. They were gobs of muck on a lens somewhere. It was Bender's fucked mind that made em look like Moms. Moms with football heads and flails of hair, mounds of bodies and dangling feet. Hovering Moms, way clear above the ground, balloon feet and stub toes set to burst under pressure if they land. Two of em black, one white, the other some fuckweird color like jaundiced grey. They weren't real. They couldn't be.

Bender turned to scan behind him for the projector.

- Look at us, Bender.

They were draped in sleeveless tents like ex-Steven's ex-Mom. Broad steel poles went floor to ceiling behind em. It's like they were witches tied to stakes. Bender stared and stared some more and figured something out. The poles were the pillars of hydraulic lifts. The Moms were on chairs that hoisted their weight from their ankles. They were sitting the other side of a wall of glass.

They were speaking.

- We are alone. The doctor's gone.

The voice, as deep as a man's and mellow as a large woman's, had no direction but came from all around him. Or inside him, who the fuck knows. The Mom near the left moved her lips to match it, like she was sucking the words in.

- This time is special to you.

Now the words matched the button lips of the Mom on the right.

- We love you.

The Mom on the left.

- We care for you.

The Mom near the right.

- Like mothers.

The voice stayed the same. Always the same. Bender stared at one Mom, then another. Each one he looked at was the one who was speaking. He asked a question.

- I'm a prisoner?

- You think we want to keep you here?

Bender stared from left to right. The voice stayed the same, and all the Moms' mouths moved in time with it.

- Who's talking?

- We have no who. We're of one mind. Nothing parts us, nothing comes between us. It's a fact of our existence. You don't need to understand it. Choose a face. Focus on one of us if it's easier for you. Turn and stare at your mother if you prefer. Her lips won't move but these words you hear are her words too. This is also her voice.

The near left Mom, one of the black ones, had sticky ginger hair. Bender focused on her.

- Am I a prisoner?

- Do you want to stay here?

- No.

- Then you are free to go. We wanted to look at you. Your mother wanted to look at you. That's one reason you're still here. Don't be embarrassed. Your mother understands. She knows what's happened to you. She accepts. She welcomes the news.

- What news?

- You're going to be a parent, Steven.

- I'm not Steven. You warped Steven. Here in Cromozone. You did something to him. You warped him so he doesn't exist. What did you do?

- You're going to be a parent, Bender.

- No way. I'm not a breeder. You want sperm go jack off Paul. He's got the breeding gene, not me.

- We're talking parenting not breeding. A special kind of parenting. You will be parent to a special child. Her life depends on you as your life depends on her. Maybe all our lives depend on her. When you go you'll take her with you. That's our promise. She's not yet a fetus. That's much too soon. She's an embryo.

- She?

- A daughter. Your child is a daughter.

- Daughters are history.

- Steven is history. You're Bender now. You've changed the world.

- The world's fucked.

- Nothing was fucked, Bender. Your mother gave birth to the last girl born of a human. You will give birth to the next. A woman of the Council gave the egg, inseminated by the donation of a high-order pre-degenerate male, that will grow into this very next girl. The embryo is female. You will parent a daughter. That much we know. The rest is speculation. We have changed the conditions of your daughter's physical birth. No womb can ever reject her because she will never enter a womb. Should she be brought to term we hope she will bear daughters of her own. Think of the possibilities, Bender. Your child may grow to be the ancestor of the rest of the human race.

- Let me out.

- You want to leave?

- Let me out.

The doorway slid open. Doc Drake was standing in the corridor outside.

- Our prayers are with you, Bender. Your mother's prayers are with you.

Doc Drake looked at the glass wall. Bender looked too. The wall was blank.

- They let you see them? the doc asked. His eyes shone wide.

- See em? Blobby as clouds and wide as horizons? Sure I saw em.

- They spoke with you?

- One voice. One sick lying voice between em.

- They don't lie. They never lie. They never speak to men. They never let men see them. This is special, Steven.

- Who's Steven?

- Bender. It's special. That was the council.

- They're just like Mom. Ex-Steven's ex-Mom.

- They've adopted her. She's joined them. One mind, Bender. One female controlling mind that runs all of Cromozone. This place is a birth factory. The world got screwed. This place is one single experiment to set the whole world right. You see these wires leading from your Mom's head?

The doc walked across to run a hand through the air around the wires. The door was unblocked. Bender could run. Run till they bothered to chase his little green bleep down on their map.

He had nowhere to run.

- Your Mom's connected to the neural network that keeps this whole place running. She is its principle feminizing agent. Each fetus that grows in this place, animal and human, reverberates to the sound of your mother's heartbeat. Now it's your turn, Bender. It's your turn to carry that heartbeat into the world.

- I can go?

- They told you everything?

- They told me nothing. Only lies. I'm no breeder. I'm Bender.

- You're to be a parent.

- They said that. They lied.

- They never lie.

- Everything lies. Everything that speaks lies. Lies are why people speak.

- You're going to be a parent. The parent of a baby girl. It's in embryo form already.

- Then give it me. Those women who never lie said I can have it. Said I can take it with me. I want it. I want it now.

- You've got it, Bender.

- It's here?

The doc didn't answer. Bender checked the room. It had no furniture. Just ex-Mom and her cushions.

- Where is it? At the end of her wires?

Bender moved across the room and reached up to snatch the wires back from their sockets near the ceiling. The doc was quicker. He swiped Bender's hand from the air and pinned it behind his back.

- You've got it. Don't you understand? Didn't they explain it to you? You've already got it.

Bender relaxed his body. The doctor released the grip on his arm.

- Where?

Bender patted his slinksuit down, held out his arms.

- Where? In these pumps? Tucked under the soles of my feet? Fucking where?

- It's inside you, Bender. The embryo is attached to the lining of your stomach.

- How?

- It was a very minor operation.

Bender dug his fingers in beneath the slinksuit's collar. The black material stretched wide as he pulled it down one shoulder then the other, pulled his arms free of it and rolled it down his chest. Over his stomach. He stroked a finger over a tiny white pinprick of a scar just to the right of his navel.

The stitches have melted, the doctor explained – It's healed. Even that scar should vanish when you get some sun on it.

- You've stuck an embryo inside my stomach?

- Not inside the stomach. We've implanted an embryo and placenta into the abdominal cavity just under the peritoneum, the stomach lining. It's attached itself to your stomach. The fertilized egg produces enzymes which allow it to feed there. It's tapping into your blood vessels.

- Fuck sake why? I'm seventeen. I'm male. What have I done?

- Your twin's a girl. The last girl born of a woman. You followed her, Bender. Steven was the last boy born in the old world.

- You got it. The last boy. Karen's the last girl. She's the one with a womb. Get someone to fuck her. Fuck her yourself.

- Any resulting child would be a boy.

- You got something against boys?

- I'm a scientist. I'm out to save the world. The world needs girls.

- This embryo's female. Take it out. Take it out of me and stick it in Karen. Stick it in her womb.

- We've tried. You saw them. Saw the women in their cells. We've got hundreds more like them throughout the building. Hundreds of women with female embryos in their wombs. Every one of them will miscarry. We keep on trying, keep chasing the offchance, but statistics are against us. They stack higher against us every day. Natural wombs reject female offspring. It's not a fact, we've discovered no scientific basis for it, but it happens every time without exception. Women want to give birth to daughters. Women's bodies refuse to do so. Women's bodies reject the possibility of bringing more of their own kind into this world. We've got to break that chain.

- You're making me into a woman?

- You're a young man, Bender. It's why this might work.

- Why what might work?

- Why you might carry a female child to term. Opposites attract. A male won't reject a female. The chain will be broken. A female born of a male might bear daughters of her own. We cannot rule out the possibility.

- You're a doctor. You know better than that. Men have no wombs. They can't bear children.

- Things change. You were in the womb room, Bender. You saw female fetuses growing in artificial wombs.

- You're saying I've got an artificial womb?

- I'm saying more things are possible than you know. No-one believed in artificial wombs but they were in development even before you were born. They were my own specialty in fact. I was a research psychiatrist specializing in the emotional constructs of alternative pregnancies. Artificial wombs would offer women lifestyle choices, their pregnancy occurring in a controlled environment while they continued their working lives. In the days of health cover, insurance companies were preparing to make artificial wombs their preferred birth environment. The fetus could grow in laboratory conditions with no risk whatsoever to the mother's life. Neither mother nor baby need face the trauma of birth for birth becomes trauma-free. Such was the theory. Artificial wombs were the stuff of vast research grants. No sustainable life has ever emerged from one, and I'm guessing none ever will. We're out of time. But to answer your question, no. You don't have an artificial womb. With you the process is entirely natural.

Bender stabbed a finger at his scar.

- You call this natural?

- The growth of an embryo outside of the womb through fetus to birth is a natural process. It's rare but it has always happened in women. The fertilized egg takes the wrong passage out of the fallopian tube and exits in the abdomen instead of the uterus. It's called an abdominal ectopic pregnancy. The possibility of male pregnancy has existed for decades but has never to my knowledge been brought to effect. It increases rather than decreases the dangers and discomforts of birth. The incitement of male ectopic pregnancies had no rational basis in science. Till now. Till you.

- You're saying I'm pregnant?

Bender's brain hit rewind. He saw images from Karen's anthead visor. Saw the bloodied mess of an infant pulled from the wound in its parent's stomach.

The doc was quick. He caught Bender before he hit the floor.

- Guess that was all news to you, huh? the doc said as Bender came round. Someone had slipped his arms back through the sleeves of his slinksuit.

They were still in the room with ex-Steven's ex-Mom as its centerpiece. She faced the window, her sealed eyes fixed on the sky. Bender tried to move. The more he tried the tighter he was bound. Straps held him to the seat of a slipcart. The seat was built for a fleshblob. Bender sat on half the seat, the doc on the other.

- Relax, Bender. You fainted. You're in shock. I've administered a mild sedative. Some wave of calm should be sweeping through you. Find it. Relax. You remember this type of constraint? The more you relax, the looser the straps become. Your body's been moving faster than your mind. You're in shock. You need time to understand. Time for your brain to catch up with the situation.

Bender tried to fling himself to one side, so his weight would bring the slipcart to the ground. The straps clutched him still tighter against the seat.

- I'll kill myself, Bender said — That what you think? You let me go and I'll kill myself? Kill myself to get rid of this thing in my stomach? Too right. That's what I'll do. I'll kill myself.

- No you won't, the doc replied — You get your flash intuitions. They're all well and good, but here in Cromozone we adopt more professional techniques of foretelling the future. We use psychological and genetic profiling. You're rare for your age, Bender. You show no disposition toward suicide. Let me tell you what you will actually do when we release you. You'll go home and sort some things out then return to us here. You'll be met at the gates and transported somewhere special. I can't tell you more. Even I don't know. Your destination is a council directive. You'll bring this child to term if at all possible, and you'll survive if at all possible.

- You say it's attached to my stomach ...

- It's an abdominal ectopic pregnancy. Such a condition is dangerous but you're strong. In good health. You stand a chance of survival.

- It's a parasite. I'll get it cut out.

- It's your child. Your daughter.

- It's sick. A sickness. I'll get it cut out.

- Who'll do it?

- My sister. Karen. She's got the fiberoptics. She's been trained.

- She's trained for delivery from abdominal ectopic pregnancies, Bender. Not for abortion.

- She'll do it. She'll cut it out.

- Fine. Your decision. Nothing's being forced on you, Bender.

- Ha.

- Nothing more. Nothing else. You're free. You have to be free. It's a council directive. Bring your sister with you when you come.

- I'll never come.

- OK. If you get what you think is a better idea then act on it. We won't stop you. We'll simply track you.

- I'm outta here.

- Are you going to say goodbye to your mother?

Bender looked round at the mound of flesh and wires that sat and soaked up the windowlight. He tried to speak twice. Words stuck in his throat like lumps of fat before he gulped down the pain and managed to speak.

- Does this slipcart move? Bender asked – Turn it around. Get me outta here.

The slipcart whirred out of the room, down the corridor, and turned left as doors slid open. They were in an elevator.

- I'll swallow something, Bender said, speaking a thought out loud, looking for the doc's opinion – Some acid should do it. Something strong enough to kill the baby without killing me. What acid would do that? What dosage?

- You've no womb, Bender. You can't miscarry. The only way this baby gets out of you is if it's cut out. Whoever does that will leave the placenta inside. The placenta will get absorbed. A fetus won't. A dead fetus will just hang around and rot. Your best bet for survival is to deliver a healthy baby. Healthy baby healthy parent. Remember that.

- I won't do it. You know that? I'll find a way. I'll cut it out myself if I have to.

- It's a baby. Just a baby. Not a demon. Your baby.

- You say women's bodies reject females. They refuse to bring daughters into the world. You think I want to do that? You think I want kids? I know Dads. I'll never do that. I'll never become a Dad. A Dad's the worst thing that can happen to a kid. Better to kill this kid than be its Dad.

The digits in the elevator touched zero then carried on down. Minus one. Minus five. The doors opened.

- You can move now, Doc Drake said – Just a little. Do it gently. The straps have loosened.

Bender eased himself forward. The corridor outside was light blue and brightly lit. Two young women dressed in white cotton gowns were sat on their slipcart. Their swelling hadn't set in so they were able to sit side by side. The elevator emptied and they rode in.

- Your Mom's lucky, the doc explained – She gets to look out on the natural world all day, every day. These women get just a half hour slot on the viewing platform. We point them at the sun. It's an attempt to tune their bodies to natural rhythms. You probably think you're locked in some artificial hellhole with crazed scientists and madwomen. The truth is we're all obsessed with the natural world. We're determined to restore it any way we can.

The slipcart built up speed as the doc worked the controls. The schedule had changed. Bender was no longer on a freeflowing tour of inspection. Glass cells lined the corridor, each with its bed and its young woman in white, but the speed blurred all the details.

- Where are you taking me?

- Outta here. Like you asked. What you want is what you get, Bender. You get to keep free will. The Council of Women decided it. A girl must be born of a man, and that man must be free. We need a girl born of a human who will then give birth to girls. It's the natural way for the species to survive. You're one unique chance of finding that natural way. We could keep you entertained in a fantasy cell. We could strap you to a table and bring you to term. We could set you free. Do you see what a choice we're giving you? Do you see just how free you are?

- Free this then, doc. Free this fucking embryo. Rip it out. Then ask me. Give me the free will then. See if I want another fucking implant.

Bender tried to stab his hand at his stomach. The constraints squeezed his arms back against his sides.

- I came in healthy. I'm going out sick. I've got a stomach parasite.

- It's a baby.

- It's a parasite. It's feeding off my guts. It's likely to kill me. You're a doctor. Cure me. Get rid of it.

- It's a life, Bender. An embryonic life. A baby girl. She exists. She's got a name in our files already, a code name. Her life is no less valuable than yours. No more, no less. I can't consent to killing either of you if both of you can live. You can both live, believe me.

- Take out my brain while you've got me. Stick it in an oxygen tent. Feed it and train it. That way you might get it to believe a word you say. Only then.

The slipcart reversed, leaving the boys behind in their cells. The corridor was like a chute of artificial light, shimmering blue with convex glass walls now opening on to workstations. The doc pressed a control as the cart slowed. The constraints slipped from Bender's body and retracted into the seat.

- Are you ready to leave?

- Just go? You're going to let me go?

- It's your life, Bender. We've hijacked your body for a while, that's all.

The doc climbed down from the slipcart. The walls of this bit of corridor were made of steel. The doc set his sightwaves on the access panel and a partition slid back. Bender waited a while, then followed the doc through. The door slid closed behind him.

- Do you recognize it? the doc asked.

The floor was made of grey-blue cement. Flat panels of the same color formed the walls. Lights embedded in Perspex formed the ceiling.

- It's decontamination zone. Where I came in.

- You're almost right. Your entry level is one floor below. Most research at Cromozone is subterranean, in the stacks, for better climate control. That panel opposite opens onto the elevator shaft. It leads up to the front gate.

The doc handed Bender a backpack, made of the same material as the slinksuit.

- Its padding molds itself to your back. The straps expand and contract with the muscles in your shoulders and chest. It should free you to run with almost no constriction. The clothes you wore to get here are inside, washed and pressed. Your old shoes. And a chicken. A roast chicken. Fresh. Cloned and enhanced with natural grain. We had it slaughtered this morning. It's not roasted of course. You moved too fast, we didn't have time. But it's particled to recreate a four hour slow roast of a six-month old free range organic bird. Sealed in uniplastic so as not to leak. You feel bitter, Bender. You feel degraded. Sit down when you get out and taste that chicken under an open sky. You'll be the first person in more than a decade to eat chicken in the outside world. You'll trust us then. You'll know we're on your side. You'll know life's only getting better from now on. And here's something else I've brought to show you.

Doc Drake reached into a pocket of his lab coat and pulled out a creature. It was white with pink ears, a pointed snout, and a long tail. It ran up the doc's arm and perched on his shoulder. He reached up to take hold of it then pinned the creature on its back, its spine curved along the palm of his hand.

- Do you see that? Do you see its little dick here? Do you see its balls?

The doc's fingernail pressed against the creature's skin.

- It's a rat. Male. Cloned. It's got a name. E513. You see this?

The fingernail moved up over the round of the creature's belly.

- This male rat, Bender, is pregnant. A fetus is attached to its abdomen. The fetus is a baby female rat. Do you want to take it home with you, so Karen can practice her delivery techniques? The pregnancy has almost run its course. Birth is due whenever we decide. A little slice, a little leverage, a little snip, a little sewing, and E513 and daughter should both be doing fine.

Doc Drake lowered the rat to the floor and let it go. The creature found good grip on the cement. It scurried round the edges of the room.

- Do you see how healthy he is, Bender? This creature is male, heavily pregnant, and running as well as you're ever likely to do. You really have nothing to fear. Take time, think things through, talk to Karen. Everything will be fine. Believe me. Have you anything you'd like to ask before you go?

Ask a question, get told a lie. Bender had nothing to ask. He just folded his fingers into a fist as his hand shot forward, and thumped it into the doc's stomach. Air gusted from the doc's mouth as he slumped to the floor.

- You like that, doc? You like that sort of doctoring? You like having stuff stuck in your stomach? Make you feel good about life, does it? There's more like that, doc. We don't have to stop there. Believe me.

Bender kept back till the doc showed sign of recovery, till the man had drawn in fresh breath and risen to his feet. Then he skipped to within the doc's range, his fists raised, his belly exposed.

- Do you want me to hit you, kid? the doc asked – Thump you in the guts? Is that what you want?

The doc clenched his right hand and thrust a jab at Bender's stomach. Bender didn't flinch. The jab stopped just short. The doc opened his hand and reached up to squeeze hold of Bender's throat.

- Nice try, kid. You reckon a smart blow or two to your guts might end this pregnancy, break a rib or two but leave you breathing. You're lucky I'm a doctor. I'm trained not to kill, not to go for the killer blow. I wouldn't try the same trick on the streets though, Bender. Not if you want to walk away.

He pulled his grip away from Bender's throat. Scooping the rat from its circuit of the walls he slotted it back in his pocket.

- Run your hand along the far panel if you ever want to leave, Bender. The elevator will come and collect you. You'll find your imprint only works on exit. This door back into Cromozone is now blocked to you. I'll leave you now. There's no need to hurry. This room is yours for as long as you need it.

The doc swiped his hand across the wall. The door slid back to let him through then closed itself again. Bender was sealed in. The ceiling lights dimmed, a slow fade to black. A voice, deep enough to be male, soft enough to be female, sounded in the darkness.

- Air remaining in this chamber for single adult human consumption, two hours, seventeen minutes, ten seconds.

The voice was company of sorts.

- Air remaining in this chamber for single adult human consumption, two hours, sixteen minutes and fifty seconds.

Bender slid his feet across the floor. He felt his way around the walls with the flats of both hands.

- Air remaining in this chamber for single adult human consumption, two hours, sixteen minutes and ten seconds.

It seemed he wanted to live. Bender pattered the wall with his hands. A motor hummed. Light sliced in and beamed wide as a panel opened. Bender jumped inside.

Doors closed off the darkness and the elevator carried him back to earth.

1.02

I'm Bender. I've outgrown Steven's feet. His whiteflashes are tight on the instep. They weigh heavy like they're rooted. My eyes smart with tears for the kid. He loved these shoes. They made running like flying he thought.

He knew little. He was so young.

The black shoes are in my bag. They've got a name. I call em skypumps. The slinksuit's in the bag too. It folded up so small it slotted inside a shoe. I've put on Steven's old kit. The shorts cling tight and the shirt sags. If his old life fits as bad as his clothes I'll run straight out of it.

I've got a mantra going. It's a running mantra. One syllable for take-off, one for landing.

Ben-der, Ben-der.

Drumming the new name home.

Ben-der, Ben-der.

Teensquad named me. Now I've grown into the name.

Ben-der, Ben-der.

I'll laugh when I see teensquad. Laugh inside. They'll shout hi and think they know me. They'll think I'm the Steven they call Bender. They're wrong. I'm not. I'm just Bender. Something new.

Ben-der, Ben-der.

Malik'll get it first. I won't explain. I'll just be my new self and wait. He'll cock his head to the side and stare at me. I'll stare back and watch for that click in his eyes as it registers. Bender's shifted, he'll see. Then he'll smile. He'll grin. Game on. He'll start adjusting till he's got where I'm at, till we're back in step. That's how we stay ahead. We keep pace with each other.

Maybe we'll swap kits. I'll wear his. He can try out the slinksuit. And the skypumps. It'll be fun to see him moving in those. Fun to keep up.

Dirt's drifted across the road but the wind's dead. I turn my head and there's a dustflurry where I've been. My footprints smudge the ground. I look ahead and town's hidden inside a brown cloud, like a bomb's just taken it out.

If only.

I stop. Kick off my shoes, put aside my bag, lay on the earth on the side of the road and face the sky.

Look into the sun and you burn out your eyes. That's what they say. It's a story. A lie. No-one's done it coz everyone believes it. Who'd be so stupid as to stare at the sun and find out? They tell us that crap so we'll look at the ground. They don't want us to look at the sun too long.

You don't go blind if you stare at the sun. You see what they don't want you to find.

That's my theory. I'm going to try it out.

What's to lose?

- Hey, it's Bender.

I recognize the voice. It's Soo. He's multi-colored and round, like a sunspot.

- That you, Soo?

- You OK Bender? What you doing on the ground?

The world's gone dark grey.

- Get out the way, Soo. I'm nearly there. I've been working in from the edge. I'm about to see through the sun.

Soo laughs. He thinks I've cracked a joke.

- You been forcefeeding, Soo? You got so fat you block out the sun now?

Others laugh. About four of em. Nervous laughs. They're glad to find me well. They think they've found me. They think they've found me well. They're not sure.

- I've lost it, Soo says - My Mom tells me I've lost weight.

- Your Mom's a liar, I tell him. Teensquad's got a lot to learn. Everybody lies. That's a lot to learn – Don't go trusting your Mom,

Soo. You even sure she is your Mom? Were you conscious when you were born or were you like the rest of us, zapped out of it?

- Where have you been, Bender? a new voice asks. It sounds like Runt. I stand up and stare. He's another sunspot but shorter than Soo. Not so round as Soo. As I stare at him his violet edges bleach away and he turns grey. My sight's coming back. It's Runt.

- In the woods. Working out. I've learned a lot. We've got a lot to do. We've got to be fit. See that?

I pull up my shirt to show my stomach.

- Hard as rock. You've not lost weight, Soo. You're the same fat fuck as ever. Three weeks starving in the woods, running assault courses till you drop, you'll never get near a stomach like this. You know why? You see that?

I point out the pinprick white scar. Soo bends to take a closer look. It takes a while. One bend is a whole excursion when you're as fat as Soo.

- I got it in Cromozone. It's a silicone implant. A new formulation. It spreads evenly around the stomach lining and hardens. Cromozone's designing a new breed of warrior male. This silicone's as tough as armor plating. It blunts knives. It reflects lasers. I've got the hardest, toughest stomach in the known world.

- It doesn't show, Soo says — You're the same skinny freak as ran away.

Good. I'm getting to him.

- Try me. Throw one punch. Right on the scar. See for yourself.

- We've come to find you, Runt explains — Not punch you. We got worried. Your brother Paul hacked into Cromozone for us. He found you'd been released. We split up to come and find you.

- You're just in time. This silicone strengthens on impact. It needs a good blow to ensure an even spread across the tissues. Otherwise it settles into pockets. Pockets aren't dangerous, they just look odd. I don't want to look odd. Do us a favor would you Runt? Thump me in the guts. It's better you do it than Soo. You're wiry.

You've got muscle. Fat fuck Soo here's turned to flab. That right, Soo? Your muscles turned to sponge?

Soo's the strongest of all but placid. It takes a lot to stir him. I'm almost there. He lifts his right fist to his mouth, spits on his knuckles, then rubs the spit in with his left hand.

- Where you want it? he asks.

- You sure you're up to it? You've come a long way from town. Not fast I know, you never run fast, well fast for a fat fuck but not real fast and it's a long way for you. This stomach needs one real blow, as powerful as a man can make it, not a fat fuck's soft dab.

- Where you want it?

I strip off my shirt and fling it to the side.

- Right on the scar. That's best. It's a tiny scar though. Are your eyes good enough to see it, fat fuck? Do you want me to mark it for you with a pen?

- You ready?

- So ready I'm bored.

I open my arms wide, slouch a little, and look down. My belly's small and soft. I'm fond of it. It doesn't deserve any of this. I watch Soo's fist drive into its flesh. He uses a twist punch he learned from karate. He's good. A fist driven like that can push right through a man. It can go in through the front and out through the back, shards of spine caught between its fingers.

That's what they say. I never believed em. Now I wonder if they're right.

I can't turn to see. The world's gone white but flashed with red. I've stopped breathing.

Their silicone's crap, Soo's saying — His stomach's as soft as, as soft as …

Soo's not at his best with words.

- As soft as Mom's bum.

- You've near killed him, Runt says.

Maybe he has. My stomach's done for sure. Parasites get no choice, they suck up life wherever they land, but if I was a parasite with choice I wouldn't leech on to this stomach. This stomach doesn't want it. Any parasite in there's just been thumped to death.

- You heard him, Soo says. He's upset – He said to hit him as hard as I could.

They all talk, like they're arguing, then they all go quiet at once.

- What's that? Runt asks.

It seems I've been speaking. I'm trying for words but I don't know what's coming out my mouth. Maybe just blood and saliva.

- Don't believe a word, is what I'm telling em – All words are lies.

If those are my dying words then that's OK. I'll never think of better ones.

You learn things from living longer. Here's something new I've learned. When you deliver a death-defying blow to someone's guts, you don't make em better by draping em over your shoulder and trying to jog along an asphalt road.

I'm a runner who can't even walk. Can't even stand. Can't even sit up. Soo kneels down and the others lift me into place. My head's cushioned against Soo's chest and my feet bounce against his back. Fat and muscle pad his shoulders but it makes no difference. Soo takes five steps, the movement jars up from the road and through his shoulder, thumps into my stomach, and I pass out.

I don't get heaven. Life ends, that's heaven enough. Another acceptable version of heaven is this. It's not a spectacular version, but it's an improvement on how life is. You wake up, day's come, and a nightmare's over. Heaven is waking up and leaving a nightmare behind. You look around and things are restored to how they used to be.

I wake up and think that I'm Steven. That's not the heaven part, that's just a mistake. Before I get it right though I look around and think I recognize Steven's garden. Years ago you could walk in that garden without treading grass to dust. Even as baked dirt it wasn't so bad. No weeds came up. You could rake the ground and have it all look neat and hopeful, as though seeds could spring life any moment.

This garden's got that baked earth look. It's the way Steven's garden looked before his Dad tore it apart. It's how a garden of just the same size and shape would look without trenches and traps and pits and platforms and barbed wire. This garden's not a crazed assault course. It's dead and quiet, the way nature means it to be. It's a peaceful place to lie.

I let my vision blur then close my eyes.

- You OK Bender?

It's Malik. I open my eyes to match the face to his voice. His head's close. His brown eyes stare into mine.

- What you do that for, Bender? Why did you make Soo hit you?

I work to bring Malik into focus. The results are mixed. I get to see him more clearly and maybe smile a moment. Pain then shoots up along that extra spurt of consciousness and smashes the smile from my face. It's like a fire that starts in some black cauldron around my balls then flames up through my guts and my chest and my throat. I guess I howled.

- What's that? What have you got down there? What are you doing to him?

For a moment I think it's Dad. I'm still thinking like Steven, like I had a Dad. I don't believe in hell. Who needs hell when you've already got life? Invent hell though and this makes a neat package, fire on the inside and the voice of Steven's Dad burning its way in from the outside world.

- Is that Steven? When did he get back? He's been in that house all along, is that it? Now you've brought him outdoors to bugger him in the open air. Have your way with him in front of his own

Dad's eyes. It's sick. You make me sick.

I turn my head toward the sound of Steven's Dad's throat as it vomits words from his system. My head is angled toward the sky. Steven's Dad appears in view, wiping his mouth with the back of his hand. He looks down from his platform. Looks down across the wall between his own garden and where I lie. I'm next door, not in Steven's garden. The madhouse of his Dad's traps and trenches still exists.

- You disgust me, Steven, he says.

Sunlight catches spittle from his mouth and makes it sparkle in the air as it rains down.

– Get up. Get some clothes on. Get back inside the house. I'll have to lock you up with Karen. Keep armed guard over the pair of you.

Here's another thing I've learned from living longer. Parents force kids into total shutdown. I feel it coming on. It's like a whistle that gets so high it's ultrasonic, the pressure builds up and gets tighter and tighter then in a flash it's gone. Your body's left for your parents to scream at but you're not there, you're long gone. I've been in and out of consciousness so much it's getting easy. Here I go. Pain easing, dream of whiteness spreading wide.

Then Bender kicks in - That fuckhead's no Dad of yours, he reminds me - You're me now. You're Bender.

Ex-Dad's talking again. His voice comes down from the platform. Now I get the difference. In Steven that voice triggered a slug of resignation. It jolts Bender with anger. My eyes open. I'm alert. The fire's in my body and my throat's burned out. The pain's reduced to a slab that thumps around my heart. Life's come back as a heartache. I guess I'm not due to die after all.

- V78we9t7, I say.

- Shhh, Malik says – You're not making sense. Cool down. Stay easy.

Seems I must regroup my senses if I'm going to get to tell more lies.

- This is how we found him, Malik says. He's talking louder, speaking to the man above the fence.

- Naked?

- With his shorts on. Like he is now. The rest of his things were in this funny black sack. We split up and took separate roads north, looking for him. Soo's group found him, by the side of the road. He's been attacked.

- He's sick?

- He took a blow to the stomach, we think.

- That what he says? Get up, Steven. Get up at once. Don't be such a wuzz. A punch in the stomach never killed anyone.

- Houdini, Furbo says — Harry Houdini, the escapologist. He died of a punch to the stomach. I read about it. He was showing off. Asked his assistant to punch him but the blow came before he was ready, before he had tensed his muscles. It ruptured his insides. He died soon after.

- I'll give him something to die for if he doesn't get up this minute. Come on Steven. On your feet.

- He needs medical attention, Malik says.

- Then we'll call Statesquad. They can take him in and examine in. Find out just what you've done.

- He's just been released from Cromozone, Malik reminds him — You know that. Paul found that out. Whatever's happened to him happened there. They dumped him on the side of the road. We can't send him back into that.

- So what do you suggest? You want me to leave him in your capable hands?

- He needs proper help. Someone who's trained. Maybe his sister. She's had medical training, hasn't she?

The sky roars. It's ex-Dad laughing. I look up inside the grey chasm of his open laugh and can smell its gusts from memory. From Steven's memory. His laugh spends itself out.

- You think I'm falling for that? You think I'll let you use my own son as bait to trap my daughter?

- He's sick, Malik tries – He needs your help.

- The whole world's sick and he's one of the sickest things in it. I might chain him up but I can't help him. He's beyond that.

- Give him his qual, Runt suggests. They've closed in around me now, leaving ex-Dad to peer from his watchtower – I found this batch in that new bag of his.

- Ring of Power, Furbo shouts. He takes the bag from Runt and counts em out – There's enough and then some. One each.

- With that freak watching? someone asks.

- He's a drek, Malik answers – He doesn't exist.

- You talking about me? ex-Dad shouts down – No drug-soaked skink gets to talk about me like that.

Ex-Dad's an empty scream. Chuck words at him and you fill him up so he can scream on. Ignore him and he soon dries up. Teensquad have all had Dads one time or another. They know that much.

- Let's do it, Malik says.

He goes to my left, Dome to my right. They ease my body into position and stretch up my arms.

- You'll be alright, Malik says. His voice is the first good thing my body's felt since coming back as Bender. It starts from where his lips touch my ear, collects inside my head and pulses down my spine – I'm with you, Bender. We're with you. We'll give you everything we have. We'll hold on, Bender. We'll hold on.

My lips are open. He reaches between em to pull my lips apart and settles a capsule on my tongue. It slides down to my throat and I swallow.

- Soo's holding the center, Malik tells me – He'll watch out for your Dad.

Everyone swallows and lies down. The fingers of Dome's left hand intertwine with my right, the fingers of Malik's right hand intertwine with my left. We are gathered in a ring with Soo as its center, our arms angled high to form the pattern of a star. I feel the power on the instant of connection. It's like blood is pumped through all of us by one giant heart, the current charging from left to right. It's electric.

Game's on. The trick is to hum when the qual kicks in. As each one starts the ride they hum till we're one voice humming, carving out time and space.

It's there. I can do it. I'm first. I find voice enough. I hum.

Hum.

Like you hum when waiting for something to happen.

I hum louder. No-one joins in. Dome relaxes his hold on my hand. The ring's breaking apart.

- Duds, a voice says from the far side of the ring — There's nothing in em. What's Bender humming for? They've been feeding him blanks.

I felt something. I still feel it.

Malik lets go of my hand. The feeling stops.

- Nobody move.

The shout comes from the watchtower. We look up and see ex-Dad. He's holding a crossbow in front of him. He's been trading this stuff since I was a kid, keeps a pile of such crap in the cellar. He's grinning like this is his big day. Like life's been worth screwing with all these years just to make this kind of sense.

- The first one to touch her gets an arrow.

It's his version of romantic. Ex-Dad's playing Cupid. The gate to the garden where I'm lying opens and a figure walks through it. I turn my head to one side and I can see it. It's dressed in yellow plastic. A plastic hood, plastic cape, and thick plastic pants that buckle round its ankles, an outfit left over from times when it rained. It crackles as it moves.

- Karen, Furbo says. He recognizes her fast. She's been playing on his mind.

- Nobody move. Nobody touch her. Just stand clear of Steven and let his sister examine him.

Karen crackles louder as she kneels close. Her face is white. Her right cheekbone's bruised.

- What's up? I ask. A sound comes out of my mouth but not the sense. Karen's face turns extra worried and she looks across at Malik.

- He got hit in the belly, Malik explains – a real hard blow.

- No talking, ex-Dad shouts down.

Karen pulls some rubber tubing out of her pocket. She fixes two ends of it to her ears and presses a suction cup at its other end to my chest.

- Can you talk? she asks.

- No talking!

- Look lay off, Dad. I'm draped in your dirty plastic in hot sunshine. No-one's getting a look at me, no-one's chatting me up. You've got the whole place covered with that fucking crossbow.

- You mind your language my girl.

- I've got to talk to Steven. Find out what's wrong. Just let me get on with it and get out of here, OK?

She waits. Ex-Dad doesn't answer back. Karen bows her head so the hood hides her face from him. She speaks soft.

- He's flipped, Steven. He's lost it. What did you come back for? I've just been waiting. Waiting for my chance. I was going to follow you.

I stare up at her.

Her face. Malik's face. Those two faces staring down at me. That's what I've come back for.

- Well Miss Doctor, you got a cure? ex-Dad shouts down.

- I'm working on it.

- I know what you're doing, my girl. You're waving your ass around in the air. Now you get your ass into gear and bring it back round this side of the fence. I've had enough of this game. You … and you.

He waves his crossbow to make his choice. Dome and Soo.

- Pick Steven up and bring him round to my gate. Leave him outside and come back here where I can see you. I'll drag him inside and Karen can help me carry him from there. You're not setting foot inside this garden, not one of you, not one step, not till I'm ready for you. You understand? I know your game. You want to carry Steven up to his room. You'll case the house on the way, and work out its layout. That was your plan. Well it's not working. If we've got to have Steven back then we'll drag him back ourselves. That's an end of it. Go on. Pick him up.

Dome grabs under my arms, Soo around my thighs, but I still sag in the middle. It creases my stomach so that I shout out.

- He needs a stretcher, Soo yells.

- You'll all need a stretcher if you don't get on with it. Hurry up. Bring him round.

- Don't worry, I hear Malik say as I pass him – We'll get you out.

I'm glad he says it. Some lies are alright.

I stand up. Ex-Dad's carrying me nowhere. I've got to practice walking for when I run from here.

- Thought so, ex-Dad says when he opens the gate – You were fine all along. It was a plot.

Karen's got my clothes and my bag. I walk barefoot along the path and in through the front door, then hold on to the railing at the bottom of the stairs before starting to climb. Paul's in the front room. I see him through the angle of its open door. He doesn't look round. He's plugged into his terminal.

- I'm going to bed, I tell Karen.

Dad's stayed out in the garden. He's the dog. Karen's followed me in. She's peeling off her plastic rainsuit and chucking it back down the cellar steps. She's in tight silver shorts and a lilac sleeveless top pouches her breasts. She shakes her head to loosen its ginger curls.

- You look good, I tell her. My voice is pinched but it's working.

- You look crap. What bed are you going to use? Dad chopped up Mom's bed for the wood and dragged its mattress down to his cellar. He's been sleeping in yours. He tried to get in to mine. He said times are hard and we've got to stick together. I turned to the wall and he held my back, pressing his dick against my bum. I kicked him out. He came back and gave me this.

She points to the bruise on her cheek.

- He got worse, Steven. I gave it him worse. He crawled away but he won't crawl again if he ever comes back. I'll kill him. I should kill him now. Kill him in any case. You're not strong enough to be back, Steven. He'll have you.

- Steven's gone. I'm Bender now.

I walk the stairs to Steven's room. It takes a while, one step at a time, some resting and some gasping. My face is wet but I'm not crying. My eyes are sweating.

The sheets are grey and marked with ex-Dad's imprint. I pull em off, drop em to the floor, and lie on the mattress. Karen comes and stands by the bed.

- You going to be alright?

- You're the medical student.

- I cut babies out of stomach's. That's it.

- You can stop that now.

- It's what I do. I'm getting good. An operation's on hold in my room. I've delivered the baby. A girl. Now I'm saving the parent. I'd better get back. You see Mom?

- Don't ask. You don't want to know.

- She alright? She like her things? Did you give her my dove?

Funny how you don't think about it. The world wants a lie and you give it to em.

- She was touched, I say - She laughed and cried. She says thank you. She says to give you a kiss. Could you bend down?

Karen bends, she puckers her lips, and I kiss her on the mouth.

- I knew she'd be pleased, Karen says – Little things still matter.

The kiss and the lie have made her life right for a while.

- You'd better get some rest, she tells me.

She smiles and goes back to her room.

I doze. I don't know what was in those capsules. Hormones. DMT. Whatever. Something's taking effect. Something's going on in my stomach but it's not all bad. It's like my guts are knitting themselves together. Beyond that, all around that, something else holds me. I guess it's chemical, a gift whisked up by my brain, but it feels like a hammock of skin which rocks me. Or maybe a boat. A round boat of skin stretched round a structure of thin white bone and bobbing on a sea of tar.

Something yelps. I listen but nothing follows. Maybe the yelp was me, a stab of pain inside a dream. I drift off again.

- Can you move?

Karen's got hold of my shoulder.

- Can you make it across to my room? I can help. Hold on to me. I want you to see this. You've got to see this. It's so weird I nearly screamed but cut it off. You don't scream in this house. Screams bring Dad running.

She's been finishing off her operation.

- I did it. I told you I'm getting good. I've kept em both alive. Baby and parent. I've left the placenta inside and stitched up the wound. I've even taken a sponge and washed up a bit. The program's kept running. I took the time to have a look around. Checked out the operating theatre. Checked out the patient. Look, Steven. You've got to look.

She fits the anthead visor over her head to adjust the image, then lifts it off and puts it on me.

- Surprise number one. Check out the sex of the mother.

The stomach's still swollen. That surprises me. I thought it would just shrink back to normal with the baby cut away from it. The wound's raw, the stitches purple. I look to the right. This new mother's got a penis. Can't say I'm surprised. It looks tiny in its cloud of ginger hairs, the way a dick shrivels after swimming.

- You get it? The parent's a man.

I'm already scanning left. I watch his chest. The patient's not breathing. The image is on hold, or he's dead. I go up to his head. For all the blood down below his eyes are closed and he looks peaceful. Like a soldier in a battlefield who's been helped to die.

- You see him?

If he could open his eyes he'd see me back. We'd be looking at each other. Looking at ourselves.

- It's you, Steven. I've just helped you give birth to a baby girl.

- I'm Bender, I remind her – I got a punch in the stomach. It ripped my guts apart. There's no baby inside me. Don't waste your life. Stop practicing.

- But why do that? Why go to all that trouble? Why make me think I'm delivering my own brother's baby? How fucked is that, Steven? You tell me.

- It's fucked, I tell her – Totally fucked.

- Totally.

I lift the visor off.

- They must have scanned me when I was in Cromozone to beam that picture in.

- You let em do that?

- Why did you let your Dad hit you?

I brush my hand across her cheek. She glares back.

- That's what I mean. You don't let em do things. They just do em. It's a battle, Karen. Like you and your Dad. You see it's a battle?

- Too right.

- Who's winning?

- Dad or me? I'll die before he wins.

Death's the final card. It's an ace. Play it and you can't lose.

Dying's a funny game. It's a spectator sport. That's the good thing and the bad thing about it.

The bad thing's not knowing when your own death's over,

so you don't get to enjoy it as much. You don't get that sense of completion.

The good thing is watching others die.

Steven was mixed on that. Death wasn't his favorite sport. Bender's much clearer. He's developing a long list of dying fixtures he doesn't want to miss. Dad's dying is way on top of the list. Bender's big on the sport of dying. He's a fan. He's me. I'm a fan. I look out through the window at Dad on his tower.

I'm getting to see the world in a few different ways. Here's a funny thing I think about houses. Live in one long enough and it starts leeching from your life. A family is parents, kids plus a house. The house is never on the kids' side. It knows the kids want to run away. In a bid to keep the family together it steals thoughts from the kids' brains and transmits em. I have these thoughts when I'm running the streets and I bet Dad doesn't twitch, lift his head, and stare in my direction. That trick only works for him in the house. It works now. I think of death. I think of the sport of watching his death. He lifts his head and stares straight in through the window and at me. He climbs down from the watchtower and a minute later he's climbing the stairs.

- You signaling to em? he asks from the doorway, then focuses on Karen – As for you, that outfit's obscene. Why not strip off the top and flash your tits at the world. Shall I fix you a red light for nighttime? Then you can keep displaying yourself at the window.

The red light's not a real offer. He's brought the wrong tool for electricity. He rips back Karen's carpet and smashes the wedge end of his hammer into the floor. Soon he's ripped up a floorboard. Another follows. He makes a gap of three boards from wall to wall just inside Karen's door. When he's finished he moves over to her window, opens it, and starts to throw the planks down. He doesn't watch the last plank fall but turns and leaves. His feet run down the stairs and out of the house like he's young and excited.

I lie down on Karen's bed. I'm tired, but there's no sleeping with this much drama about. First we get the sounds of Dad sawing, then the clatter of a ladder hitting the outside wall. Dad appears at the window. His mouth is filled with nails. He lifts a board to the top of Karen's window and hammers a nail into the frame. He's a quick worker. Three more nails, the board's fixed, and he's off to the ground for the second.

Karen's ready when he's back. Hers is a sash window. She pushes it up but then she'll have to let go and shift her hands before pushing Dad back, off the ladder and to the ground. That's the flaw in her plan. Like I say, Dad's quick. He reaches in and grabs her hair with his left hand. Pushing her head down then pulling her forward he jabs her head against the sill then throws the board aside to bring the window down. It slams against her hair and traps her.

He's kept the nails in his mouth. Pulling the hammer out of his belt he taps the nails more gently than before for fear of breaking the glass. He's nailing the window shut.

I wait till he's finished, till the window's boarded and the room's lost its light. Karen stays still. I know what's happened. It's ultrasonic whistle time. The pressure's built up and she's left. They've got her body but she's broken free. That sort of thing. I go to her dressing table, open a drawer, and pull out her scissors. They're nail scissors but they'll have to do. Snip by snip I cut her free, as close to the window as I can manage. She turns her head to keep some pressure on her scalp. As soon as I cut the last strand she knows she's loose. She leaves her hair hanging outside and goes and sits on her bed, her feet scrunched up against her body.

- Call that winning? I ask her.

Her hair sticks up in tufts around her head. Her eyes are rimmed red and glare. She's shaking. She looks sick as hell. She looks like me. That's one trouble with twins. They reflect each other too much. I shudder and step across the hole Dad's ripped up inside her bedroom door.

He's crashing about in the cellar. I stand at the top of the stairs and wait. He soon comes up, stacking two gas cans on top of eight others by the front door.

- Mom's a blob with wires streaming from her to machines, I tell him – They prop her on cushions to keep her upright. The fat's swollen her eyelids shut and she just sits and cabbages in front of the window. But at least she's kept her hair.

Ex-Dad turns to face me.

- Did you cut your sister free?

- She had great hair. It was like Mom's.

- It was a fire hazard. Any spark would set her head alight. She's better off without it.

I close my eyes. Screw em tight. Hold on to the banister and let myself down to the ground.

- Do you see it? Are you getting one of your visions?

- No, I lie. Flames lick round the inside of my skull. Faces peer through em but they're too charred to recognize. I wait for the colors to fade to black and open my eyes again. Ex-Dad's still in the hall, grinning and staring up at me.

- It's coming isn't it?

- It's the gas. The fumes from those gas cans made me dizzy.

- You're lying, Steven. You're a lousy liar. You see it. That fire you see, it's on its way. It's soon, isn't it? Your scum friends are coming for you. For you and your sister. I know. I've not got your sense Steven. I don't see things. I smell em. Your teensquad's coming. They're coming for you. And I'm ready.

He opens the door and shifts the cans onto the path.

- You're mad, I tell him, but he's already closed the door. The lock turns.

Karen comes out of her bedroom.

- I heard what you said, she says – Heard what they've done to Mom.

- They didn't do it. They just took what they got and plugged it into their system. He did it. Your Dad turned your Mom into a freak.

- She's your Mom too. He's your Dad.

- Not mine. Steven's. He's ex-Dad now. She's ex-Mom.

-You talk like Steven's gone.

- He has. He's ex-Steven. His Mom's ex-Mom, his Dad's ex-Dad.

- And I'm ex-twin?

- I'm still working on that.

- Call yourself what you want, Steven. You say you're Bender, I'll try and call you Bender. But you can't wipe out your past like that. It goes with you. I go with you.

She crosses the landing and goes into my room. A moment later she comes out with my cutthroat in her hand.

- That was hidden, I tell her - You can't find that.

That's what I thought. I got one thing out of Dad's gift of the cutthroat razor. The fact that Paul wanted it, I got it, and Paul didn't, made the razor worth having and keeping. I used its blade to slit a small hole in the mattress, the side that faces the wall, and poked the razor inside. No-one would find it there. Seems I was lying to myself. This house allows no secrets. Someone always ferrets em out.

- I'm the older twin. I got special powers. You want me to stand here blabbing more of your secrets?

Karen rubs a hand up through the remains of her hair then nods toward the bathroom.

- Come on, she says. She throws me the razor and walks to the bathroom.

- You've got a choice with that thing, she offers – Slit your wrists, or shave me.

The razor's sharp. Dad must have stropped it. Beads of blood stud Karen's scalp as I work, sliding the blade through the lather of foam. I try not to smudge em. The blood beads are dark and pretty.

- Nobody would think you were a girl, I tell her - Your head's too complex.

I wet my finger and run it across her skullscape of bumps and dips and veins, between the beads of blood. She's watching me in the mirror, watching her new shape emerge.

- Was you hair just a disguise to make you look dim?

- I look like a cat, she says.

- A wildcat.

She smiles. Catching sight of herself in the mirror she stretches the smile into a grin, baring her teeth.

- They still trade cat pictures on girltalk, she tells me – Some of em cute. All of em wild. They say no-one ever tamed a cat. That's why we girls like em. Cats could be locked up in houses but never tamed, just like us.

- Miaow, I say.

Karen hisses, and scratches at the air in front of her reflection. Staring closer she reaches up and pushes her fingers through the blood beads on her head, then streaks three bloodlines down each cheekbone.

- You think Mom can be rescued? she asks.

- Mom's gone. What they've got is just a hulk. Mom's floated away somewhere.

- Is that what you think about women, Bender?

She punches my new name through her lips.

- You think a woman's body is something she floats out of? Mom grew. She kept on growing. Still no-one ever noticed her. You saw Mom in Cromozone, Bender. She was there alright. You just didn't recognize her. No wonder she sealed her eyes shut. She's sick of looking out at a world that pays no regard.

Karen reaches down to the cabinet under the sink and pulls out a bumper pack of crepe bandages.

- Do you remember her using these? she asks.

I don't.

- It was in the early days, when she first started to swell. She bound her thighs tight, from the crotch down to her kneecaps. She thought it might keep her in shape.

She puts down the bandage pack, grips hold of her lilac sleeveless, and starts to yank it over her head. Her breasts bulge up as she pulls, then they spring free. I've not seen em so clear for months. The moons around her nipples are large and almost purple. The nipples are sticking out for a licking. She's enjoying herself.

- Bind me up, she says.

She reaches a crepe bandage up from the floor and winds the first loop around her chest.

- I can't do it myself. You've got to help me, Bender. As tight as you can.

- Don't be stupid. You're being like Mom, I tell her – Breasts swell. It's natural in girls. You can't stop it.

We've been talking to our reflections. Now she turns from the mirror, stands up, and faces me direct.

- You think I want to stop em growing? she asks. She cups a breast in each hand and raises em toward me – They scare you, don't they?

- Course not.

- You like big tits?

- Tits aren't where it's at.

- The world's not changed that much, Bender. Boys like big tits. That teensquad of yours has been staring up at my window for days. They stand in the gardens to either side, open-mouthed, jerking off. We're twins, you and me. We like the same things. We both like boys. It's lucky there are enough to go round. Come on. Bind me tight.

- What for?

- How far do you think I'd get, running this pair of breasts through those streets?

- Stupid question. You're not running anywhere.

- So you've come back home to stay have you, Bender?

- I'm different. I'm a runner.

- You want to see a runner? Set me loose of this trap. You get out of here again, little brother, and you've got me as a shadow. A shadow so fast you'll be in its shade. Come on. Flex those silky arms of yours and bind me tight.

Her back's well muscled. I get her to relax. She wants this bandage tight, she'll get it tight.

- That's crap, she says when I've finished – I can still breathe.

- You want it tighter?

She runs her hands across her chest. The bandages are beige, like make-up on skin. I've bound twelve loops round her. She's lost the shape of a full-breasted girl without getting much to replace it. She walks through to my bedroom and takes my full-sleeved crewneck from my drawer, a blend of red and blue hoops. She can't have that.

- That's a favorite.

- Good.

She drops it over her head.

- You can't just take it.

- You've become Steven again, have you? Clinging on to the past? Keeping hold of what used to be yours? You can't have it both ways, Bender. You've either changed or you haven't.

She drops her own silver shorts to the floor, pulls thigh length grey ones out of the drawer, and puts em on. I follow her back to the bathroom where she's standing in front of the mirror.

- Bender, she says to my reflection – Meet Steven.

It's a joke. Like pulling out someone's teeth and arranging em into a happy smile is a joke. A joke that's funny if you forget that it's real. Bald-headed Karen, Karen in men's clothing, flat-chested Karen with her naked blood-streaked face and grey-blue eyes just staring and staring, so like Steven she could be Steven back from the grave. Some zombie Steven come to haunt me as a twin.

- Not Steven, I tell her – You can't be Steven. If you want some new name, then choose one. But you can't be Steven.

- I'm not like you, Bender, she says – I'm running away from this place, not from myself. I don't want a new name. I'm Karen. I'm still Karen.

- Whatever.

I head to my room and lie down. The window's shut, my room's baking, the sun's sinking and chucking the last of its flames through the glass. I close my eyes, sweat, and play a game. Bit by bit I'm melting, oozing into the mattress. Inside my head goes dizzy, a shimmer of orange, sleep coming at me like sunset-touched waves. A memory of Karen's face comes through, bald and blooded, then breaks apart. I'm gone. I'm out. My body's on the bed and I'm in dreamland.

Even when dreamland's stocked with nightmares it's a better place to be than this house.

Ex-Dad wakes me. Not by a sound, coz he's silent. Not by a smell. He wears faded jeans and a thick black cotton shirt buttoned at his neck and down past his wrists, his forehead's streaming sweat, but he doesn't smell. It's one of his quirks, one of his disguises. He should breathe out gusts of garbage, he should stink of spilt guts, so you know what you're dealing with, but he gives no such clues when he's not lickered up. He's as sneaky as the onset of dysentery. The lack of stink lets him draw real close. He's on you before you know it. Give him an hour to turn drek, whisky seeping from his pores and rolling off his tongue, you'll smell him then. For now just one thing gives the game away. Just one thing shows he's worse than an aimless ageing fuckhead. Just one thing hints at the weird psychotic twisted fury brewing deep down in his bowels.

His stare.

His stare wakes me. His pupils are the average cosmic rush of veins that dance around a slit, and through this slit a slice of black beams out.

I don't see the slit. I feel the black. It prods me awake.

You stink, he says – This room stinks.

He steps across the room and pushes open the window. It's a new window that flaps open. The glass smashes against a gang of moths. They fly in a curve to sweep inside and batter against the bare lamp on the landing. They smash shadows against its white light. Orange light comes in from the street to show me ex-Dad's face. Look at ex-Dad's face and you see the skeleton inside. The face is all skeleton, old skin and bristle.

- You're such a waste, he says – Times I've slipped off a rubber and weighed the come in the palm of my hand before flushing it away. I think of all the millions and millions of sperm I've pumped out just to let em die. It's enough to repopulate the whole planet Earth with seed left over for Mars. I think of that, of all that potential, then I think of you. I look at you, lying there like a long streak of piss. I wonder what devious quality you had in your little sperm brain to wriggle your way to the top. Whatever it was, it must have dropped off with your little sperm tail, for you've sure got no quality now. You shame me. You're like vomit. I look at you and wonder how something so slimy and yellow ever splattered out of my insides.

He's talking filth, but it's poetry in its way. Words often fail him and he hits out. Now he's gushing. He's on a roll.

- You know why only boys have been born since you poked your head into the world? I've got a new theory. It's to make up for you. You're evolution's end, Steven. Evolution got to you and found itself at the dark end of a blind alley. It cut its losses and started again. Like Eve was a rib ripped out of Adam, it had to get its first building block right. You were the template for everything that's wrong about a man. Starting from you it had to build an opposite. It had to produce a real man.

He's speaking faster. Air begins to whistle round the edges of his voice. I get it now. His words are like moths and the lamp.

They're flapping round some glint of an idea in that blacked-out mind of his. Hell is ex-Dad's imagination. Hell has fires. The fires are ex-Dad's ideas. He catches sight of one of em and gets a warm glow. Everyone else shivers. This idea's a big one. He can't contain it. Mom's gone. Karen scares him. Paul doesn't give a shit. He's left with me. The words are beginning to fail him now. He's got one gust or two left. His revelation's close.

- You were odd when you crawled. Then you started to walk. No happy tottering for you. You picked up your feet like they were stuck to the ground with honey. You're not normal, Steven. You make me sick. You've always made me sick. The only thing good about you is that you don't look like me. That's what kept me going. That's what made me want to try again. That's how come we got Paul.

He moves closer. His stare had gone but now it's back, like he's checking out a stain.

- How's your stomach? Still poorly?

I tense. The tension shifts muscles that hurt. The hurt shows in my face. Ex-Dad spots it. Like you spot a fly you're waiting to slam as soon as it buzzes its wings. His hand strikes down. I hear it, a flat slap of skin on skin. It's a funny sound, far away like it's underwater. My knees kick out and my head tries to lift but he's got me pinned. His hand presses down on my stomach, around and around. It feels like the touch of dry bone. I yell once and that's it. My breath's gone. Tears cover my face but I'm not crying. It's just ex-Dad squeezing my eyes dry. Soo punched me and it didn't hurt like this. Nothing's ever hurt like this. Ex-Dad's good at what he does.

- Thank God for Paul, he says — You're fainting into your mattress, he's still plugged in downstairs. He's smashed every record, broken through every barrier and still he keeps on going. He's a star, and this is countdown. He turns sixteen at midnight. We'll know what Statesquad plans for him then. I expect the world. I expect the world for my boy.

The thought turns him mellow. He takes his hand away without a final punch and leaves the room.

Now's all there is. Lie down sick and I lie down forever. This house is no place to be. Walk from here then I can run.

I tread the stairs one step at a time, where they're firm at the edges and don't crack. Ex-Dad's in a chair in the front room, his back to me. His head dips down toward his glass. His eyes are on Paul. Paul's eyes are flashing responses to the vidscreen. I reach the hall.

Two minutes to blastoff, ex-Dad says without turning round – Good of you to stir yourself, Steven. Have you come to sing Happy Birthday to Paul?

I turn the handle on the front door. It's locked.

- Don't worry, Dad says – The place is secured. You're safe in here. Safe as houses. That streetscum of yours won't get at you tonight.

I head for the kitchen. I'm not hungry or thirsty, but some unknown masterplan says I should eat and drink. It'll distract my stomach. Give me energy.

- Here, ex-Dad says as I pass him. He holds out his whisky bottle – Pour yourself a glass of that. Be ready to join in the celebrations.

I stare at him. He's better at staring than I am. He just grins at my effort.

- Paul's been joining me, he says – We've been sharing a nightcap.

- You're both dreks.

- You think so? Then dreks win. We're the future. Here's to dreks. Here's to the future.

He lifts his glass toward Paul, downs it, then bends to pour himself another shot.

- I've got to keep this glass charged, he says – We're set to celebrate.

He checks his watch. It's a relic, an heirloom thing, with a face and three hands. The second hand spins around like it's accurate but it's always playing catch-up. The watch is always slow but it suits ex-Dad. It sets him in the past where he belongs.

- Here it comes, he says, eyes on his watch as it ticks the way to midnight in his own screwed up little world.

In real time he's locked into yesterday. Midnight's past on any clock but his. The newday's already started, taking Paul along with it.

1.03

- Twenty, ex-Dad says – Nineteen, eighteen…

Paul's juddering on his chair and his eyes flare wide. He couldn't give a fuck about Ex-Dad's countdown. Ex-Dad's voice is like the rattle of pipes before gunge spews out the taps. You ignore it. You want the result, not the noise. Paul's as keen to get away from here as anyone. He's just not a runner. He's following a different route.

His hands grip the table and shake it so the computer shakes with him. His chair spins back on its wheels and falls on its side. Paul drops to his knees but keeps his eyes on the screen. I move round to see what's exciting him.

- Six, ex-Dad says, near shouting – Five, four…

He's shouting out the seconds from his retard watch, but the realtime birthday's already struck. What's going to happen to Paul's already happening. The screen's a mess. Waves of grey are flashing down it. I don't get the fascination. Moving closer I see the waves are made of numbers but they're too small and flowing by too fast for me to make em out. No way Paul can be making sense of this. No way.

- Three, two, one, BIRTHDAY. Happy Birthday Paul! Happy Sixteen!

Dad fills his glass so he can set the bottle down, then drains the glass so that both hands are free. He lurches across to grab Paul by the shoulders. The hold steadies him. Paul stays kneeling, gripping the table, as Dad leans over his head and peers at the screen.

- What's this then, Paul? Are you making sense of all this? Is this why you're so excited? This is your assignment from Statesquad, is it? Your reward for being the highest-scoring sixteen year-old of all time?

Paul says nothing. Only stares. The waveflow down the screen stops. A message appears.

Upload complete. Press any key to continue.

Dad reaches forward and presses the space bar.

A blue H appears from the right of the screen. It's made to look like it's twisted together out of balloons. The H bounces off the bottom of the screen then floats up to the top left corner. A red A appears. A green P. Another P, this one in pink. Paul's face begins to relax. His mouth was slack, his cheeks and jaw rigid. Now his face eases back into a smile. The balloon message fills the screen.

Happy Birthday Paul

16 Today

The balloons in the message suddenly pop. Tatters of rubber stream into the middle of the screen then merge and swell into a large yellow blob. The blob rotates as a sphere. Dots of eyes appear, the one-line slash of a mouth and two quick curves for cheeks. It's a smiley face.

Paul giggles.

- What is it Paul? Dad asks.

I put Paul's chair back on its feet and sit on it. I don't want to believe what I've seen. Dad acts like he hasn't even seen it. He reaches for the spacebar again and presses it. The smiley face shrinks till tiny then floats around the screen. It bounces off the bottom wall, the left wall and the top. When it touches the right-hand wall it evaporates like an explosion and the speakers go oink.

Paul giggles again.

- What's it doing? Dad asks Paul, Paul the wonderson, but Paul can't speak.

- It's rebuilding his basic motor skills, I tell him.

Ex-Dad looks back at me like I'm the one insane. Paul reaches his hands to the keys. He puts the index finger of his right hand on the up arrow, the index of his left on the down. He's chosen the right keys. At least they've left him that much.

- They've downloaded him, I explain.

Paul presses the up arrow. A small bar shoots up the right of the screen. The yellow smiley blob floats slowly to the right, steering itself so Paul can bat it away. He gets excited and his bar goes shooting past. His hand-eye coordination needs work but he's happy enough. He laughs as the smiley blob shatters and goes oink.

- Paul? What's up? Stop playing. Tell me what's happened.

Paul hates being touched. Dad tests the reflexes on the uploaded version. He pulls Paul's hands from the arrows and Paul puts em straight back. His back goes extra rigid but his eyes stay on the vidscreen. Dad yanks Paul's chin round and bends down to looks him straight in the eye. He's giving the stare from close quarters. It's one of his favorite tricks. Or it used to be.

He's an old dog. It's an old trick.

Paul's eyes are blank. Nothing stares back.

Dad should have looked away. He should have turned Paul's chin back to the vidscreen and let go.

The last time Dad did what he should have done I missed it.

I've heard stories about animals. Chop off a cockerel's head and it kept running around. Spill the guts of a slaughtered pig into a bathtub and they writhed and tried to slop over the sides. That's how Paul is. They've leeched his brains but his body's still running.

He snaps his head back out of Dad's grip, then smashes it forward. He stays on his knees and keeps low. As his forehead cracks against Dad's jaw I can watch Dad's eyes. They bulge like boils ready to pop. Pull the wings off flies and that's Dad's eyes, spinning round in a panic unable to fly. I'd have laughed more but my stomach still hurts.

Ex-Dad crumples. His legs fold till he's kneeling then he keeps on falling. He's ripped up the carpet by the wall and rolled it back to get at the boards. His skull's hit the carpet. That's what saves him. The carpet's old and pink and rosebudded. I hate it. Now I hate it more for saving Dad.

The smiley blob on Paul's vidscreen drifts to the right and goes oink. Paul's headbutt snatched the cord from his ears. He hears the smiley's call but looks the wrong way. Clip the umbilical cord and drop the baby to the floor, that's how he is now. He drops his hands to the floor like he's going to crawl but slides to the side. His left cheek's on the carpet, his ass in the air. He tips over till he's on his back. His arms wave and his hands kick, but not hard.

The front room's not big. Two men flailing fill it. I slide my chair back to the kitchen door and watch.

Ex-Dad's lips are moving. He's not making sense, not even making sound, just practicing. Seeing what bits of his body are still working. He opens his eyes, looks at me, then looks away. I'm not interesting enough to look at. His head still sideways on the rolled up carpet he shifts his eyes to locate Paul. He sees Paul's bare feet kicking the air. Ex-Dad screws up his nose and sniffs. He smells the air. Gags on the air. Sits up so he doesn't gag himself to death

He stares at me. Not a bad stare. It's got pressure and focus. He's coming round.

- It's not me, I tell him - Paul's shit himself.

The shit's leaking down both legs of Paul's shorts. He spreads it on the carpet as he rolls around. It serves the carpet right. That carpet's going to have to go. Ex-Dad pulls himself across the floor to stare down at Paul's face.

- Statesquad downloaded him, I explain. Stuck here in this house all his sad old life Dad doesn't get to hear the stories that buzz the streets – I've heard about it. Never seen it before. They set you eye-recognition tasks. Promise rewards for high scores. Slip braincode into the programs so all you live for is your next plug-in to vidscreen. They build levels within levels till your eye-trigger response-time matches the fastest rate of input, then gets still better. You get to the stage where your eyes don't just react to the program, they write it. That's when they upload you.

- You can't upload people.

Dad speaks like it's a command, like you can turn your ignorance into a truth if you shout it loud enough.

- They don't want bodies, I say, and point to Paul – They don't want the body called Paul. They've left us him. They've uploaded his neural capacity. It's been sucked into the computing network. Next time you log on for biofeedback, a little bit of Paul at his best will be staring back at you. That's what's left to be proud of. Now Paul can restore his neural capacity. Starting with the smiley blob game. Sit Paul in front of that and he'll build up his old skills. Another year, all his waking hours plugged into vidscreen, and he'll be uploadable again. Maybe in time for his seventeenth birthday.

- He's shit himself.

- You shouldn't have jerked his head from the screen. They sent happy birthday letters and a smiley face. They were bringing him back gently. Grabbing his head like you did, that's like slapping a sleepwalker awake. You shouldn't do it.

- Are you saying this is my fault?

He nods down at Paul's body.

- Are you saying I've turned my own son into a moron?

You reap what you sow, I could have said, but it's a lousy time for a chat. I just watch instead. Dad rolls back the carpet to get at new boards and tugs at one of em. Nails screech and one end splinters but what the fuck. The board's long and weighty enough. He brings his feet together, like he's learning to stand, and sets the board swinging. His weight's behind it as it curves around. The board smashes through the glass of the vidscreen and keeps on moving. The terminal flies and explodes on the wall.

I guess Dads work from instinct and sometimes it's right. Paul's body shudders at the crash then changes. He doesn't sit up and take an interest. Nothing like that. He just stops flailing and lies still. Ex-Dad drops the board and kneels beside him. He cradles his head then tucks an arm under Paul's legs.

- Let's clean you up, eh Paul? he says – We'll carry you upstairs, give you a bath, and put you to bed. You get some sleep and you'll be better in the morning. OK?

He lifts Paul into his arms. Paul's head flops back but his muscles aren't gone. It's just his brain can't work his neck and mouth at the same time. He sees me, some upside down version of me, and smiles.

Paul only smiles for one thing. He's saved up for this sixteenth birthday. He got a Statesquad rating I'll never be able to match. I can read that vacant, hanging smile. I know what he thinks.

He thinks he's won.

I drop parsley flakes into a can of lima beans and stir em round. It's a cooking trick Mom taught me. Fresh is in the eye, she said. Make it look green and it tastes green. Green like fresh is green.

Tears wet my face as I think of Mom's cooking. Cry for the past like that and I'll melt.

I bite my tongue.

A little blood slips down with the next spoon of beans. Mom's gone. Green's gone. Ex-Mom and ex-green. A taste of blood, that's what fresh is now.

My tongue bleeds and my tears change from soft to hard. Tears like that are juicy. I bite my tongue again.

Dad's stripped Paul and set him in the bath. Paul's slid down till he's flat on his back. His legs are levered at one end and his chin's in his chest at the other. Dad skims his hand and pools up water to pour down Paul's body.

- You've used up the water, I say – I could have washed myself down before you filled the bath with Paul's shit.

Ex-Dad looks up at me. It's not a stare. More like twin plugholes. Paul ripped from his terminal, Dad ripped from his bottle, their eyes are the same. It's like a pebble's dropped inside em and all you get is ripples.

Dad's in full drek mode, teary-eyed and vicious all at once. No point talking to him. The only thing dreks get the point of is a knife.

The front of his shirt's streaked with Paul's shit.

- You stink, I tell him.

There's as much sense in talking to a sewer, but at least it's not a lie.

I'm dreaming when Karen comes in. I know coz I feel good.

I wake and the dream's gone. Dreams don't work in daylight. All I get now is a warped nightmare. I get Karen as me. Karen with the bloody nicks on her shaved head.

- Where's Paul? she says. The bandages squeezing her tits inside her chest have forced her voice higher.

It's crazy she's still called Karen. It's like she tried all these years to grow into the name and then gave up. I'd call her Egg. It's what her shaved head looks like and one sharp crack could see her shatter. But she says she's Karen and I can't point out every lie. It's not worth it.

I look across at Paul's bed. It's empty. More than empty. His sheets are piled on the floor and the mattress has gone.

- Statesquad uploaded him.

Karen tips her head to one side at the news. She blinks, and opens her eyes too wide. Turtles are doing alright, they say. They'll outlive the last humans by decades. Rip a turtle out of its shell and this is how it'll look. Like shavehead Karen, bugeyed and confused.

- Someone pull you out of a hole? I ask her – They shake you at the sun?

She tips her head the other way.

- We're twins, I tell her – You look like a sick me, you dress in my cast-offs, but that's it. Step out on the streets and you'll die. They'll kill you just for the surprise on your face. And that's OK. Like it's OK to catch butterflies coz they don't live long in any case and what the fuck else comes bright and delicate like that with wings you can stick to your skin like technicolor tattoos. Teensquads will rip that gawp from your face. Then they'll stamp it into different expressions. It'll be fun.

- I'm leaving, Karen says — I thought you might want to come but you're nothing but a coma. A teenage coma. You're too much to drag. I'll leave you here. Where's Paul?

- Did you hear nothing last night?

- I stuff my ears with wax.

- Statesquad uploaded Paul's neural capacity. It was great. A shit-hot sixteen year-old with a hard-on for his birthday treat one minute, his lips blubbering and spraying the screen like a baby the next. If you think that was funny, you should have watched ex-Dad. He was lickered up and leering like he does, smug with that at-least-I've-got-one-kid-who's-got-what-it-takes look, when this shudder goes through him. It's like his whisky's turned to piss. He stands up like there's volts shot through his ass. He gets to Paul, hooks his fingers into his shoulders, and yanks at him. The cable breaks, the connection's broken. Best-loved Paul the terminal-boy, the home fucking genius streaking to glory through his mainframe, gets jerked loose from it all. He falls to the floor as soft as a turd. Where is he now? Last time I saw him ex-Dad was spooning the shit off him in the bathroom. Paul's wasted. He won't come round again till he's plugged in and that won't happen coz ex-Dad's gone and smashed the computer.

Karen stands like she's thinking, or like her brain's shot some thought into the empty cosmos of her head and she's waiting to see if it connects. She's vacant. Nothing happens.

- We should check in on him, she remembers, switching through some go-back function to a time when she still had a clue — Before we head off.

-Where to?

It's not a clever question, I'm not out to stump her, I'm just curious, just a bit, don't even much care, but she flares like I've gone and pissed on some fresh wound. She flashes out a hand to point at me, finger quivering. The movement sends a gust of rosewater my way from where she's dabbed it on her wrist. It's synthetic, there's no water for roses, some chemist in some lab fixes molecules into some stink for girls like Karen to splash around in memory of childhood. The smell's a lie. Just the whiff of it makes me dizzy.

- You think you're the runner in the family, Steven? You call what you do running? All you do is go round and round. Even when you get away, even when you get right out of here, you crawl back. You think Paul's wasted? Take a look at yourself.

She heads out.

- Dad must have kept Paul, she says — I'm going to wake him. See if he wants to come.

She creeps across the landing and edges open ex-Dad's bedroom door. I follow when she doesn't come back, slide into the room and stand beside her.

Seeing is believing, they say. It's a lie. The brain decodes what the eyes see and brains are fucked. No-one's run their own brain in my lifetime. I see the two heads on the one pillow and my brain says it's cute. Ex-Dad's dragged Paul's mattress through to his room. He's got his arm round Paul's chest, relaxed in sleep but still holding on to his one loved son. Both their eyes are closed. They're breathing and snoring together, soft snores that flutter lips, Dad's lips thin and Paul's lips fatter. Dad's snores blow air into the nape of Paul's neck. It's a love scene, two blanked out bodies spooned in sleep, as innocent as death.

Karen decodes it different. She treads the room in time with their snores and folds her fingers round for a grip on the sheet that covers em. Then she pulls the sheet hard and high so it flaps like a grey sail above her and falls in a heap behind her back.

- Steven? ex-Dad says. He looks like he was dreaming too but snaps out of it. He presses Paul face-down into the mattress as he slides his own body across him. I think he's reaching for the sheet like he's gone shy but his hand reaches to the side of the mattress as he controls his roll to the ground, and as he turns a shotgun's held in both hands and the bolt drawn back.

- So you've let your scum in the house have you, Steven?

His voice is quick and calm but he's talking to Karen. He turns his gun to the figure in the door. To me. His head tilts to one side.

- Steven? he says.

One Steven was already too many. Now he sees two. I read his mind. He's deciding whether to laugh or to shoot.

Shoot, he decides. Shoot one of em, bring things back to normal. Now he's got to choose which one.

Karen solves the problem. She speaks. Her voice gives her away.

- What have you been doing, Dad?

She doesn't give a fuck about the gun. Ex-Dad wheels the barrel back toward her but she looks at his groin instead. It's understandable. For all that she lives in a male world she's not got to see much dick. Ex-Dad's body's pale plus grey patches of shadow and hair. His dick pulses lower as Karen stares at it but its erection's still blazing.

So Dad's got an early-morning hard-on. It's not pretty but it's no surprise. I've heard him jerking off in the night. Karen looks away but she's roused. She steps round Dad and leans down to examine Paul. Paul turns his head but he's too dopey to do more than blink. Karen looks at the white rounds of his ass.

- This is Mom's bed, she says — What kind of monster are you? You've been fucking your own son in Mom's bed.

- Karen?

Dad recognizes her at last. He sets down the gun and scrabbles on the floor for his underpants. They're off-white and baggy, and hang off him like a diaper. He stands straight like he's respectable again and points at Karen, his arm quivering.

- You come in here dressed like a boy. Pull off the bedsheet so you can get yourself an eyeful of your own father and your little brother. That's sick. Don't you ever go judging me, my girl. Don't you ever.

It's Karen's turn to point. She holds a finger just above Paul's ass. Semen's crusted around the crack, and the crust is streaked with traces of blood.

- Today's my little brother's birthday, she says – He's just sixteen. Look. Look what you've done to him.

Ex-Dad's not interested. He stares at her instead.

- Look at his face, Karen. Take your dirty eyes off his backside and look at your little brother's face. This is his big day. This is his payoff for all those hours and days and months he's put into his onscreen work. Months in which I've stood behind him, supported him. What kind of sister were you to him all that time, locked in your room, chewing your mouth off like a bitch on heat? I've cared for him, stood by him, and look what they've done. Scraped out his head like it's an icecream tub. What is he now? He's a discard. Look into his eyes. Do you think he's got any memory of what happened last night? If Paul can't remember it why should it trouble you? The boy's good for nothing. It doesn't mean I can't love and protect him as much as ever. The way I choose to do that has nothing to do with you. If you're so concerned about what happens in this bed, get in it. You don't have to be jealous. I've got love enough for two.

Karen just stands. Her face is a wipeout, like a screen that goes blank as a program's loading. The Karen of a week ago would have run to her room, slammed the door and shouted some brave obscenities from the other side. She still might. She might leap at ex-Dad and squeeze her nails inside his eyes. She might become Egg and just stand there and cry. There's no telling. Even doing nothing she's got the power. Ex-Dad and me just watch and wait.

What she does is sit down on the edge of the mattress. She moves slow, easing her weight onto the mattress. I catch the jink of interest in Dad, that brainbuzz that sends messages to his dick and turns the hair on his neck to bristle. He thinks Karen's got onto the bed to take up his offer. The stupid fuck. She's coiled for something but it's not that. If he pulls his dick out now she'll swallow it and bite.

- Paul, she says. She takes his left shoulder and heaves it up off the bed. Pushing hard she wheels him round so he's flat on his back. Ex-Dad takes a step closer. His brain's decoding what he's seeing and he's loving the lie it's spinning him. He watches Karen manhandle Paul's naked body and thinks she's making room for him. Thinks he knows her next move. She's going to lie on her back and call him over.

- Get up Paul, she says instead – Come on, sit up.

She moves behind him to lever him upright and hold him there.

- Come on Paul. I can't do everything for you. Move your legs. Put them on the floor and I'll help you stand up. You're going to walk. Steven and I will help you. We're going to walk you to your room and get your clothes. We'll help you get dressed. Then we're leaving. Steven who's Bender now, you and me, we're all leaving. We're walking out of this house and never coming back. It's over Paul. None of your life will ever happen again. You've just got to get up and walk away.

Here's what a fantasy would look like. Paul gets to his feet. Ex-Dad drops to his knees and begs forgiveness. That's the two sides of the miracle we all leave room to happen for a moment. It's got all the miracle ingredients, a sick young man in bed and his sister pleading for him. It's even got the right lighting effects, early morning sun shafting through the window. It's just that miracles are a lie that none of us believe in.

- Have you finished? Dad asks – Coz if you've finished groping Paul he could do with some sleep. I don't know if he'll ever mend but it's clear he's going nowhere for a while. If you want to get naked with a brother try Steven. He might fancy you now you've dressed up like a boy.

She grips Paul under the arms and wrenches him round, so his ankles rest on the floor.

- Come on Steven, she says – Take his feet. We'll carry him out.

- You could never do it, ex-Dad says – You'd drop him down the stairs.

- That's better than leaving him here to be your little fuck machine. Come on Steven.

- I'm Bender, I remind her, but start to move round in any case. It's a mistake. Stay where I was and I could have jumped back through the door and away. Ex-Dad moves for his shotgun.

- That's far enough, Steven, he says – One step more and you'll be scraping your leg off the wall.

His gun's pointed at my right kneecap.

- It's tough for a father, choosing between two sons, he tells Karen – But I've done it. I've chosen. You move Paul and Steven loses his leg. He'll lie on that mattress till his stump heals. It's your choice now, big sister. You get one brother or the other. Pick.

Give Karen a choice of two things though and she'll always opt for a third. Toss a coin and she'll bet that it lands on its edge.

- Sit up, slob, she yells right in Paul's ear.

He blinks and shakes his head. She grabs hold of the flesh at his sides.

- I can't help you, she tells him, but the message is for ex-Dad as much as Paul, letting him in on her gameplan – I help you, Dad shoots Steven. You get up on your own though and I don't have to make a choice. Go on slob, get up. I'll give you ten. A count of ten then I'm going to tickle you.

Paul hates being touched. He'd smash everything in a room then start on your bones sooner than let you tickle him.

- Ten, Karen starts – Nine

- Five, ex-Dad shouts to interrupt her. I'm getting a bit sick of her game myself – Steven loses his leg on zero if you've not let go of Paul. Four. Three. Two.

He's not going to mess with one and a half. Karen scurries back across the bed, taking her support away from Paul. He topples backward, his body flat on the mattress and his feet still on the floor. I hope his neural capacity's happy wherever they've streamed it to. I hope he likes his afterlife as a virtual computer. He's smiling now but it's no more than a baby's burp as his fall knocks the wind out of him.

- Now get to your room.

Karen pauses. She can stay. She can go to her room. She makes up her mind. It's option three, the one she wasn't given. She runs out of the bedroom and down the stairs.

- Which leaves you, ex-Dad says – You saw what happened to Paul last night. Do you plan on staying home to look after him?

His gun's still pointed at my kneecap. That's all that interests me right now. He gets the point, shifts the safety lock back in place, and leans the gun against the wall.

- It's fucked, I tell him – What you did to Paul. That's fucked.

He pulls a clean shirt from a drawer and puts it on, switches his underwear for clean ones, gets out some fresh jeans. He even stands in front of the mirror and brushes back his hair.

- Are you going to get dressed? he asks me – This is a special day. You might as well.

- And Paul? Are you going to stick clothes on him or keep him naked?

- Like you care?

He puts on his glasses and turns to me, then leaves the room. He comes straight back with a shirt and shorts for Paul. He takes the shorts first, and bends to slide em over Paul's feet and up his legs. Bouncing Paul off the mattress he fits em in place then sets to work on the shirt. Paul makes his limbs easy to maneuver. That's the best he can do to help himself.

- Paul looked after you. He helped your streetscum find you yesterday. It was his last day for racking up scores, but he took time out. He searched deep inside the Cromozone database till he found your details. Maybe that's why they uploaded him. Maybe he left a trace. Maybe he touched a nerve.

He shifts Paul's legs back onto the bed, and plumps up a pillow to slot under his head.

- He found out you'd been released and ran straight off with the news. Ran next door to your streetscum's new base. He was gone a while. Too long. When he got back he was agitated. He plugged himself straight back into his terminal. Didn't come off again till you saw him. It must do your head in, being raped by a gang of thugs. Something like that must show in your eye-trigger responses.

- Raped?

- Don't play coy Steven. You know that scum. You can barely stand up for what they've done to you. They buggered Paul so hard he was almost witless when he got back home.

- You did it. You.

- Karen's on heat. Her head's flush with sex. She sees sex everywhere. Her imagination needs smothering.

- You told her to get on the bed. Said you'd fuck her like you fucked Paul.

- That's what you heard? I thought I said I had enough love to go round. You know nothing of love. It's before your time. I was dreaming of your mother when you came in and woke us. Dreaming of a time when we were both young. OK I had a hard-on but I was dreaming of love.

- Your hard-on was pressed against Paul's butt.

- He started shaking in the night. I held him still.

- You gave him a bath. His ass was clean when you took him to bed.

- Your streetscum pumped him full. His ass leaked. Is that what happens, Steven? Does your ass leak for hours after you've serviced your scum?

- You're lying. You fucked Paul. Rolled him over and fucked him.

You don't do that with ex-Dad. You don't lay too much on him at once. Not at close quarters. His left hand slashes out to slap my face but it's only a feint. It stops short and he wraps his hand around my left ear.

- You're in this house, you're on my side, he says into my face.

His right hand gathers into a fist and thumps into my stomach. I fall back against the wall. That's OK. Ex-Dad's just finishing off what Soo started. Making sure. I can cope with that.

He moves across the room.

- I'm doing this for you, he tells me. He sounds calm but there's a catch in his voice, like he's choking on some emotion – For you, for Karen, for Paul. For the family. The future.

He picks up a deodorant, lifts his shirt, and sprays under his arms. I'm crap around sprays. They trigger things. He trades the aerosol for his gun and the spew of words keeps steaming from his mouth but the whole picture of him wobbles now, like in a heat haze, lines of shivers passing up from his feet and out through his head. His mouth goes still a moment, but I don't hear it go quiet coz a roar's gathering. It's like Mom's planes are flying from Heathrow again, roaring to bust my skull from the inside, the bricks and wood of the whole house shaking. Ex-Dad's speaking again, at least his mouth's making shapes, but I can't hear the words for the noise. The shivers gather him up coz one moment he's there then he's gone. The door takes up shivering where he used to be. Then the door goes too, the whole room disappears. Darkness swamps it, the room's just this black and roaring square with orange burning in around its edges.

Seeing the future's like a punch in the guts, only it's in the head. Some fist comes flaming in, burning up the present. Time doesn't stand still, it runs away with everyone else, and you're left behind seeing where they're headed and able to do fuck all about it.

My lungs stop. They're choked. It's like all the clean air's trapped inside a bubble in my throat and I can't gulp it down. My head hurts. It's more than hurt. It's like all my feelings contract into bone then pulse and buck and break. All goes dark and flashes orange then skullbreak comes and light bursts in. The light's white, a glare of strobe, and then the future's here. Stick a pin through time, that's what I see, one static moment still to come. My eyes stay shut but it's like they're seared, images etched into em. All color's gone but black and white and shades of grey between, like the future's already sealed and this image of it's an afterburn. I know the place. It's here. Outside. This hell realm is the garden. I know the people standing, too. It's teensquad. Ant Soo Skink Skel Dome all of em. Their feet and hands are sticking out like they're dancing but not together. They're not dancing and not together. They're bursting and alone.

I get down to the floor and stay low. Some air's got stuck down here, squashed beneath the heat. I'm breathing. I crawl. I've got to get to teensquad. Got to get to the garden and those etchings on my eyes before teensquad can reach em. Why get to see the future if you can't get there first? If you get to see the future you can stop it.

Seeing the future comes. And then it goes. My skull knits together and I'm looking at the inside of my eyelids. Next thing I know the floor's shaking. Karen's back in the bedroom, ex-Dad's gone. I look up. I've been dragged to the landing. Paul's mattress is at the top of the stairs. Karen comes out of the bedroom, walking backward, dragging Paul from a hold under his arms. She sits him on the mattress then swivels him round before laying him down.

- What are you doing? I ask, close enough to speak softly.

- You're having a turn. Your stomach's bad. You can't lift. This way I can get Paul down on my own.

She steps over him and stands on the stairs, grabbing hold of the mattress. It slides toward her and she lowers it. It lands at an angle, the bottom of the mattress wedging itself against a step. I get the plan. She means to toboggan Paul down the stairs, the mattress protecting his head and body from any knocks. The plan half works. The mattress sticks and Paul slides off it. His body's relaxed so it snakes down the steps.

- Great work, I say — Kick him when you're down there so he really knows you care.

She hurries down.

203

- Fuck your stomach, she says – Get down here, grab him by the legs and we'll do the rest of this together. Get him down the cellar.

- That's not our job, I tell her – That's Dad's job. That's what he wants us to do. It's a bluff. Paul's always been his favorite. Dad's worked it so we carry him to safety, then he lets rip. He won't do anything while Paul's around. If we carry him anywhere it should be back upstairs. We can prop him up in a window. He's our hostage. Dad won't do anything till he knows Paul's safe. Danger for him means safety for us.

- What did they do to you in Cromozone, Bender? she asks. She says my name like it's an in-joke, punching out the syllables like it's something to laugh at – Trade your brain with an amoeba's?

Karen's got spirit. Shooting insults is good but I need to stand up again before joining in. Karen sees the pain and comes running up the stairs to help me. She takes me to my bed, sits me down, and chooses me some clothes. A white skintop with thin pink hoops, matching shorts, and stale whiteflashes. The window's open and the choke of kerosene's coming through. Ex-Dad's in the garden, bending down the other side of a kerosene haze, pouring the stuff out of a can into his blue-lined trench.

- He's doing it, Karen said, helping me on with my clothes – He's going to burn us down. I'm the bait. You're the bait. He'll wait till your teensquad's come to get us, then burn us all.

- I thought you'd be gone, I tell her.

- Dad's taken the inside handles off the doors. Anyway we can't just leave Paul.

- They'll bring him a new terminal. That's all he wants. He'll be fine. Dad'll never burn Paul.

- You think you can outsmart Dad, she says – You're wrong. He knows you. Whatever the secret, sickest part of your mind is, even if you haven't discovered it for yourself yet, he's been there before you. He's sussed it out and tabbed it. He knows you don't give a toss for Paul.

I look up at her.

- Don't just let Dad worm his way into your sick brain. Get into his. We found Dad buggering his youngest son. You commit a crime like that, you get caught out, what's the best thing to do with the evidence? Burn it. You're not interested in saving Paul. Dad's played around in the sick part of your brain so he knows that. He's relying on that. He gives you the chance to save Paul. You can't be bothered. Paul dies. It's your fault. Dad's conscience is clear. The evidence is burned. Come on. Get up. We've got to get Paul down the cellar. Dad's thought it through. The cellar door's gone but bricks are piled in the hall. And a bucket of mortar. We've got to get down there and brick ourselves in. It's the only way. See you downstairs.

Standing hurts. Walking feels impossible. But then a father locking up his kids and dousing the house with fuel isn't too likely either. I make my way downstairs, heading through the front room to the kitchen. I've got a plan. Fight fire with fire. I try it out but get nowhere then head down the cellar. Natural light gives out at the bottom of the stairs. I sense Karen breathing, and just make out the shape of her bent over Paul.

- The kitchen stove's blown a fuse, I tell her — It must have happened when ex-Dad exploded the terminal last night. I thought I could leave paper on the hotplates till they caught fire, but that won't work. And I can't find any matches.

- You want to set fire to the kerosene trenches.

That's a trouble with having a twin. You think you've had an idea but she shares it so quick it might as well be hers. A special trouble with Karen is that she won't leave it there. She carries your own ideas forward then presents em back to you as masterplans. She does the same thing now.

- You set fire to the kerosene rather than leave it to Dad, and that way the house goes up in flames before your teensquad gets caught in his trap. Is that right?

I nod. She goes on as if she can see me.

- Maybe Dad gets caught in the flames and that's a bonus. That's what you've seen in your visions all along, Dad going up in flames. Right?

- I see flames. I see Dad. He's at the heart of em.

She carries on.

- You've thought through all the alternatives. You've thought of the other ways of keeping teensquad away. Right? Like write a message. *It's a trap – stay away.* Tie it to a brick and chuck it over the fence. That's not an option?

I think it through.

- Dad's got the front garden covered. I just checked. He's up on his tower. The front window's unbreakable. Your window's boarded. Smash out the boards and he'd be waiting with his gun. He'd shoot my arm before I threw.

- Agreed. It's the only other idea I've had. The fire's the best thing I've thought up too. It saves the others and gets rid of the fence so we can get out ourselves.

- Exactly, I say, like I've thought of that bit for myself – So let's just get on with it.

- You've checked all the kitchen cupboards for matches? she asks.

- It's like ex-Dad's seen the possibility. Like he's hidden em.

- You and him, Bender, you're the same. He's just had more practice. Whatever bad thing you think of doing, he'll have got there first. You think he'd pour kerosene around the house and not hide the matches? He's a parent for fuck sake. All our lives he's tried to think of the worst things we could do just so he could stop them. Sure he's hidden the matches. You search the shelves, I'll search the table.

I can't even see the shelves, but Karen goes straight to what must be a table and starts picking up glass jars and banging em down.

- You can see, can't you?

- Kind of, she says – You got to run the streets, I got to stay indoors. I get this house to myself at night. I developed night vision to make the most of it. But this is dark even for me. Maybe this'll help.

I hear a scratch. Smell sulphur. A glow of orange light illuminates her face as she bends to look across the surface of a table.

- No matches, she says — But this jar's got a candle in it.

The candle flames up inside the jar. I can see around the cellar now but don't bother. I just stare at Karen as the candle casts shadows round her eyes.

- You had matches all along?

- In my bedroom. I've got things hidden all over the house, just in case.

- Give em here.

I reach out but she ignores me and climbs the steps.

- You any good at bricklaying? she calls back down. She lines a row of bricks up along the base of the cellar doorway then starts slapping mortar around — I figure if we build the whole thing but leave mortar out of one section, then we can push those bricks out to make a hole. We set fire to Dad's trenches, leap back in through the hole, plug the bricks back inside it, and that's about the best chance we've got. Come on, get some bricks in place while I fetch water.

She heads for the kitchen. I come out to the hallway and set to work. I've laid three bricks before she's back. It's good work, the mortar even, spillage trowelled from the sides.

- Beautiful work, Karen says — I'd make you a bricklaying diploma only it'd go up in flames with the rest of us as we scream ourselves to death. Come on, Bender. Cut the neatness crap. Slap it on, pile them up. Take five more minutes, max.

She's carrying the bucket from under the sink, filled near the brim with water. Mom's collection of kitchen towels is tucked under her arm.

- I'll take this lot downstairs, she says — The water and towels will give us something to work with if smoke gets through. Then I'll give you a hand. I'll spread, you lay. It'll soon be done.

I don't stop to listen. She waits for my response but I simply build fast and high. She has to step over a height of three bricks just to get back into the cellar. She leaves the bucket down the bottom, comes back up, and I'm on my fifth row. She waits the other side. When I'm done I push in the few bricks from the middle that I've just slotted in without using mortar. Karen works on the inside, catching and stacking em. It leaves a hole the width of my shoulders and about the height of my waist.

- So I chuck a lighted match in the trench, jump back in through the hole, and brick it up before the house burns down, I say.

As a checklist for a mission it's simple. Paul could come up with a mission as simple as this as soon as he learns to gibber. Karen passes her box of matches through the hole.

- Strike it in the kitchen, away from the fumes, she says — Light something you can throw so you're not hanging over the kerosene when the whole trench blasts.

She runs down the stairs and comes back up to reach a box of nails through the hole.

- This should do it. The cardboard's old. It'll flame well. Leave some nails inside to give it weight.

She's popping out ideas like she's mainbrain. That's my role. She's stuck me in the dumb role of all-action hero. Life's a twist. I take the nailbox to the kitchen and strike a match. It's pink head goes spinning off the end of the wooden splinter and fizzes to death in a spill of water on the floor. Great. Five matches left. I press a finger over the head and hold it down against the matchbox's side as I strike again. It spits into flame.

Karen's right about the nailbox. The edge of the lid catches light at once. I'm not thinking straight. I've now got to carry a ball of flame to the only open window. My bedroom. I start forward when the front door slams back against the wall.

\- That you, Bender?

A flame touches my fingers and I drop the nailbox. The rush of air as it falls sees the flame spurt up then die as it's rolled on the floor.

\- Malik?

I know it's him. I just make it a question like what the fuck are you doing here? He's wearing my slinksuit and skypumps, grinning like being alive is excuse enough to be happy. The black slinksuit's tight to his body and his hair's tight to his head, sweat streaming down his face and neck. He looks good. His right hand grips a steel bar, like he's got the baton in a relay.

\- I told you I'd come and get you. Didn't expect it to be this easy. Good to see you on your feet.

I grab his left arm and pull him down, jumping back so he crosses the threshold, pulling hard so his head crashes against the inside wall. We hear the crash of splintered wood and look up to where his head would have been. The bolt from ex-Dad's crossbow would have pierced his neck and pinned his throat to the door. Instead it's buried in wood.

Malik spins his body to roll inside. I push the door closed with my foot but check out the garden as the gap narrows. Ex-Dad's just to the left of the gate. A stack of splintered wood in front of him works as a hide. He'd ducked behind it to reload the crossbow but his head sticks up as I watch. He catches sight of me. The door slams shut to cut him from view but it's too late. I've seen him. Seen his grin. It's stretched wide across his face like he's the front of an astrojet. The cull's started. He's taking out the young ones. - Where are the others? I ask Malik.

\- They're coming. We were out for a run. Wearing these shoes of yours I shot ahead. They'll be here in a minute.

The lid's burnt off the nailbox but the sides are still clear. I rip one side a bit loose so it'll catch light and take it back to the kitchen. Mom's oven glove's still hanging by the stove. It had a lamb on it once, dancing in a field of daisies, but washes and burns over the years have wiped all the picture away.

- Get through that hole, I tell Malik, pointing at the cellar — Karen's down there. And Paul. I'll join you in a minute. I'll explain then.

- What's happening?

- Get through that hole!

He's never been great at taking orders. He watches me. The match light's first time. I hold it to the torn strip of the nailbox which flames right up. Mom's glove will help. I wear it on my right hand and set the box down on its palm. I've got one chance. It's got to ignite the trench first time. The fire's got to blast round the trenches and take ex-Dad with it, before he gets the chance to reach the gate. We'll see what his grin looks like then. See how his lips flame red while his teeth shine to black.

The box's sides aren't just cardboard any more. They're blue and yellow and orange licks of flame. The heat reaches down through the oven glove. The nails on their own will glow enough to fire the trenches. My hand's burning. That's good. It's time. I put my foot on the stairs, starting my run to the top. Now or never. Ex-Dad's right. Now's now. Now can open up and swallow everything whole. You see the future and it's now. It's unleashed. You can't snatch it back.

Malik smashes the flaming box from my hand. It hits the floor and burns there.

- You stupid fuck.

His breath touches my face. It's the scent he carries inside him. It's moist and alive. His eyes go blank, like he cares for me but there's no hope, I'm just some lobo spouting headshit.

–Teensquad's coming. Dad's going to burn em. Burn em alive. All of em. I've seen it. Gotta stop it. Fire the house before they get here. Stop em getting in. It's a trap.

Malik turns to the front door.

- Where's the handle?

He beats the door with the flats of his hands and kicks at it. Those skypumps aren't made for kicking.

- Where's the fucking door handle?

He kicks at the door with his heel then turns and heads for the front room. Out through the window he sees the cans of kerosene upturned and scattered round the garden. Ex-Dad's got another can of the stuff in his hands. He pours a line of kerosene along the outside window ledge then moves out of view. The splash of liquid hits the front door. Then we see him again, striding over the first of his trenches and heading for his tower. He's put on a silver suit. It's new but it crinkles. The legs are tucked inside large silver boots. A large silver hood hangs down his back. He looks good. Ex-Dad's coordinated for the first time in his life. The suit catches the light like a shaken pool of water, and even his hair now looks silver.

The air above the trenches shimmers. Both trenches. The one near the house and the one inside the fence. The window ledge shimmers. Looking some more I see the whole ground shimmers. The garden's like a desert after dawn, morning sun sucking up the traces of dew. The light brown dust is dark in big patches with lines of dark reaching between em.

Malik picks up the computer chair. He comes running the chair at the window then lets go. The cushioned seat and back hit the glass. The window doesn't even shake.

Ex-Dad's climbed his tower. He's looking down, over the fence and into the road. I hear shouts from the street but they're muffled. Ex-Dad's voice is loud and clear. He's calling down into the street. It seems teensquad's arrived.

- Stop fretting, scum. Your Malik tried. He sneaked in and tried to fuck my daughter. Thought she was hot. Thought she was asking for it. Well she's not. Not while her father's still around. I dragged him off her. Dragged his little boy's quivering body off her while he was holding her down. Poor Malik. He's not up for it any more. He's got a headache. I say ache. His head's kind of caved in. So she's still intact. My daughter's still a virgin. And she's staying that way. I'm sick of you young pups spilling around every time the bitch goes on heat. Run off home, all of you. Run off home to your mummies and daddies. Go jerk each other off in the woods. Do whatever the fuck you want, only leave my daughter alone.

Malik plucks the backrest off the chair so that its steel pole sticks out. Hoisting the chair up, he rams the pole into the window. The pole glances to the side. Malik's body judders with the impact. A slight round mark shows where he's scratched the glass. That's it.

- It's armored plate glass, I tell him – Dad got a legacy from Gran years back. He used it to change the downstairs windows. I guess this was why. He's been thinking ahead.

Malik leaves the window and heads for the kitchen. The windows are armored glass there too.

You can't smash a rock through armored glass, but words pass through it. Ex-Dad's talking again. It's talking not shouting, but it's loud. He's getting personal. His arm's rigid. His finger points down to pick off each of teensquad one at a time.

- You, yes I'm talking to you dwarfbrain, you who's all mouth and no dick. You I could let in. That'd make Karen's day. She's a medical student. She could strip you naked and have a good laugh trying to sex you. Is it a girl or is it a boy? she'd ask herself, picking your dick up with her tweezers. And you, yes you with your mouth hanging down, you who's all gums and no bite, you I could let in. I've never seen a more obvious little cocksucker in my life. Girls frighten you don't they, babyface. You need a cock in your mouth for comfort. Waaa. Baby needs his cockdummy. Give him his iddybiddy cockdummy. Now you, you're really dangerous. I'm not talking about that little knife you're waving. That's a toy. Your knife's not dangerous. I mean your face. Those boils could erupt any time. They should put a bag over you. Spare us the ugliness and spare us the puss. You, yes you, standing there scratching your balls. Don't bother. You won't find em. They've not dropped yet. And you. How old are you? Seven? Six? What's your role? You must be the mascot. They bring you along for luck. You're the mascot and this is the team. What's the sport? Skipping? You all fresh from coming a valiant last in the neighborhood skipping contest? Or maybe you're the sewing circle. The neighborhood boys' sewing circle. They call you the Needledicks, coz your dicks are too tiny to thread. Well bad luck, Needledicks. Put your mascot back in your pockets. He won't do you any good. This isn't your lucky day. You want my daughter to come and play, but I'm sorry. She's too old. Too old for the likes of you. She doesn't play with dolls any more. Run off and play with each other. Go on, all of you. Fuck off. Fuck off before your pimples burst and mess up the street. Fuck off before I faint from the stink of you. Is that your secret weapon? Your juvenile stink? It makes me sick. You make me sick. Fuck off before I vomit all over you. Am I making myself clear? Are you receiving me? Who's the one with the brain cell? Who's the one to get the message and pass it round. F-U-C-K-O-F-F. But you can't spell. I'll put it together for you. Fuck off. Fuck off.

This is what ex-Dad does. It's a skill of his. He's got nothing to say but he keeps on saying it, words words words like your brain's turned to shit and a fly's buzzing round it, till all you can do is swat at him.

Someone shouts. A rock comes over the fence. The shot's not bad. It's at the level of his face but a meter wide. I hear a cheer from the street but Ex-Dad doesn't duck. Another rock comes flying. The shot's good. It hits the rail around ex-Dad's platform.

- Miss. You missed. That was a girlie throw. Go back to your sewing circle, Needledicks. Leave proper sports to the big boys.

Steel glints in the sun. A knife spears the air above his head. Ex-Dad turns to watch it rise and rise then fall.

- Here's a lesson for you, Needledicks. A throwing lesson. Speed plus trajectory plus aim plus strength plus intent. You need intent.

You've got to really want to hurt someone.

He stoops down, then straightens himself with a rock in his hand. It's the size of a fist. He holds it a moment by the side of his face then jerks his hand forward. The rock flies.

I hear a cry. It's a yelp. It's got to be Furbo. He's had it coming. You don't let off at ex-Dad like he did then stand in range. Furbo's got a rock in his mouth. Ex-Dad never misses with cheap shots.

- Ha! Ha!

It's not laughter. It's a war cry. Ex-Dad opens his mouth like that to make his face a target. You've got to live with him to know it. Like you live with a disease. You know what it's doing, you just don't know how to stop it.

A steel bar comes next. It spins around. Ex-Dad snaps his head to the side so just the breeze of spinning steel hits his face.

- Ha! Ha!

A rock comes. A knife comes. A bar comes.

- Ha! Ha!

He dodges. He shifts. He jumps sideways at a knife that snags his silver suit then tumbles to his platform. He doesn't duck. He waits. Waits for a whole arsenal to come flying over the fence in all its bits and pieces. A rock hits his shoulder and bounces up to scrape the side of his face.

- Ha! Ha!

Then nothing. For a moment nothing.

Then a can. An empty can. They've run out. Ex-Dad's thrown nothing but the one stone back. They're scraping the street for litter. That's what they're reduced to. Litter.

This is when he ducks. With nothing worth dodging coming over the fence, he crouches on his platform. He picks up a plastic-coated wire. It leads to a broad staple hammered into his fence, and threads through that to loop around a bolt on the front gate. He doesn't tug. He just pulls gently. The bolt edges loose.

Malik and me are mainbrain. Without us teensquad isn't

teensquad. It's not even undertow. It's mindless. Dad's coiled himself around every friend we've ever had and is throttling em dry. Malik and me could have stopped it. We could have known what to do and done it. Dad knows that. He's separated us. We're locked in the house and they're on the street. He's got away with it. He's disarmed em.

Ex-Dad stands up on his platform again.

- You want your toys back? Come and get em. The gate's open.

His arms rise, his hands go wide. He's opening the gates of hell. Click. I don't hear it. I don't even see it through the wobble of fumes that rise from the garden, but I feel the latch move inside my head. The click of the latch connects with the back of my brain. The future's coming to pass. I know it.

The gate eases open.

Soo's first. Poor sod. His polytext shirts always creep above the waistband of his shorts. This shirt's his favorite, with its narrow orange and green stripes. He's painted the same orange and green on his hand-me-down trainers. He fills the gate a moment. He looks up at Dad.

Dad's kept to his platform. He's getting ready to receive his guests. His left hand's in a silver glove that matches the rest of his costume. His right hand's sliding into the other glove.

Soo checks the garden for the weapons. They've mostly landed in the far corner. Soo could go and grab hold of Dad's tower, grab hold of its support, and rip it from the ground. He's capable of that. Dad would come tumbling down. It's the best thing Soo could do.

It can't happen. Soo does the best thing that's suggested to him and no-one's suggested bringing ex-Dad down. Ex-Dad's let him in to run and collect his weapons. That's what he'll do. He'll jump over the fuming trenches, hurdle the fallen cans, run round the barbed-wire traps. He'll pick up what he can.

I raise my arms. Malik raises his beside me. We beat the flats of our hands against the glass. We scream so loud each word is like a punch in my guts and then scream some more. Get out Go back Get out Get out Get out.

Soo smiles. The poor sod smiles. Creases of worry ease from his face. He recognizes me. The friend he punched coz he thought it would help is up and by the window and waving at him. He thinks I'm waving at him. He lifts a hand to wave back, and starts coming my way.

- Get out Go back Get out Get out Get out.

I ball my hands into fists and beat at the armored glass. I stand back a pace and make pushing away gestures as I keep on yelling.

Soo turns his head. Is he going?

Runt stands behind him. The same polytext shirts have nothing to grip to on Runt. His is lime green and it sags. He's in shorts, his legs like pins. Go back Runt. Go back.

Runt turns. Now the gate's open I hear him shout.

- It's Bender. Soo's found Bender. He's in the house. He's waving to us. Come on. Quick.

In they come. They bunch at the gate, squeezing side by side, and burst in. Mulch Pint Roach Skel Furbo Zeb Melba Kes Jok Dome Rasp Skink Parch Ozie Mug Toast Saf Flint Scud Ant. They're dressed for the undertow, dressed for heat, bare feet stuck in old trainers, bare legs, bare arms, bare heads too, coz who gives a fuck about cancer from the sun and who gives a toss for headgear laws coz we're all dying the planet's dying and since we're dying let's die free with the wind of our running blowing on skin. They're dressed for the sun but not for flames. Dressed for heat but not for fire.

Furbo's bare chested. His shirt's in his hand, smeared with blood he's wiped from his mouth, the blood from the hit of Dad's rock, and the blood's now dripping to streak down his ribs, the mouth bleeding but grinning, his arms held wide, dancing a little circle dance of his trim buff body for Karen to see and to choose. He's made it. He's come for Karen. He's in the garden. He's on his way.

Kes leaps to the right and runs, his arms flapping, heading for the knives and bars and stones in the corner, re-arming for the ex-Dad wars.

Roach looks to the door then the window then the weapons then the tower, his legs going all ways at once but somehow forward.

Dome holds his bare hands toward me, the sun folding a shine of light round his head, smiling his simple smile.

Skink blinks, standing still on the edge, choosing his move.

Scud falls. He was charging the door. His feet are in the air somersaulting round his head. I see the trap that got him before he lands. The dull white of Dad's paving stones are sleeked brown. Dad's coated em with oil. The random mess of his paving, stones scattered round the front, has a purpose after all.

Pint's headed round a patch of barbed wire coils. His foot's found a stone. Another oiled stone. His arms reach forward like a low dive in water, his head set to scrape the dust.

A bottle arcs high from Dad's silver arm. It rises from his tower, glowing amber.

- Go Get out Go Go GO

I mouth the shout. Malik joins in. Our hands are up, we push the undertow back, we signal em back, but we're on the inside and they're on the out. I'm inside watching.

I look for flames from the bottle, a flaming bottle, but it's just a bottle. Mulch is in the group between the back trench and the front. He catches sight of the bottle and swipes it aside. It smashes on the bakehard dust, exploding in shards, its liquid splashing high.

A shard of bottle glass cuts into Furbo's leg. The liquid springs up and hits his chest. He wipes his left hand over it and smells. His face curls up. He hates this smell. He shouts.

- Whisky!

Furbo scoops up the bottle neck and shakes its zags at Dad

— Drek! Fucking drek! We'll zag you!

Furbo's body's coated like it's in a whisky sweat. He steps out, raising his foot to start the charge, him against ex-Dad, him and his trim buff newly flammable body ready to shake down the wooden tower.

Kes gets to the tower first. He snatches a knife from the ground and holds the blade between his teeth as he leaps for a high right handhold on Dad's ladder then flexes his arm to reach up with his left. He looks good. As Dad holds a bottle over his head and shakes whisky down into his face, Kes looks good. And as Dad swings the bottle round to connect with Kes's jaw, Kes looks perfect. His jaw clamps the blade tight in his mouth, his arms beat fast against the air, and he's backward flying. It's good.

I'm saying this with no more Kes but he did it. It's good I saw it and good to say it. Kes did it. Kes took flight.

He's in the air when bottles join him. Kes comes down to earth as bottles fly high. Dad has a case of twelve. His aim looks wild but it's good.

Kes thumps to the ground. He's light. He's made for flight not landing. His head twists to one side and he crumples. His body's still. The first bottle lands beyond him, in front of Furbo's charge.

Furbo swerves. Glass and whisky chase him.

Bottles explode, undertow scatters, the glass is nothing coz cuts only bleed and blood won't burn but whisky's different. Whisky sticks to the skin where flames will find it. A bottle spins round and smashes loud on the brick over the door as Scud thumps against the wood. Scud's now bruised and wet and flammable.

Ex-Dad's crouched on his platform. He flips the hood from off his back to silver over his head. He's looking out now through a reflective visor, looking at his hands. One bottle's left. It's between his knees, a rag stuffed into its neck. Dad reaches left to something I can't see but I know what it is. I know.

He's reaching for his lighter.

I'm frozen. Frozen inside the picture of all I'm seeing. The voice of Karen shakes me loose, yelling from the hole in the cellar door. Yelling at us to get down there.

- No, I yell.

I think I yell. The yell's so loud it sucks in the air and blasts round the house as a roar. It's like yelling can't stop things but only join in like the rattle in throats at death. I see Dad set his lighter to the rag that's stuffed into the end of his final bottle. I see the light catch hold and the bottle whirl in his arm before sailing its flame towards the front of the house. I hear it land against the brick and scatter its liquid fire.

A moment. Teensquad had one moment. Turn for the gate and some would have made it. But they stare. I don't blame em. Skies don't collapse every fucking day. This is too good. The air thumps down from the sky to suck at the trench then blasts back as a roar. Flames are yellow and orange and blue but first it seems they're white. The blast is white. It shoots in white above the house and then the faces turn.

Some turn just a fraction to the right and some turn to the left. They're watching the white of flame. It shoots wide just as it shoots high, speeding from the front garden along the trench and round to the back. The kerosene was liquid fuming on plastic. Now it rises from the trench as a wall.

Dad's planted a wall round the house. The faces go white as the flames rush toward em. Ant knows what it is. Death's coming. Fuck off death. He spins around to head for the gate. Spinning's easy. His foot's on a stone that's coated with oil. His feet run behind him as his body tips forward.

The wall closes. White flames collide outside my window. They bulge against the house. The plate glass cracks. Four lines zig from the corners. Heat and light turn all things white. My eyes are burned but still I see. I see the future as it happens.

Ant reaches down to break his fall. He runs with his hands as well as his feet, scuttling clear, making for the gate. The feet jump forward with the fire at their soles. The fire jumps too. It crosses the dust from where Ant was then leaps ahead to meet him where he's going. He can't shout but I hear his head. It explodes above the outer trench, snatched up in the blast. Its blood and tissue go like a volcano, upward stream of liquid fire.

Dad's stepping down his ladder. The flames turn orange round the ladder's wood. His boot falls through the charcoal of the last two rungs but he stands on landing. His suit won't burn but the earth's hot. He lifts one boot up then the other, jumping into quicktime spotrunning. His silver turns gold coz the suit reflects fire. He wants to stick around. I know that though his face is just flame in the mirror of his mask. He wants to watch us burn but his body says breathe.

Two steps take him to the outer trench of flame and he leaps it. He crashes through the fire of fence and is gone. He's out on the streets to earth that won't melt. He's running for air that won't scorch lungs. The fucker's still breathing.

Dome breathes too. Flames lick high from the whisky splashes stuck to his back, blue and yellow flames like wings. His jaw lets loose his final breath. It burns from his mouth like a tongue of flame and is gone. All air is gone. There's nothing to breathe but fire. Dome's body drops as heavy liquid to coat the dust in tar. Toast plucks the flames from his face. His fingers sink in past cheekbones. I catch a smile on Mug as the fire licks his face into shape. Then the face and the smile are gone. Pint and Flint run against each other. Their arms fold round like they're a dancing couple. Their bodies melt and fuse. Scud charges at the house and hits the door. His body's a ram, a battering ram, a flaming battering ram. The door holds though flames pass through it. Scud's legs kick as he burns down to carbon. Ozie must have farted. Flames rocket the ground from out his ass then shoot up to take him as fuel. Furbo's olive skin goes darker, darker, olive turning oil. Parch's skin goes white red black gone. Skel goes up like a wooden stake, arms stretched like a cross. Runt flares, those matchstick legs pumping up a wind but there's no wind coz there's no air only blast. Looks like Soo had fat in him. His skin bubbles and spits. Mulch slaps at the craters on Soo's skin while bubbling himself. Jok's black hair, Melba's blonde, both turn to ginger as they stand side by side. Their hands make fists and they both stand still. They make beautiful fires. Roach's left leg catches fire before his right one, and then the right one catches up. Zeb sits and folds his head inside his arms. Flames fold a ball around him. Saf opens his mouth, shaping a word, some dark round hissing word. His fingers point high like birthday candles. Rasp jumps through the trench and presses his nose against the window. His face slips a smear down the melting glass. The smear is red and smokes to black.

That's it.

- Shut the fuck up, Bender.

- Malik. Where are you?

- I'm here. Open your eyes.

- They're open. It's bright. So bright. I can't see. Only light. White light.

- Open your eyes.

- Karen? Is that Karen?

- Yes. Put down the voicecard and open your eyes.

- I've got to see. I've got to tell it. See it and tell it as it happens. It's all gone if I don't see it, don't tell it. Dad's gone. They'll say it didn't happen but I saw it. I saw it.

- It's over, Bender. It's over. You're in the cellar. We dragged you down. Karen took care of you while I slotted bricks into the gap in the cellar door. You passed out. Then you came round. You've been babbling since. Just shut the fuck up, Bender. Shut the fuck up and open your eyes.

- What do you mean open my eyes? They're open. It's bright. Too bright.

- I'm Karen. It's OK. You're safe. I'm here. Malik's here. Paul's here. We've got you safe. I'm going to bathe your eyes. Keep em closed and I'll bathe em with warm water. We haven't got cold we've only warm from a bucket but it'll do. Then you can open em. You'll see where you are. You've said enough, Steven. Just go quiet. I'll bathe your eyes, and then you can take a look around.

- He got away. Dad got away. The fucker had it planned. He sucked us all in then put on that silver suit and walked out through the flames. I saw it. I saw it all. I saw it so I'll get him. He thinks he ...

- Shhh. Here. I'm bathing your eyes. Go quiet, Steven. You've said enough. Let's have some quiet. Stop recording. I'm turning your voicecard off. Come on, give it here. Let go. Let me have it.

The light in the room's dull orange and even. It doesn't dance through shadows the way candlelight does. The bricks in the walls each give off a glow. I look up and make out the cracks in the ceiling. Heavy beats thump across the floor above. Maybe it's just timbers falling. The cracks shoot forward through the plaster and widen. Flashes of bright orange shine through em. I turn my head to look across the floor. Paul's in his pajamas lying on his mattress. His body's flat but I watch his right hand. Its fingers are arched and tapping.

- He's working a keyboard, I say.

Karen rolls across and checks his face. She looks close.

- His eyes are doing their thing too, she says – All those tiny shifts and dilations they made in front of the screen.

She waves a hand in front of his face.

- He's not here, Steven. He doesn't see me. He doesn't know where he is. You know what he's doing? He's watching some re-run of an old program. His head's still in front of that computer, jazzing up his scores.

- Better there than here, Malik says. Malik's never been so hot on living the now. Now's fucked, he often says. Anywhere but here he says. It's one of his mantras. It's what keeps him running.

Maybe he's right. I close my eyes and give it a go.

I dream up a blue sky. Plant a branch across it and coat it with green leaves. Have the leaves dapple the sunlight so I get both brightness and shade. Try for the touch of cool breeze, some scent of living flowers.

Maybe that's how I'll go when I die, snatching up scraps of nature like this, kidding myself that life was worth living. Maybe I'll give in at the close like everyone else and end on a lie. Right now orange light burns slivers of moons below my eyelids. My lungs are made of black cracked leather and pumping and hurting and gasping. My face was a shell that's opened and now it's burning to the bone.

Karen screams. She used to go ultrasonic as a kid, screams so sharp and high they scratched patterns in the plaster over her bed. Where I was a runner she was a screamer. I ran the streets, she pierced the neighborhood with screams.

Then she stopped.

She's been storing this scream up for years. It belts out of her like she can use it to blow the heat away. I think she's looking at me. Think her scream is a measure of what I look like now with my face burnt off.

She's not looking at me though, not looking at Paul whose fingers keep tapping coz loud as Karen screams he's not heard a thing. She's staring up the cellar stairs. She lifts her hands to protect her face as fragments of brick spit down to hit her but still she stares.

Two sledgehammers hit our brick wall with one more single pound and the bricks hurtle down the stairs. It's Dad, I think. Ex-Dad. We're dead and this is the underworld. Dad's bursting in to claim us.

It's weird the crap your mind thinks up in an instant so small no time passes.

A white blue light flashes into the cellar and stays there. I watch a cloud bulge through the hole. It spills off the stairs and hits the walls. Malik's gone. Karen's gone. Instead there's nothing but cloud. It washes my eyes and streams in through my mouth and nose. It's a white cloud but filled with rain that coats me. My hands slip in the moisture that lands on the floor and I fall back. My only move is to shiver, to shiver so fast my body won't freeze and turn direct to ice.

It's Dad's breath, I think. Ex-Dad's breath, as I catch the stink of sulphur. He's gusting down the stairs. I hear his steps, and the crash of the table as he pushes it out the way. A jar with a candle in it splinters on the floor. A figure stands above me, grey within the cloud. It crouches lower, and presses a tube of cold black metal against my head. An electronic beep shifts to keener and higher, as high-pitched as Karen's early-teen screams.

- Got him, a voice says. It's a male voice in electric mode, clipped and hollow – Entering chill. Demist now. Repeat, demist now.

The cloud is sucked away. The figure is revealed. It's dressed in the full black fibogear of a Statesquad trooper. A trooper on detox maneuver. A fire trooper. The cold light sparkles as he flashes out a silver blanket and drapes it around me, crinkling it to my sides. My shivers stop as my bodyheat turns back inside.

Operation code SG17, the voice reports – Item number 5HP3 ready for evacuation. Incapacitated. Unconscious. Request flatbed assistance.

If this is unconscious then alert's a firework of psychodrama too intense to shit.

2.0

Steven carved his initials on his headboard when he was nine.

— You want to turn your headboard to a tombstone, his Dad said when he found out — Then I guess I'd better kill you.

His Dad had a canvas shoe with a rubber sole. The canvas was worn but he kept it for these special moments. It was his punishing shoe. The sole had imprints of stars that he left on the bare flesh of Steven's little-boy ass.

— That'll teach you some respect for furniture, he said when he'd done.

Now the bed's burnt to black and landed in the hall. I look up to where it fell from. The bedroom's a smudge of sky.

Vibrations reach up through the flatbed's padding as firetroopers stretcher me out of the house. Motors are at work, beaming my body image to a diagnosis lab. Other troopers work the garden as I pass.

Fiberglass bubbles stud the earth like farts coming up through a bath. Some are tiny. It's crazy to think even Runt or Pint would burn down to a tinderpatch that size. One's so huge though that ex-Mom could roll around inside it. It's in the middle where teensquad clustered. Its bubble shell is frosted but still I see through it somehow. Inside is a mixture of fleshmelt and dust. I see what looks like a hand, then another, then another. The hands are black and the fingers are straight and stretched, not gripping but letting go. When we ran as undertow, when we ran as teensquad, we ran as one body with one supermind. We ran as one animal. This animal's not that one. It's got too many hands and no feet that I can see. Maybe this mess is just a skin. Maybe the feet of my dead friends aren't crumpled out of sight but kept on running. Maybe I'm crying even though my eyes are dry.

The fence has gone. The troopers step from burned earth to asphalt with only a charred rim in between. They fit my flatbed to a trolley and hoist it up to the back of a van. I'm slid inside and the trolley is bolted in place.

- You hear me OK Bender?

I know the voice.

- It's Lester. Dr Lester Drake. Remember me?

I try to lift myself, to look around.

- Stay still Bender. The scans show no breakage but we need to be sure. You're immobilized. Your body's sucked on to the flatbed as safe as a vacuum. Your head's contoured in a flexigrip. Blink your eyes. Shut your eyes. You'll understand.

I do as he says. I shut my eyes. It makes no difference to the light that comes in.

I practice some more, shutting and closing my eyelids. It's a new experience. It takes getting used to. Shutting my eyes makes a difference to what I see but not how I see it. What I see is myself, my head fixed to the flatbed as my eyes open and shut. So if my head's fixed, how the fuck can I be seeing it from somewhere else? How can I watch from the outside as my own eyes shut?

- Shall we take one last look at your old house, Bender?

From inside my head I stare through a tinted window reinforced with wire netting. A thick vaporhose trails across the garden but it's idle. It's done its job. The fire's gone out. It's a new house now. The door and windows have been knocked out from downstairs, the outer walls and roof are gone from above. Everything's turned to black. Doc Drake laughs, a low chuckle.

- That was quite a blast. Your neighbors have got your fence in their front rooms. Fence posts flew in through the windows or straight through the brick. You want my advice? Don't ask for those fence posts back. Did you help your Dad or did he do it on his own?

I've got no Dad.

- OK Bender. You can't talk but I register your emotions. You just showed anger not guilt. When you took your first look at your burnt-out home you registered relief. I'm a psychiatrist. I trust emotions more than words. That's why we're working through this little exercise. You're linked to my field of vision, Bender, but the reactions to what you see through my eyes are purely your own.

I look from the house and back inside the van. Malik is strapped to a shelf that runs along a steel wall. I look down on his face. He's relaxed. His eyes are closed but I sense movement behind the lids. A slight smile touches his cheeks.

- Ah-ha. A hard emotion to label but let's be unprofessional. Let's call it love. Don't worry Bender. Your friend is in good hands. We've got him sedated.

No way. No fucking way are they going to do to Malik what they say they did to me.

Doc Drake laughs.

- Don't worry, Bender. We've got no designs on your friend. We have plans for him maybe but ultimately we've only got his wellbeing at heart. You did well to lend him your slinksuit. He's come through that experience unscratched.

My view turns away from Malik and takes in Paul. He's strapped into a chair, seated to face the wall of the van that backs the driver's section. The sight doesn't interest me. Where's Malik?

- You want to see more of your friend? You've not exhausted that emotion yet?

Malik comes back into view. He has the thickest eyelashes I've known, even in pictures. He's beautiful when awake too but that's different. Then the beauty's in the motion, in the flow of his body streaming through life. Awake he's alert and that's what grabs you. The rest of life finds a mirror in his face. Nothing passes by when you're with him. Everything excites. In sleep though he's gone soft. He's gone gentle.

A hand reaches in to stroke his cheekbones. A black-skinned hand. It runs a fingernail along the outer line of Malik's nose, around his lips, and down to his throat.

- You surprise me, Bender. You're more refined than I knew. I was sub-labeling your love-emotion as a teenage lust thing but it contains several underlying components. One is aesthetic, a real appreciation of beauty. And this one ...

The hand goes out of sight then returns to press the flat of a short steel blade against the skin of Malik's throat. My look turns away, to a monitor scrolling green numbers across a black screen while a red line at the bottom jags high.

- That's a real maternal protective thrust you're showing there. I label it maternal because of its ferocity. You sense vulnerability in the one you love, you see the presence of danger, you flash out a stab of violence. What now, Bender? As I insert the blade you see a thin line of blood stretch across your loved one's throat ...

I see nothing. The doc gives a commentary of flesh parting and blood streaking across Malik's throat but doesn't let me see it. All I see are more numbers that spurt across the screen as the red line scrawls a dense scratch of panic lines along the graph.

- Interesting.

My vision turns from the screen and across my body, reaching toward the other side wall of the van. Someone else is strapped there. I find I'm looking down on Karen. How's Malik? What's he done to Malik?

- Don't be stupid Bender. Do you think I'd hurt Malik. I'm a doctor. Look.

I see back across my own body to Malik. He's smiling still. His throat is intact.

- You see? He's alright. Calm as a baby. Is that OK now Bender? You've settled down? Let's get back to business.

My sight now shifts to linger a while on Paul. His chest is strapped to the chair and another belt wraps round from the seat to bind him round his thighs but his hands are free. His fingers are working a keyboard though he's facing no screen, simply the rear wall of the van. Anything he sees is through the visor clamped round his head.

- You see his mouth?

His mouth's open, the lips stretched back across his gums to show his teeth. I hear nothing but it seems he's laughing.

- He's happy. We've made him happy again. We're doing what we can for all of you. You're all mending. Paul was ripped too soon from his reconstitution program. If you'd left the program to run its course you'd have noticed little difference in his behavior now from the Paul you've always known and loved. We only download excess neural capacity. It's like piercing a boil and letting out the pus. He's better for it. We leave full social and animal functioning. He could have enjoyed a perfectly happy birthday. Indeed that's what he's doing now. Happy birthday to Paul.

My sight drifts round to the wall on my left and to Karen. Her eyes are shifting behind her closed eyelids, much as Malik's were doing. Her cheeks are touched by a similar smile. Even though that's what I see it's not where I look. It's not where I focus. Instead I glimpse a reflection of Doc Drake in the shine of the steel wall. He's looking down on Karen through a pair of clear plastic goggles strapped round the back of his head.

- Now that's interesting, Bender. I catch a spike of aggression more usually associated with intense male rivalry. Is this your usual reaction to your sister or only when she's made up to look like you?

I get it. I'm learning how to play this game. It's like watching a movie but only focusing on the bottom left corner of the screen. The camera's working to grab your attention, to show you something else, but you say fuck it. Fuck your entertainment schedule. I'll see what I want to see. So you focus on some little scrap the camera's just passed by. You screw attention to a touch of world they expect you to ignore. You decide what's special. You make something special just by seeing it. That makes you special too. I've watched movies that way. It works. You get a buzz of creating something instead of just a brainwipe.

I try it now. I only get to see where the doctor's looking, but inside his field of vision I can focus where I want. I spotted his reflection. That's what got me going but he doesn't even see it. He's staring down at Karen. He wants me to react to what he's doing to her. Well fuck him.

- I worry as a doctor that you've bound her chest too tight, Bender. I'm concerned about her breathing.

His hands reach out to fold around her breasts. I focus on the perimeter of what he sees. The silver bag containing me is reflected in the steel wall. He looks up to check the monitor and gauge my reaction. I take the chance of this shift in visual angle to focus on the back of the driver's head glimpsed through a window at the front of the van.

The view changes. I look down at myself for a moment, then out through the window at the burnt ruin of home. In the bottom left corner of the view two firetroopers have sliced the ground below one of the smaller fiberglass bubbles and are setting it down on a thin sheet of steel. The van begins to move and the image to recede. Bye bye house.

My view turns back to Malik. The flat of the blade presses into his cheek this time. It's a small variation, an old story. Slice away if you want, doctor. There's fuck all I can do about it. I check the reflection in the section of wall above Malik's head. I'm getting to see what I'm not meant to see. It seems the body of the van is empty of anyone but the doctor and us four.

- That's impressive, Bender. You've shifted to steady analytic mode. How have you done that? Time to abort this experiment, wouldn't you say?

I'm looking down on myself from up close. I'm looking into my own eyes. I shut em.

- Ah-ha. Got you. I've got your full attention. There's still a little vanity left in you I see. Don't worry, your eyelashes should grow back in time. Till then you'll have to live with the blink of a newborn rat. The blemishes to your skin are just that. It's nothing to concern you. The flash of heat dried your skin but didn't truly burn it. We'll have you looking fresh-faced again in time for your release. Now let's slip forward your protective headshield, shall we?

His hands reach down and a black Perspex hood arches up from behind my head.

- Your attention's become too keen Bender. As a doctor I'm concerned for your state of conscious equilibrium. This particular emotive program is designed for work on the subconscious mind, but you've grown too excited. I'm switching you back to your own vision. What you'll see is the inside of this hood. What you'll see is blackness as wide and as high as you can look. Now this will hurt just a bit but don't worry. It's an injection of nothing stronger than I've already administered to your sister and your friend. You've been through trauma. This is a sedative. Sweet dreams, Bender. Sweet dreams.

The Book
of the Father

Answers to an interrogatory

You say you want a testament not a confession. Well fuck you. If it's a testament give me a keyboard and I'll type it out but never sign it. It stays anonymous. You think I'm some young dumbfuck with a ball for a brain? Don't ask for a testament and stick me on oral. Oral's fed to voice patterning. Voice patterning smears my DNA over every fucking word I preach. You're not getting a testament out of me. Testa-fucking-testicle. You're not getting a confession either. I've nothing to confess.

Steven? He's a fucking mutant. You say you're keeping me in this holding tank to keep me safe from Steven? You say he's got loose? He's out to get me? Let me out and we'll see who gets who. Sneeze on him and he cries for his mummy. If Steven's a problem let me loose. I'll sort him.

Don't son me. Don't lay Steven on me. There's nothing mutant about my sperm. Test it. My sperm swims straight. Steven happened after I shot my sperm. It was a twin thing, ripping the egg apart. One part turned out a girl and the other turned out girlie. A girl with a prick and an available ass. Don't lay Steven on me. I donated the sperm. That's all I'm liable for.

Don't lay that one on me either. It's you that fucked Paul. He was a decent lad. On top form. Then you got him. You warped him. He was meat when you finished with him. Who cares what you scraped out of a piece of meat. Who cares what your fucking analysts worked out in their stupid fucking labs. You fucked Paul. Fucked his brain and left him limp. That was sick. So sick. Maybe I fucked a slab of meat. Maybe I did. So fucking what.

That brown wanker pal of Steven's led him on. I like timber, I love timber, I know timber. When we had timber we had wisdom. We knew the dangers of niggers in woodpiles. You want to know what fucked up the world, go scrape the brown skin off that little wanker and investigate his junk DNA. You're all too fucking correct to crawl back down the midden of history and face the truth. We had Y chromosomes by the fucking bucketful before brown wankers got into the country. Letting brown wankers in like that, it's like the Antichrist sneezing out snot, it's just shooting out virus. A burst of virus slam in your face. Aids started in monkeys, black men ate monkeys, you rolled out a fucking red carpet at the airports and showered those monkey blacks with money, our fucking money, and now we're fucked. The virus is in. You want a confession, you get that little brown wanker fucker Malik pal of Steven's to spill. I should have got him. He should be dead.

You're like that woman you got in here. 'Do you think it was right to use your daughter for bait?' she kept on, spinning maggots on a line like I'm pike enough to bite. Karen's a whore. She was gasping for it. I was protecting her. 'How many do you think you could have saved?' you ask me now? As if I was going to run through the flames, pick Steven's pack of fuckbuddies up in my arms and carry them safe to their mummies. Well what about you, you fuckers? You were there. You were waiting. You filmed it all for fuck sake. You picked me up. Whose fucking side are you on? We're samesiders, you and me. You know it. Urban scum's on one side, you and me on the other. Pick your nose, you stupid fucking imp, pick your fucking ass, but don't pick a fight with me.

Testament? You want a father's testament about Steven? Steven's a lying little prick. Words from his mouth are like pus from a boil. He's a fucking invert. Take what was good when I was a kid and turn it inside out, hang it from some butcher hook and let it fester, and you know what you've got? Steven fucking no son of mine Bender.

Bender in Paradise

2.01

- What day is it? I ask.

  - Tuesday, Doc Drake says.

  In the beginning is a word, the word is Tuesday, and it's a lie. Even if he's struck lucky on a guess, even if somewhere else on the planet people wake and their calendars say it's Tuesday, it's a lie. It's a lie to wrap something up in a word before you understand it. Whatever this day is it's not Tuesday. The world's not sequenced like that. You blink your eyes open, light comes in, and you get on with it. It's not another fucking day of the week. It's not a Friday follows Thursday kind of day. It's just another space of light and time to run through. You keep on running till you fall off the edge or you're pushed and all goes dark for a while. You wake up and you start again. On the seventh day God never rested. He just gave up counting and took off, left us to muddle through the day on day shit. Weeks are never wrapped up, we get no rest, Tuesdays don't exist. Bombs never drop on a Tuesday. Kids don't die on a Tuesday. Teensquads aren't flamed alive on a Tuesday. If days need names they can be horrordays. Whoever suffers the fiercest horror gets to name the day. Maybe today's the day a mother watches a virus eat her baby's flesh down to the bones. If that happens and she feels like talking she can name this day what the fuck she wants. It can be her day to name.

  A doctor in a picnic chair doesn't get to call it Tuesday though. He's got no right.

  - Where are we? I ask.

  - Eden, he says.

  His picnic chair's got a seat and a back of blue and white striped canvas. It's got a foldable aluminum frame. Three matching chairs are set around the other sides of a picnic table. The table's got stainless steel knives and forks either side of empty white dinner plates. Four glasses and a pitcher are empty too.

  - Come on, the doc says. He pushes his chair back, stands up, and moves his hands wide apart in front of him like he's setting loose a butterfly. I'm meant to look where he's looking and find it wonderful. I've had my fill of seeing though his eyes.

I see trees with green leaves. The leaves on branches near the top move in shivers. I check the air against my face and feel heat, not wind or breeze. The picture doesn't add up.

- We'll take that path, the doc says — I'll show you a secret. Show you round.

He points to a path of baked mud. Its surface is cracked, but the land to either side of it is green, two stretches of green each so wide and yet so narrow I could roll through it and flatten it all, once up once down. The green that is nearest has huge flowers on top of long stems, dark at the core with a mass of surrounding yellow petals. I'd call em sunflowers only sunflowers turn to face the sun. Here the sun's over to the left. The flowers aren't interested. They're facing us.

I turn away and climb back into the van. Its doors are wide open.

Malik's lying on the left, Karen on the right, but Paul's chair at the back is empty. If Doc Drake's going to feed me lies I'll ask him something I don't care about.

- Where's Paul?

- Don't worry. He's safe. He's in a secure unit, working a terminal linked direct to Cromozone. Your computer access here has no download capacity. Perfect though this place is it's no good for him. His functions are coming back. He's happy where he is. I left him grinning.

Happiness is an odd thing. It sits on the strangest faces. He tells me Paul's wired in to some terminal like it's a dream come true, like life's just found a meaning. I look down at Malik and though our teensquad's burnt to tar and ashes, and Malik's body's been dragged from its senses and carted fuck knows where, yet scanning his face for his take on life I'd swear he's another happy punter. Not gulp-me-down happiness, not a heart-thumping thing, just the slightest curve of his mouth into his cheeks. Some drama's still flicking at the inside of his eyelids. His clothes have been changed. He's wearing a slinksuit of his own but where mine was black his is white.

A black version has been slipped over my body again. I smell the armpits to see if it's the one Malik was wearing, to try and catch his scent on me, but the smell's neutral. My outfit's been cleaned or it's new.

Ex-Steven's old clothes have been taken off Karen. The bandage wrap's gone from her breasts. She's in her own slinksuit that lets em bulge. The fabric's cream rather than white. It shows the rings and points of her nipples but without transparency. Wherever she is inside her head she's happy to be there. Her eyeballs are dancing under her lids like Malik's are. She wears a similar smile. She's shaved her head and she's my twin but she doesn't look like me now. I can't smile like that.

They're not restrained by belts. They're free to get up off their tables if they wake.

- Are they drugged? I ask.

- In strict neuropsychopharmacological terms, the answer's no. Their condition is infinitely more advanced than drugs alone could ever achieve. I call my own method psychopressure. Electronically pulsed stimulation of the neuro transmitters. Drugs facilitate the process but they're simply one ingredient in a sophisticated cocktail. The fundamental factor is the client's own store of memories. We access what they know and advance the tale of their lives into the future, incorporating our own incomparably supreme data on the state of the world. I see it as aiding clients to achieve their potential before they've even conceived of its possibilities. Understand it this way, for simplicity's sake. Their bodies took a shortcut to get here. Their consciousnesses had more to experience along the way. They're still travelling. They'll be here soon. They'll begin to stir as though they're waking from a night of sound sleep, and they'll be hungry. Come on. Let's go and find some food for them to eat. Let's pick us a picnic.

He heads for the path between the not-sunflowers. I head round to the front of the van. The cab's doors are both locked. I look in through the window but see no driver. Being alone without running is crap. Doc Drake's the only company I've got. I'd choose better but I've had worse. The company of a pathological psychobutcher isn't as boring as life gets.

The doc's sat himself on the dust of the path to wait.

- Get yourself down here, he says as I join him.

I crouch low.

- What do you notice?

- Lettuces. Planted between sunflowers that don't turn to follow the sun.

- All these are new breeds of plants, designed for high-density growth. In this instance an added bonus for the lettuce is the shade protection of the sunflowers. Pick the lettuces like this …

He twists a young plant of about eight leaves to break it just above the ground …

- leave the roots behind, and they'll rot into the soil to improve the next crop. This stretch of planting is the most experimental real-earth garden our bioengineers have ever achieved. Follow the logic of their plantings and you'll come to understand their method over the seasons. You'll be able to replicate it, maybe even improve on it. But that's not what I expected you to notice. Go back to the van, stand there for a couple of minutes, then come back here. Tell me what you notice then.

I take the chance of being back at the van to look in on Malik and Karen. They're still sleeping, or whatever their state is. Malik's hair is thick and flops around his head. I climb into the van and examine Karen's scalp. I see no obvious sign of implants, but I left so many small cuts with the razor it's hard to tell.

I start checking the ground around the van for footprints.

Either Doc Drake drove us in or the driver dumped us and legged it. I see no obvious tracks.

- Do you never stand still? the doc calls across.

I slap a mosquito against the sleeve of my slinksuit. Blood spurts out of its body and across the black material. Doc Drake's blood maybe. The suit seems to give me protection against insect bites. I slap at the back of my neck. I'm quick. Anticipate that first sting of bite, strike when the fuckers are hooked into the vein, and I get em. We used to play games in undertow, stripping down and using our bodies as bait, swatting the biters against each other's flesh. Everyone wanted to pair with me. I'm the best.

My neck's out of the suit and exposed. My slap was fast. The bulk of a horsefly is now squashed against my neck but two legs have stuck to my hand. I brush em off, then reach back and wipe my neck clean. A smaller fly lands on my left leg but it's sucking at my sweat and not biting. I let it ride. I've had enough of standing still. I head back to the path.

- So what's the difference between standing here and standing over there? Doc Drake asks.

- Here there's only one path and you're blocking it. From over there I'm free to go any way I choose. I guess I made a mistake in coming back.

I turn and head back toward the van. A horsefly lands on my left shin. Shins are the worst. Bites there tend to swell like boils. The best way of protecting shins is to run. Instead I slap at the horsefly but miss and stumble.

The doc laughs.

- You can't do it, he says – You just can't stay still. You're either running or you're swatting.

A mosquito lands on my hand. I kill it.

- You'll note, if you bother to look, Doc Drake says, spreading wide his arms – No flies on me. None landed on you while you were on the path either. Much of this Eden is as nature intended but we're not stranding you in pre-biblical times. Nature attracts insects, some that pollinate and others that serve no useful purpose whatsoever. In this stretch of garden scientists have moderated nature. You'll have no need to spray on pesticides. Pesticides are coded into the genetic structure of the stock. This garden's an insect-bite-free zone. This path is a great place to lie on your back and admire the sky. Spend time here, Bender, and you might even learn to be still.

He heads off down the path and plucks a red fruit from a plant staked on canes to his left.

- Catch, he calls, and throws it.

My body's quicker than my brain. My hand's stretching out as my brain's computing. Brain recognition one. It's a tomato. Recognition two. The tomato's going to burst in my hand. This is some sick joke. Recognition three. Life's screwed. What's a squashed tomato on top of everything else?

I make a perfect catch. The fruit stays intact.

- It looks like a tomato. It tastes like a tomato, the doc explains – But instead of a skin it's got a shell, somewhat like an avocado. We work on one premise at Cromozone. The world can be a better place. Not better than it is now. Better than it's ever been. Mankind's had a huge effect on the planet. Now nature is weeding us out. Here's how nature wants us …

He takes the stalk of the tomato in his hand and twists it away from the body of the fruit. He then inserts a fingernail into the resulting hole and slices it down the sides. The skin peels back in four sections.

- Naked and vulnerable. We've destroyed the natural world as it was before we came. Now we have nature's response. The natural biological process gives us no more female children. Humans face extinction. Nature has us where it wants us. And this is what it will do, left to its own devices.

He folds his hand around the peeled fruit, and squeezes. His

241

hand contains it as it explodes. He opens the fingers slightly to let the juice pour down to the dust, then tips the pulp after it.

- We've changed the rules, Bender. We can't expect nature to get us out of this mess. Nature's wiping us out. We have to conquer nature to survive. We have to adapt it to our own design. Humans are the dominant force on the planet. It's time we accepted that fact. Nature has been a great teacher but we've surpassed it. We have the skills. We have the raw ingredients. Now we need to apply them. We need to take responsibility for our own future. Who needs make do with tomatoes that bruise and rot under pressure? Who needs accept that male humans can't give birth? Who needs ever to think in terms of limitations? Not us, Bender. Not us.

He pulls out his palmpad and checks details.

- The consciousnesses of your sister and your friend are being separately introduced to their slinksuits right now. They'll slip them on in what they take to be privacy and settle down on their transport beds. Their consciousnesses are about to catch up with their physical forms. Allow ten minutes for journeying and they'll be with us. You can catch up on each other's stories. We'd better hurry if we're to have a meal ready. Come on, Bender. You're a runner. Let's see you run.

He turns on the path and kicks up dust. It's the kind of invitation I'm used to. His speed surprises me. For a bulky man he's nimble. The path's straight but the man's obscured by cloud. I can't see him for dust, he can't see me. I could run the other way and leave him to track me down. First though I need something from him. I need him to tell me one more lie. I listen for the rhythm of his tread and run to match it, lengthening my stride.

The dust cloud's dropping by the end of the path. I see the outline of his figure, kneeling down. I stop and wait as the dust settles and the picture clears. His hands are held in water. He's rubbing the tomato from his skin.

- You're impressed, he notes – Good. I was wondering what it would take to wake you to the wonders of this place. We dug this pond mechanically but it's filled by an underground spring. One more improvement on nature, Bender. And it's all for you.

He stands, shakes his hands dry, and walks to the band of crops that grow around the pond's perimeter. I look out across the water. The pond's no lake, it's maybe eight times my own length across, but it's full. Two ducks are swimming near the far edge, pushing their beaks through the grass that grows on the bank. They're white with thin orange crests and orange trim to their wings.

- They're both ducks, Doc Drake explains – We could manufacture drakes but breeding would follow the same male-only rule. These ducks are layers rather than breeders. It's a new species of duck. Name it what you will, Bender. The birds are here for their eggs but even more they're here for the scenery. Every Eden needs a little wildlife. Your daughter can grow to love them, Bender. They'll be company for her.

He's picked a bundle of salad and brings it in two fistfuls to wave in the water of the pond, cleaning it of soil. Now's the time to ask him for my lie.

- You know better than that, I tell him – You had me on the flatbed scanner. You know my stomach took a real blow. It was a hellhole inside there. The blow nearly killed me. You know nothing as fragile as an embryo would have survived. Your plan's over doc. I'm giving birth to nothing. You get that, don't you? You've gone and built a playground, but I'm not going to play.

He nods back along the direction of the path. The dust of our run has settled back down.

- You ran well, he says – You were fast. Just like the Bender of old. There didn't seem much wrong with you. When was this blow you're talking about?

- Yesterday.

- You're sure of that? You lost consciousness, Bender. It wasn't worth the trouble of bringing you round. Whatever we let you see of our procedures you'd swear it wasn't true. We kept your consciousness on hold and treated your body with microsurgery. We did well, as you've just discovered in running. You're a healthy animal. Surprisingly but pleasingly the embryo implant has held. It's secured itself to a blood supply and is developing normally. Your daughter's going to make it, Bender. She's a fighter.

It's a lie. It has to be. I know it in my gut. My head goes faint. I fall to my knees and churn the lie out of my system. Vomit spews from my mouth and coats the grass. The sound startles the ducks. They flap their wings but they're not designed for flight. The flapping helps em keep balance as they scramble their webbed feet onto the bank. They run quacking over the grass rim and onto bare earth.

- Not to worry, the doc says — Nausea's to be expected. You'll get over it. Come back to the van as soon as you're recovered. I'll have that meal ready for us all.

He goes and I crawl to the pondside and stare at my reflection. The image of me stares back. I look normal.

That's not a lie. It can't be.

I dip in my hands to wash the image away and carry water up to my face. It feels good. I stick my whole head underwater, then slide my body in after it.

I work my way round from the pond, along the far edge of the planted garden. The slinksuit steams dry in the heat, the skypumps too. Beyond the garden the ground is dust.

One logic to the planting is that everything is within easy carrying reach of the water from the pond. The spur of plants along the path is high enough to form a shield if I bend when I walk. I hear voices. Malik and Karen are up and out of the van. It sounds like they're settled, probably seated around the picnic table. In the music of their conversation the doctor's voice is a low rumble, Malik's is somewhere above that, and Karen's voice is low for a girl but still high. I can't make out the words.

I lie on my back, on the dust but close enough to the not-sunflowers to keep the insects at bay. The sky's still beige as much as blue but I guess it's cleaner than in town. I stayed underwater in the pond as long as I could before bursting up and gasping at air, but now my chest feels tighter even than that. My heart's a rock that thinks it can breathe. It squeezes out a sharp thin pulse. My twin and my mate are in earshot, sitting round a picnic table.

It's simple, strolling over to check in with em, kickstarting whatever this new life is. Hey, we all got through. Let's celebrate.

It should be easy to do that.

But it's not.

My heart's not hurting for the thrill of reunion. It's not busting itself in excitement. It's something else. I've never had this sense before but I've felt it in others. I've seen inside a drek as teensquad was closing in, after the drek's run for his life and run and run and found his life's not there. The sense there's everything to run for but nothing to run to so in the end all you've got is the running and you've no heart left to run. That sense.

Before mice became extinct in the wild people made traps. Inside the traps they put cheese or best of all chocolate. Mice loved chocolate. They'd run in to take a nibble, what's so wrong with that, a mouse has got to eat, then wham. A wire bar slammed down to break the creature's spine. Doc Drake calls this place Eden. It's filled with wonderful things. It has plants and salad and ponds and ducks and insect-free zones. Listen to him now. The good doctor's installing my best mate and my twin sister in this wonderland of his.

I know what Eden means. This place isn't Eden. It's a trap. That's all it is. If the trap's as big as a world then the world's not big enough.

- Bender?

It's a low voice. The voice of Doc Drake. Not even shouting. He knows I'm close enough to hear. The trap's calling.

- Finish admiring those sunflowers and come and join us. Dinner's ready.

I stand up, see em through the flowers, and step forward. Malik pushes his chair back and runs toward me. He's smiling.

- Hiya, freak, he says.

He hugs me, then holds my shoulders to stand back and inspect what he sees.

- You're looking good, Bender. Not bad for a freak.

He holds the flat of his hand to my stomach and rubs it around.

- The doctor's told us the news. Says you're doing fine. They showed me round the Technosheds in Cromozone. I'm clued in, Bender. It's cool. Babies are cool. You've got to feel weird but it'll end. You'll be yourself again. We'll take care of you. No worries.

He takes my arm and leads me to the table. Pulls out my chair then pushes it in as I sit down. The doc piles salad onto my plate. Karen stares at me.

- It's a lie, I tell her.

- Yeah, she says – Like I've not seen the scans. Like I don't know your abdominal wall better than my own navel. Like I don't know your abdominal wall better than anyone's ever known any abdominal wall in history. You know what strikes me as a lie, Bender? That you never told me. That you saw me struggling through all those ectopic delivery programs and didn't let on what it was all for. It would have made it a hell of a lot easier to carry on if I'd known what was at the end of it. If I'd known I'd be delivering my own niece. My own part-sister. I've told Mom by the way. She's OK with it. She's OK with everything. She just sits there pumping out love and OKness.

- You haven't seen Mom, I tell her.

She takes it as a question, like we're having a conversation with questions and answers that all add up.

- I've just left her. About an hour ago. I said goodbye, got changed, and they brought me here. Mom sends her love.

- You've been here all the time. Both of you. You've been drugged and lying on tables in the van. I stood and watched you. The only trip you've been on is a braintrip. Ask him. Ask the doctor.

He admits it. You've been hooked up to some psychomanaged dream program. It's all a lie. Everywhere you think you've been, everything you think you've seen, it's a lie.

Karen looks away from me, like she's embarrassed.

- Is Mom still staring out the window? I ask. It's a test.

- She faces the window. She doesn't stare though. Her eyes are shut. They've swollen like the rest of her, bulbous eyes that have rolled her eyelids out of sight. She faces the window and her eyes have swollen shut but she sees plenty. She sees you.

- You know that's a lie.

- She doesn't so much see you, Steven, as see where you are. She sees through your eyes. The whole women's council is tuned in through your eyes. You're their world, little brother. You're their future.

- No-one can see through someone else's eyes, I say.

I catch Doc Drake's stare. He's going to do it again. He's going to blank out my vision and make me see through his.

Then he changes his mind. The stare was enough. He's reminded me of what's possible.

- Believe it or not, those women do see through your eyes, Karen says – Mom sees through your eyes. Whatever you look at is what she sees. She's praying for your daughter, Bender. Her mouth's swollen but I see the lips move. It keeps her alive as she keeps hope alive. She's praying for your daughter and the future of the world.

- Mom tell you all this, did she? She suddenly got lucid and spouted this crap?

- They wired me in to the council's vision. Just for a while. I saw through your eyes. I saw as you looking at me as I lay on the table in the van. Mom held me in her arms and my heart beat in rhythm with hers as we looked down on her daughter. We both looked down on me. Don't tell me what's real, Bender. I feel what's real. I'm not wrong.

Karen gives me her wide-eyed stare. Her focus must be crap for her eyes are full of tears but she doesn't need focus. Storms don't need focus, they're just broad and high and knock you flying. Karen collects her tears so she can wash me with em. Flood me with em. She uses wet eyes to show that she's right and I'm wrong.

I stare her out. She doesn't blink so her eyes dry in the end. She picks up a fork, spears a leaf of lettuce, pushes it in place with her knife, and then looks up again.

I stare back. My eyes never shifted while my hand picks up food. My mouth churns salad and my fingers roll the salad mixture into a thick wad and stuff it into my mouth. My Mom's in fat meltdown in an institution, my Dad's a psycho who burnt down my home and slaughtered my friends, I'm fucked if I'll sit here and show manners. I'm not domestic. I'm wild.

- That's gross, Karen says.

I flatten the rest of the salad against the plate with my fingers, lift the plate up, and slide it all into my mouth. Still staring at her over the edge of the plate.

- Glad you liked it, Doc Drake says. He reaches his own plate up from the ground and passes it across – Here. Finish mine. Maybe you can take a moment to appreciate the citrus dressing this time. Oranges, tangerines and limes have been grafted to grow on a single tree in your garden. Mixed together I find the pressed fruit adds a certain tang.

Malik stays quiet and watches but he's already taken sides. He's picked up his knife and fork. I let some of the chewed wad of leaves spill from the corners of my mouth as I speak.

– Everything in this garden's warped. That's not a plate of food in your hand, doctor. It's a bioengineering freakshow. Come on, Malik. Let's run.

- Where to?

- Out of here.

- We can't, Malik says – It's not allowed. This place is surrounded by a forcefield. They explained it to me in Cromozone. The perimeters are marked with orange flags that go luminous at night so you can't miss em in the dark. Three steps beyond the flag you come up against an electronic barrier. Reach that you get a shock. Try and run beyond that you get stunned. They've built this place up into a model of everything that's best on Earth, Bender. They call it Eden. The world out there gets more fucked every day but in here it can only get better. They're making new animals all the time. It's beautiful, Bender. It really is. They gave me two lambs to play with in the Technosheds. They're going to bring em here, Bender, and set em loose. Rabbits too. I sat in a pen full of baby rabbits. Everything we've fucked up in the world they're putting right here. Only here. You're carrying a daughter. She's going to grow up in paradise. This is as good as it gets, Bender. They've put up a barrier to protect it.

- You're a runner, Malik, I remind him – We do long distance. Pain sets in after an hour or so. You remember that? You remember what we do with it? We run through it. It hurts, hurts like your heart's being crushed and your brain's got cramp, then it all bursts open. You remember that? You kick your heels and the pain's gone, it's left behind you in the dust, the world opens in color and light and the breath of it all just fills you. We don't stop at the barriers, Malik. We don't stop at the pain. We run through it all. We always get to the other side. Are you coming?

- What do you think? he asks Karen – Do you want to explore?

I check for the sun and turn so it casts my shadow right in front of me. That's my direction. I'll aim to land on the shadow of my head with every stride. Keep on going till I'm outta here. Far away from where my mate asks my sister for advice.

- You explore, I tell em – I'll run. When you get bored, come and find me.

Doc Drake reaches for his palmpad and starts tapping at the keys.

- They've shown me the layout to this place, Malik says – I got to study it. They built a house and planted trees all around it. This place is so big you can't see it from here but I know where it is. Let's go there. Let's run till we find it.

- You've gone domestic, Mal? You?

I like to play a game with the sun on my back. I think of it as a power source. It burns my neck but it never burns me out, it just burns me faster. I use that power now. These skypumps are new ones, not the ones Malik borrowed. I feel em correcting as I stretch through the first steps of my run, remolding my soles to straighten my gait. Tussocks of grass stud the earth but the running's clear enough. My shadow forms my path. My tread reaches beyond it but the shadow extends as I come back down to earth with each step. I stop looking at the ground and look ahead.

I don't see much. Tears ache behind my eyes. I blink to let em loose. The hot air dries em to a stain on my cheeks as I run up a wind. I don't get sad but sometimes I cry. I cry to be running and alone. It's not me that's crying, it's just old life caught inside me. Tears and sweat are the same thing. Crying's just a way of sweating old life out of your system. Keep on running and those tears dry out in time. The way ahead goes clear.

Right now the way is smudged a bit, sweat and tears soak the view, but what the fuck is there to see? Baked earth. Bleary sky. Orange pennants. They hang limp at ankle height. I know what they're there for. They're back-up to a lie. If forcefields were that good they wouldn't put a fence round Cromozone. They wouldn't man it with armed guards. No way have they planted a forcefield round this place. In Malik's fucked up head maybe, they've lodged some plan of a killer forcefield inside his skull, but that's what he wants. That's easy. It's easy to make people believe in what they want. Mal wants a forcefield to keep him in paradise. He wants Karen to himself. Fuck him. He can have her. She can have him. I'm leaving.

Speed, Bender. Speed up. That pennant there's your marker.

Land your right foot on it and leap. Take to the air. You'll land on the other side.

You will. You will.

- You're lucky, Malik says.

Malik smiles. His hand's cool. It lay on my forehead but he takes it away as I open my eyes.

Maybe he's right. Maybe it isn't a lie. Maybe I am lucky. Malik's here, he's smiling, he tells me I'm lucky. Maybe it's just him and me. Maybe that's what lucky means.

- You see? I say – There's nothing we can't run through. Thanks for coming. Thanks for following.

- The doctor drove us, Malik says – I would have run but the doctor said not to. He said you'd need some of the equipment in the van. You were fast but he was faster. He reprogrammed the co-ordinates. He guessed you'd take a leap at the fence and shifted the second shock curtain back some lengths. You were stunned and fell before you got to it. That's lucky, Bender. Two shocks of that force could have killed you.

I sit up and look around. I'm not in the van. I'm not on the ground at the far side of any forcefield either.

- You're in the house, Malik explains – The house they built for us. The doctor gave you a sedative to ease your system through the shock. He said it was important you came round gradually. You've had enough shocks for one day. Stay cool, Bender. Lie down.

He puts his hands on my shoulders. My shoulders are bare. I'm naked. Someone's peeled me out of my slinksuit. I'm lying on a single bed, covered by a white sheet. Malik presses me down onto the pillow. Some things I fight. Some things I don't. Malik wants to press me down onto a bed, that's OK. I can take that. I stare up at the ceiling in this new house. It's made of logs, still covered in their bark.

- So you brought me back? I didn't get away. You didn't follow.

- We put you on oxygen. Wrapped you in a foil blanket. The flatbed scanner diagnosed your condition then heat got to work. That's how I understand it. Heat and light are targeted through and around your body to regenerate stunned and shredded tissue. The doctor says it's no different to the natural healing process, only infinitely faster. We don't have to wait on nature, he says. We don't ever have to do that. We can make it work for us. Left to nature you'd be dead. Your guts would be fried inside the electric perimeter. The doctor's taken the van with him. You run at that forcefield again, you won't survive. We can't pick you up and set you right again. You understand that, Bender? You're going to stay easy for a while? You're not going to run?

- Are you going to stop breathing? I ask him – It's dusty out there. You don't want dust in your lungs. You'd better stop breathing.

- Are you OK, Bender? Are you OK in the head? The doctor said you'd be OK.

- I'm a runner. Don't tell me not to run, Mal. I've got to run.

I either say those words or think em as I drift back into sleep.

2.02

Karen sits on the edge of my bed. Her weight makes me roll toward her.

- How are you feeling? she asks

I look up at her. She's got bags under her eyes.

- Mom used to come in to my bedroom in the mornings, I say. I don't say ex-Mom. Names are made for shortening – She pulled on my nipples. Wanted to give me big tits. She wanted me to be a girl. Did you know that?

- I'm not Mom, Karen says.

- It's a shitline, all that stuff about me being pregnant. It's a lie. You do know that, don't you?

- You're Bender. You're my twin. I'm the girl, you're the boy. It doesn't matter what they've done to you. It doesn't change that.

- You believe em. You believe the lie. You think I've got a girl growing inside of me.

- There's a lab attached to the house. It's filled with cages and pens. A rat's in one of the cages. A pig's in a pen. There's a sheep too. I've only examined the rat so far. It's male. It's pregnant. They've left me notes. I'm meant to slice into the creature, deliver the baby female rat, then seal the father up again. It's practice, they say. With any luck the female offspring will bear females of their own. If you've got a baby in there we'll get her out. We'll get her out and life will go on. We've got a solar computer in the house. My surgical program for ectopic births is loaded into it. I've just practiced. I'll keep on practicing. I'm getting past step three every time. The baby lives. The parent lives. No problem.

- It's sick. You're as sick as Mom. You'd slice anything open to find a baby inside. That's antique, Karen. That's some primeval instinct playing itself out inside you. Forget it. Boys are born instead of girls. Fact. Why change it? It's great. Get used to it. You know what it means? It means there's no second chance. Parents can't have kids to live their lives for em. This life is it. It ends here. We've got to live it for ourselves.

- For each other, Karen said.

- You think this is Eden? It's just one more extension of Cromozone. They've installed us in a breeding program.

- The doctor calls it Project Naamah. Naamah was the wife of Noah.

Some things you can take lying down. Some things you have to sit up for.

I sit up.

- He told you that? I ask her.

- He confirmed it. My ectopic birthing program has that same title for its master file. Project Naamah. Call it that. Call this Eden. Call it the Ark. Call it what you like it's a big deal, Bender. We're it. You're carrying one possible future of the whole human race.

She stares at me. It's enough having a sister that looks like a mirror. This is worse. Fuck knows how she does it, her eyes are just eyes, just that average crazy complex of a cosmic journey stuffed into a pupil that everybody has. Maybe the trick's in the whites that surround it, maybe the whites are whirling and revolving to suck me in, maybe that's where the intensity lies. It's some blend of compassion and intelligence. She means well but those looks are killers. They break me up.

- It's your baby inside you, she steams on – Some other geek's sperm and some weird wannabe Mom's egg but it's in you so it's yours. Your daughter's going to come out of your body. She'll have babies. Maybe daughters. That's not some parasite you're carrying, Bender. It's the future. The whole future of the world is going to trace itself back to you.

I shake my head. I close my eyes. I open em again. She's still staring. I get out of bed. I see it shocks her. It's not that I'm naked though I am. She's used to seeing me naked. She's used to stitching up my wound and flipping her anthead view to a distant perspective so she can take in my whole body. My body's something she takes apart and puts together again. I'm the virtual naked being that lays on a slab while she flashes her fiberoptics around. Laying on a bed is close to how I should be. She can whisk out her fiberoptics and cope with that. Walking round the room is playing it all wrong. It's virtual reality run amok.

- You should rest, she tells me – That's what the doctor said. He said you should rest.

My slinksuit's folded on a wooden chair at the end of the bed. I pick it up and let it hang like shed skin, then start climbing inside it.

- The doctor says rest, I tell her – Then I'll run. Run till I drop.

I fit my arms inside the sleeves of the slinksuit then slip the skypumps onto my feet.

- Whatever, Karen says – You've got to do whatever you want. That's part of the deal. They didn't choose you for your perfect body. Your body's not that hot. They chose you because you're you. They had a choice of anyone in the world and they've gone for Bender. You've got an electrical implant in your brain. The doctor explained it to me. They can emit a signal to paralyze you. They've done it before, he tells me, when you were trying to cut open your own head. Is that right?

It's not right and it's not wrong. It's part of a story. Who knows what the fuck to believe. I stay quiet.

- They knew you were going to run through their electric curtain. They could have stopped you in your tracks. They always can. They can go as far with you as they want. They can keep you numb on drains and dripfeeds and grow baby after baby in your abdominal cavity till your body gives out. There's so much they could do with you, Bender. And they don't. Ever wondered why?

She waits for an answer but not for long. Not even for a second. She's got her own answer so doesn't need mine. She heads to the door and opens it. A smell comes in. Lots of smells, a package of smells, but wrapped in the smell of fried onion.

- We've cooked dinner. We'll talk at table.

She walks out. It's an old trick of hers. She walks out of a room so fast she leaves a wake, a wake that sucks you into it.

The room I'm in is as simple as rooms get. Logs for ceiling, logs for walls, two single beds, two wooden chairs, no lights but one small window. The view takes in trees. A few light green leaves hang on the branches.

I follow Karen out of the room, but only because she's gone first.

I was going in any case.

The food smell comes from the left, along a narrow corridor.

I cross the corridor and open a door into a room like the one I've left. It's got the same ceiling, walls, chairs and beds. The same window with what looks like an identical view. One of the beds has been slept in. I smell the pillow, pull back the sheet, then go back to the second bed in the room where I woke and do the same. Smells are mixed on the pillow but I see no stains, find no pubes.

- We all slept in here, Karen says. She's come back to find me. She could always move around a house like hot breath. She didn't need skypumps to float to where she wants without you hearing her. Now she's got em she's going one better. She's ghosting into my thoughts without a sound – We took it in turns to sleep with you. One in this other little bed, one with you.

She knows what I'm thinking. I may as well say it.

- Have you fucked yet? You and Malik?

- Get real, Bender. I'm your sister. Don't warp me. I'm not you. Don't mix me up. You've fucked. You and him. Not him and me. Do you remember what real is?

She stares at me. I stare back. Then the stare breaks. I hold out my arms and she walks into em.

- This is fucked, I say – All fucked.

Her shoulders shake a little like she's crying. We hold on, quiet, then she presses home a gentle hug and steps back. The tears are drying on her face. She tries a smile.

- We'll get through, she says.

The house is a log cabin. The kitchen's made of the same barked wood as the bedrooms. I call it a kitchen coz I walked toward its smell of food but it's just a big room. The house has two bedrooms and this room. Two shutters are drawn back from a hole in the back wall. The food smell is coming in through that hole, sliding out from under a lid that rattles on top of a single pot. The pot sits on a rack above a wood fire. The smoke from the fire goes straight up into the air.

- That's our new stove, Malik says —We're in a hi-tech, low-tech world. That stove's the low. They've left us a supply of matches. Over here's the high.

The room's got two tables. One is a dining table in the middle of the room. The other is smaller and set against a side wall, away from the window's light. It's more like a desk. Malik shows it off. A vidscreen hangs on the wall above the desk, and the desk's surface is filled with chrome. Chrome racks, speakers, a keyboard and computer.

- It's solar powered, Malik explains – A solar computer. The panels are fixed to the outside wall. It's the best, Bender. This machine could run whole nations and still sell off spare capacity, but you know what it gets to run? Us. That's it. It's dedicated to us. You see this little bank of chrome? It's a library. Take the British Library, shrink it, streamline and update it, make it user-friendly, and it comes down to this. It's got no transmitter and no receiver. What the old world knows is already here. Anything new that we learn, we get to keep. This machine is God. We want to know something, it has to tell us. And when God sucks, when we don't want the answers, when we know better than God, we can tell him to shut the fuck up. It's our pet house-God, Bender. We turn him on, we turn him off.

Malik presses his thumb on a button on the keyboard. The screen on the wall goes blank.

- Who was that? Karen asks.

- Who?

- On the vidscreen. That morphfile. It looked like a kid but kept changing. I thought I knew him. Then I didn't. Who was it?

- You want to see? Malik asks.

A face forms across the vidscreen, eyes first. They're the eyes of a baby. They start blue, but as the face morphs the eyes change. The baby becomes an infant and the eyes turn brown. I focus on the eyes and I could be looking at Malik. The face could be his too, him when he was young. I see traces of his cheekbones, and olive tones to the skin. But the cheekbones aren't as high as Malik's, the skin isn't as dark as his. The face is too long. It's more like mine. This young boy's nose isn't straight like Malik's. It bumps a little at the end like mine.

- What have you been doing? Karen asks.

Malik smiles, a happy smile that flashes teeth.

- You know that rap of Bender's? he says – The future's now, now's all there is, all of that shit. Well that picture's it. It's the future. The future's us. It's a picture of you, of me, of Karen.

- Are you on qual? I ask him.

- We've got no qual. We're set to be self-sufficient. There's a patch of shrooms out back though. I wanted to stick em in the soup but Karen said no. She wants to get to know me sane first, so she recognizes crazy when it happens.

I go closer and stare at the vidscreen.

- Is this your kid? I ask, and the answer's obvious. The machine's running a DNA spawn program. These things are a feature of girlchat, girls rubbing their DNA up against the DNA of a celebrity mate and drooling over the results. I never thought I'd catch Malik at the game.

- Sex is random. The results aren't accurate. Tweak this DNA program and I come up with a different screenkid each time. Some look more like you, some look more like me, but they all look like each other. That picture's not our boy. It's like our boy

- Our boy?

- Karen's and mine, but with the twin thing you and Karen are the same so it's ours.

- Get a brainwipe, Malik, Karen says. She lifts the pot onto bricks in the middle of the table and slops soup into three blue bowls – You want a baby you might as well keep fucking Steven. I deliver babies. I don't do em.

– She needs time, Malik says, and pulls a chair up to the table – She had a bad role model with your Mom and Dad. She's not used to playing happy families. Look at this! Veggie soup with tin beans and too much salt. It's crap but it's our crap.

The empty bean tin is in the middle of the table. It's filled with water, and a flower full of red petals sits in it. I pick it up and hold the flower while I pour half the water into my soup.

- You've not tasted it, Karen says.

I stir it up and test it with my finger. It's cool enough. I pick up the bowl and drink in gulps from its edge.

- So? Karen asks.

- It tastes like piss. Great. Thanks. Great piss. Just what I needed.

I take hold of the flower, bite off its head, chew it round my mouth till it's pulp, then swallow it down with the rest of the flower water. I don't do domestic. I'm wild. I want em to see I'm wild.

- Great flower too. Thanks.

The image on the vidscreen keeps changing. A label at the top says it's seventeen years old. A face stares out. It's not me, it's not Malik, it's not Karen. It's its own thing. It doesn't smile.

- Is that kid of yours into girls? I ask Malik - Does he grow up to fuck the girl that's leeched on to my stomach? Do their kids grow up to breed more of themselves? Is that the future of the human race, fucking and breeding and fucking and breeding?

- Sounds good to me, Malik says – What's up with you? Why so moody? It must be the hormones talking.

- What hormones?

- They pumped you full of em in your qual rations, so the pregnancy would take hold. Now the embryo inside you has taken over, it creates all the hormones it needs to grow. That's bound to affect you

- Shitline. There's no embryo. No hormones.

- We fucked. You got pregnant. It happens all the time.

- Not to boys. Not to men.

- Boy, girl, man, woman, get modern, Bender. You're into difference all the time. We're all just people.

- You're people, I say.

- And what are you?

I am blank.

- You've not changed, Malik says – Whatever they've done to you, you're still you. I see you. You're Bender

I laugh. The laugh comes out higher than I mean it to. It bounces off the ceiling then it's gone. I hold my hands high in the air, like my body is something to show off. Karen looks at me and Malik looks at me and their eyes are shiny but not bright. They're shiny with tears.

The big room has a door to outside. I open it but no air comes in. The air's heavy. It's not moving. I take one step, then another. It's not running, but it's a start. The air begins to stir against my face.

- Bender calling Cromozone. I'm out and running, Cromozone. This is my final transmission. Sixty-one seconds from now I'll be running at your wall. Not fast, not slow, just steady as I am now. You hear I'm not breathless. I'm in good voice control. I'm steady. Steady enough to run right at your wall.

- Can you see? Can you really see through my eyes? Is that true? Then you see this earth coming to life. You see the dust speed toward my feet. Hold yourselves in check. If I get through this wall you'll see things you never wanted to see. Stay watching and you'll see me die but before you do you'll see me live. I'll live and fight and fuck and sleep and rise just where the running takes me. You can track me, you can see through my eyes, but you'll never stop me till you see me dead.

- I'm turning. Running myself into a straight approach.

- Note the pennants. See em coming nearer.

- The earth's alive. I'm running it alive. See how it's rushing toward me.

- Five seconds.

- Three.

- I'm at the pennants. I'm past the pennants.

- I'm running. I'm running.

Thought so.

Soft doesn't work. It never has, it never will. What doesn't kill me makes me strong.

Here's what I reckon. Karen can abort this thing. It's not so hard. Not so much harder than birthing it. But she needs more practice. The longer I stay alive, the more practice she gets, and the more chance I have of surviving the operation.

So if this thing in me gets to live, it's a by-product. OK? It's like a gallstone. I want it out. That's all. I want it out.

I'm going back now. Don't pen me in again, OK? No more of that electric fence stuff. I'm a runner.

I'll get this out and you won't see me for dust.

According to Karen

'He's a good kid,' Malik says. His eyes go damp which means they're burning. He turns from me back to the vidscreen. Steven's in the chair and Malik's stood behind him, reaching his arms around, tapping at the controls. I watch Mal with Steven and I think some day I can love him. Love him enough.

Steven smiles his dim smile. He watches the figures on screen. One's him, the other's Mal. They run side by side, sometimes on a road, sometimes through a forest, sometimes across meadows, and they even run through cloud and over mountains when Mal gets bored. Steven doesn't get bored. He doesn't get anything.

Mal and me run for real, but not together. One of us sits with Steven, the other does laps of the fencing. The fence buzzes. I've seen two bodies the other side of it, but no-one living. The forcefield is too strong. I run a few laps then come home again.

I think Steven's free. The last time he spoke we got his words on record. His body was wrecked but he thought he was fit, he thought he was leaving. He ran through the fence and away.

We change his clothes. We bathe him. We feed him. He lies down, sits up, and can walk some steps when we guide him. I thought he'd get better. Doctor Drake said he'd get better. He went on overload, he said. Empaths do that sometimes. They see the future, and when it happens and it's too sick to bear it's like they change channel. They don't live in the world any more but they're still living. Life's still real for them. I like to think Steven's still running. I blow soft air onto his forehead and cheeks sometimes, like it's the wind of running against his face.

His body's shrinking. We dampen soft cloths and run them round his neck and over his ribs. His stomach swells but not so much and his cheeks suck in against his teeth. We wonder sometimes if his smiles are real or if it's just the way his skin is stretched.

They've left me morphine. I'm glad of that. He likes running. Maybe with the morphine he can run until he flies.

Malik strokes my breasts. I'm glad of it and sometimes let him suck. I don't like the breast pump. I want the natural way. I'm using fenugreek. We have a bush outside the cabin and I chew it and swallow three times a day. I think it makes me sweat but then we're all sweating all the time. The breast's a modified sweat gland. More sweat, more milk, such is the thought. It seems to be working. That and Malik's mouth. And of course the intramuscular injection of depot medroxyprogesterone acetate. Nature needs a little help now and again.

It's working. My milk's running. It's time.

We didn't need to use the straps. Malik held Steven down. His legs kicked but he smiled so I think he was running. It was hard at first with his muscles tensing. I didn't expect spasm. Then he was still. I had some morphine left and gave Mal a shot. He's lying down and smiling. Maybe he's running. Maybe they're both running.

I'm not professional. I threw up. My eyes were blind with tears. It didn't matter. It didn't fucking matter. I put on the visor and the gloves worked themselves.

She's beautiful. Cutting her out of the gore like that, lifting her out, it's like a miracle pulled out of hell.

I call her Wanda. I think her skin is dark, but maybe that's the blood. She's feeding at my right breast.

I won't say she's worth it, Steven. I'll never say she's worth it. But you're my twin. I know you. I know that you would love her.

Off you go now Steven wherever you are. I'll clean all this mess up later. You run and play.

ACKNOWLEDGEMENTS

This book was seeded as an idea by Trevor O'Neill. Many have touched it in different drafts and incarnations since then. The PhD process at the University of Lancaster, supervised by Graham Mort and Lee Horsley, helped me break through the final bounds and bring the book close to its final shape. Sara Maitland gave it a reading at that point. James Thornton was there in full support through its final years. Now it's yours. Thanks for reading.

Author website: MartinGoodman.com

9 780956 336453